Stories from the Faerie Queene

"She nigher drew, and saw that joyous end:
Then God she praysd, and thankt her faithfull Knight
That had atchievde so great a conquest by his might."

With Introduction by
John W Hales

Drawings by
A. G. Walker. Sculptor.

NEW WEST PRESS

ISBN 978-1-64965-131-0

New West Press
Phoenix, AZ 85085
www.nwwst com

Ordering Information:
Special discounts are available on quantity purchases by corporations, associations, educators, and others. For details, contact the publisher at the listed address below.

U.S. trade bookstores and wholesalers: Please contact New West Press:

Tel: (480) 648-1061; or email: contact@nwwst.com

Introduction

THE object of this volume is to excite interest in one of the greatest poems of English literature, which for all its greatness is but little read and known—to excite this interest not only in young persons who are not yet able to read "The Faerie Queene," with its archaisms of language, its distant ways and habits of life and thought, its exquisite melodies that only a cultivated ear can catch and appreciate, but also in adults, who, not from the lack of ability, but because they shrink from a little effort, suffer the loss of such high and refined literary pleasure as the perusal of Spenser's masterpiece can certainly give.

Assuredly, when all that cavillers can say or do is said and done, "The Faerie Queene" is deservedly called one of the greatest poems of English literature. From the high place it took, and took with acclamation, when it first appeared, it has, in fact, never been deposed. It has many defects and imperfections, such as the crudest and most commonplace critic can discover, and has discovered with much self-complacency; but it has beauties and perfections that such critics very often fail to see; and, so far as the status of "The Faerie Queene" is concerned, it is enough for the ordinary reader to grasp the significant fact that Spenser has won specially for himself the famous title of "the poets' poet." Ever since his star appeared above the horizon, wise men from all parts have come to worship it; and amongst these devotees fellow-poets have thronged with a wonderful enthusiasm. In one point all the poetic schools of England have agreed together, viz., in admiration for Spenser. From Milton and Wordsworth on the one hand to Dryden and Pope—from the one extreme of English poetry to the other—has prevailed a perpetual reverence for Spenser. The lights in his temple, so to speak, have never been extinguished-never have there been wanting offerers of incense and of praise; and, to repeat in other words what has already been said, as it is what we wish to specially emphasise, amidst this faithful congregation have been many who already had or were some day to have temples of their own. We recognise amongst its members not only the great poets already mentioned, but many others of the divine brotherhood, some at least of whom rank with the greatest, such as Keats, Shelley, Sidney, Gray, Byron, the Fletchers, Henry More, Raleigh, Thomson, not to name Beattie, Shenstone, Warton, Barnefield, Peele, Campbell, Drayton, Cowley, Prior, Akenside, Roden Noel. To this long but by no means exhaustive list might be added many of high eminence in other departments of literature and of life, as Gibbon, Mackintosh, Hazlitt, Craik, Lowell, Ruskin, R. W. Church, and a hundred more.

Now, of course, the acceptance of a poet is and must be finally due to his own intrinsic merits. No amount of testimonials from ever so highly distinguished persons will make a writer permanently popular if he cannot make himself so-if his own works do not make him so. Of testimonials there is very naturally considerable distrust—very naturally, when we notice what second-rate penmen have been and are cried up to the skies. But in the present case the character of the testifiers is to be carefully considered; and, secondly, not only their words but their actions are to be taken into account. Many of our greatest poets have praised Spenser not only in formal phrases, but practically and decisively, by surrendering themselves to his influence, by sitting at his feet, by taking hints and suggestions from him. He has been their master not merely nominally but actually, and with obvious results. If all traces of Spenser's fascination and power could be removed from subsequent English literature, that literature would be a very different thing from what it is: there would be strange breaks and blanks in many a volume, hiatuses in many a line, an altered turning of many a sentence, a modification of many a conception and fancy. And we are convinced that the more Spenser is studied the more remarkable will his dominance and his dominion be found to be. To quote lines that have been quoted before in this connection—

> "Hither, as to their fountain, other stars
> Repairing, in their urns draw golden light."

"The Faerie Queene" is one of the great wellheads of English poetry; or, in other words, Spenser's Faerie Land has been and is a favourite haunt of all our highest poetic spirits.

And yet it is incontrovertible that this poem is very little known as a whole to most people. Everybody is familiar with the story of Una and the Lion, and with two or three stanzas of singular beauty in other parts of "The Faerie Queen," because these occur in most or all books of selections: in every anthology occur those fairest flowers. But the world at large is content to know no more. The size of the poem appals it. "A big book is a big evil," it thinks, and it shudders at the idea of perusing the six twelve-cantoed books in which Spenser's genius expressed itself—expressed itself only in an incomplete and fragmentary fashion, for many more books formed part of his enormous design. "Of the persons who read the first canto," says Macaulay in a famous Essay, "not one in ten reaches the end of the First Book, and not one in a hundred perseveres to the end of the poem. Very few and very weary are those who are in at the death of the Blatant Beast. If the last six books, which are said [without any authority] to have been destroyed in Ireland, had been preserved, we doubt whether any heart less stout than that of a commentator would have held out to the end." And

Macaulay speaks truly as well as wittily. He is as accurate as Poins when Prince Hal asks him what he would think if the Prince wept because the King his father was sick. "I would think thee a most princely hypocrite," replies Poins. "It would be every man's thought," says the Prince: "and thou art a blessed fellow to think as every man thinks. Never a man's thought in the world keeps the roadway better than thine." Even so is Macaulay "a blessed fellow to think as every man thinks," and no doubt his blessedness in this respect is one of the characteristics—by no means the only one—that account for his widespread popularity. He not only states that people do not read "The Faerie Queen," but he shows that he himself, voracious reader—*helluo librorum*—as he was, had not done so, or had done so very carelessly; for, alas! the Blatant Beast, as at all events every student of the present volume will know, does not die; Sir Calidore only suppresses him for a time; he but temporarily ties and binds him in an iron chain, "and makes him follow him like a fearful dog;" and one day long afterwards the beast got loose again—

"Ne ever could by any, more be brought
Into like bands, ne maystred any more,
Albe that, long time after Calidore,
The good Sir Pelleas him tooke in hand, p. xii
And after him Sir Lamoracke of yore,
And all his brethren borne in Britaine land
Yet none of them could ever bring him into band.

So now he raungeth through the world againe,
And rageth sore in each degree and state
Ne any is that may him now restraine,
He growen is so great and strong of late,
Barking and biting all that him doe bate,
Albe they worthy blame, or clear of crime
Ne spareth he most learned wits to rate,
Ne spareth he the gentle Poets rime;
But rends without regard of person or of time."

And Spenser goes on to declare that even his "homely verse of many meanest" cannot hope to escape "his venemous despite;" for, in his own day, as often since, Spenser by no means found favour with everybody. Clearly even Macaulay's memory of the close of "The Faerie Queene" was sufficiently hazy. But even Milton, to whom Spenser was so congenial a spirit, and whom he acknowledged as his "poetical father," on one occasion at least forgets the details of the Spenserian story. When insisting in the *Areopagitica* that true virtue is not "a fugitive and cloistered virtue, unexercised and unbreathed, that never sallies out and sees her adversary," but a virtue that has been tried and tested, he remarks that this "was the reason why our sage and serious poet Spenser, whom I dare be known to think a better teacher than Scotus or Aquinas, describing true temperance under the person of Guion, brings him in with his Palmer through the cave of Mammon and the bower of earthly bliss, that he may see, and know, and yet abstain." But the Palmer was not with Sir Guyon in the Cave of Mammon, Phædria having declined to ferry him over to her floating island. See "The Faerie Queene," ii. 6, 19:—

"Himselfe [Sir Guyon] she tooke aboord,
But the Black Palmer suffred still to stond,
Ne would for price or prayers once affoord
To ferry that old man over the perlous foord.

"Guyon was loath to leave his guide behind,
Yet being entred might not back retyre;
For the flitt barke, obeying to her mind,
Forth launched quickly as she did desire,
Ne gave him leave to bid that aged sire
Adieu."

So Macaulay's lapse must not be regarded too severely, though, as may be seen, much more prominence is given by Spenser to the fact that the Blatant Beast was not killed, than to the absence of the Palmer from Guyon's side in Mammon's House. It seems probable, indeed, that Macaulay mixed up the fate of the Dragon in the eleventh canto of the First Book with that of the Blatant Beast in the twelfth of the Sixth. But we mention these things only to prevent any surprise at the general ignorance of Spenser, when such a confirmed book-lover as Macaulay, and such a devoted Spenserian as Milton, are found tripping in their allusions to his greatest work.

Now this ignorance, however explicable, is, we think, to be regretted. A poet of such splendid attributes, and with such a choice company of followers, surely deserves to be better known than he is by "the general reader"; and we trust that this volume may be of service in making the stories of "The Faerie Queene" more familiar, and so in tempting the general reader to turn to Spenser's own version of them, and to appreciate his amazing affluence of language, of melody, and of fancy.

Clearly, Spenser does not appeal to everybody at first; we mean that to enjoy him fully needs some little effort to begin with—some distinct effort to put ourselves in communication with him, so to speak; for he is far away from us in many respects. His costume and his accent are very different from ours. He does not seem to be of us or of our world. "His soul" is "like a star": it dwells "apart." We have, it would appear at first sight, nothing in common with him: he moves all alone in a separate sphere—he is not of our flesh and blood. What strikes us at first sight is a certain artificiality and elaborateness, as we think. We cannot put ourselves on confidential terms with him; he is too stately and *point devise*. His art rather asserts than conceals itself to persons who merely glance at him. But these impressions will be largely or altogether removed, *if the reader will really read "The Faerie Queene."* He will no longer think of its author as a mere phrase-monger, or only a dainty melodist, or the master of a superfine style. He will find himself in communion with a man of high intellect, of a noble nature—of great attraction, not only for his humanism, but for his humanity. To Spenser, Wordsworth's lines in "A Poet's Epitaph" may be applied with particular and profound truth

"He is retired as noontide dew,
Or fountain in a noonday grove;
And you must love him ere to you
He will seem worthy of your love."

The very opulence of Spenser's genius stands in the way of his due appraisement. There can scarcely be a doubt that if he could have restrained the redundant stream of his poetry, he might have been more worthily recognised. Had he written less, he would have been praised more; as it is, with many readers, *mole ruit sua*: they are overpowered and bewildered by the immense flood. The waters of Helicon seem a torrent deluge. We say his popularity would have been greater, if he could have restrained and controlled this amazing outflow; but, after all, we must take our great poets as we find them. In this very abundance, as in other ways, Spenser was a child of his age, and we must accept him with all his faults as well as with all his excellences. Both faults and excellences are closely inter-connected. *Il a les défauts de ses qualités.*

He said that Chaucer was his poetical master, and more than once he mentions Chaucer with the most generous admiration:—

"Dan Chaucer, well of English undefyled,
On Fames eternal beadroll worthy to be fyled."

"That old Dan Geffrey, in whose gentle spright
The pure well head of Poesie did dwell."

And Chaucer too may be said to suffer from a very plethora of wealth. Chaucer is apt to be superabundant; but yet he was a model of self-restraint as compared with Spenser. One cannot say in this case, "Like master, like man," or, "Like father, like son." Their geniuses are entirely different—a fact which makes Spenser's devotion to Chaucer all the more noticeable and interesting; and the art of the one is in sharp contrast with the art of the other. Chaucer is a masterly tale-teller: no one in all English poetry equals him in this faculty; he is as supreme in it as Shakespeare in the department of the drama. In his tales Chaucer is, "without o'erflowing, full." The conditions under which they were told beneficially bounded and limited them. Each is *multum in parvo*. They are very wonders of compression, and yet produce no sense of confinement or excision. Spenser could not possibly have set before himself a better exemplar; but yet he so set him in vain. The contrast between the two poets, considered merely as narrators or story-tellers, is vividly exhibited in the third canto of the Fourth Book of "The Faerie Queene," where, after a reverent obeisance to his great predecessor, he attempts to tell the other half of the half-told story.

"Of Cambuscan bold,
Of Camball and of Algarsife,
And who had Canace to wife,
That owned the virtuous ring and glass,

And of the wondrous horse of brass,
On which the Tartar king did ride."

It is not without some misgiving that he adventures on such a daring task:—

"Then pardon, O most sacred happie Spirit
That I thy labours lost[*] may thus revive,
And steale from thee the meede of thy due merit,
That none durst ever whilest thou wast alive,
And being dead in vain yet many strive.
Ne dare I like; but through infusion swete
Of thine own Spirit which doth in me survive,
I follow here the footing of thy feete,
But with thy meaning so I may the rather meete."

But it can scarcely be allowed either that he follows the footing of his master's feet, or that he caught the breath of his master's spirit. There are "diversities of operations"; and Spenser's method and manner were not those of Chaucer, however sincere the allegiance he professed, and however sincere his intentions to tread in his footsteps and march along the same road. He wanted some gifts and some habits that are necessary for the perfect story-teller—gifts and habits which Chaucer, by nature or by discipline, possessed in a high degree, such as humour, concentration, realism. The very structure of "The Faerie Queene" is defective. It begins in the middle—at its opening it takes us *in medias res*, seemingly in accordance with the precedent of the *Iliad* or of the *Æneid*, but only seemingly, for both Homer and Virgil very soon finish the explanation of their opening initial scenes, and their readers know where they are, But the first six books of "The Faerie Queene" are very slightly connected together; and what the connection is meant to be we learn only from the later of the poet to Sir Walter Raleigh, which it was thought well to print with the first three books,

[*]Spenser thought that the latter Part or Parts of the "Squire's Tale" had actually been written but been lost—been "quite devoured" by "cursed eld," and "brought to nought by little bits," as he quaintly expresses it. But it may be taken as certain Chaucer left the tale as we have it, that is, "half told." The closing lines of what we have are clearly unrevised. For some reason or another—trouble or sickness, or his growing infirmity—what would have been one of the most brilliant works of the Middle Ages was never completed, and, like "Christabel" and "Hyperion," remains only a glorious fragment.

no doubt in consequence of some complaints of obscurity and disattachment. This letter is significantly described as "expounding his" (the author's) "whole intention in the course of this work," and as "hereunto annexed, for that it giveth great light to the reader for the better understanding." Certainly a story ought not to require a prose appendix to set forth its arrangement and its purpose, even if only a fourth of it is completed. The exact correlation of eleven books was to remain unrevealed till the Twelfth Book appeared. In fact, had the poem ever been completed, we should have had to begin its perusal at the end! Thus "The Faerie Queene," as has often been remarked, lacks unity and cohesion. It is not so much one large and glorious mansion as a group of mansions. To use the metaphor of Professor Craik, to whom many subsequent writers on Spenser have been so considerably indebted, and often without any at all adequate acknowledgment, it is a street of fine houses, or, to use another metaphor of Professor Craik's, which also has been freely adopted by other critics, it is in parts a kind of wilderness—a wilderness of wonderful beauty and wealth, in. which it is a delight to wander, but yet a wilderness with paths and tracks dimly and faintly marked, often scarcely to be discerned.

Such was the abundance of Spenser's fancy, and so various and extensive was his learning, that he wrote, it would seem, with an amazing facility, never checked by any paucities of either knowledge or ideas. His pen could scarcely keep pace with his imagination. His material he drew from all accessible sources—from the Greek and Latin classics (his sympathetic acquaintance with Plato is one of his distinctions), from the Italian poets (not only from Ariosto and Tasso, but Berni, Boiardo, Pulci, and others), from the old Romances of Chivalry (especially the Arthurian in Malory's famous rendering, Bevis of Southampton, Amadis de Gaul), from what there was of modern English literature (above all, Chaucer's works, but also Hawes and other minor writers) and of modern French literature (especially Marot), from contemporary history (all the great personages of his time are brought before us in his pages): but all these diverse elements he combines and assimilates in his own fashion, and forms into a compound quite unique, and highly characteristic both of the hour and of the man. No wonder if the modern reader is at first somewhat perplexed and confused; no wonder if he often loses the thread of the story, and fails to comprehend such an astonishing prodigality of incident and of personification. Figure after figure flits before his eyes—the cry is still "They come"; one seems to be n the very birthplace and home of dreams, knights, ladies, monsters, wizards, and witches; all forms of good and evil throng by in quick succession, and we are apt to forget who is who and what is what. Probably some candid good-natured friend complained to Spenser of this complicatedness, which is certainly at its worst in the Third and Fourth Books; and in a certain passage in the Sixth he makes some sort of defence of himself for what might seem divisions or aberrations in the story of Sir Calidore. He compares himself to a ship that, by reason of counter-winds and tides, fails to go straight to its destination, but yet makes for it, and does not lose its compass; see VI. xii. I and 2.

We are sure that for all young readers such a version of Spenser's stories as is given in this volume may be truly serviceable in preparing them for the study of the poem itself. And with some older readers too—and it is to them this Introduction is mainly addressed—we would fain hope this volume may find a hearty welcome, as providing them with a clue to what seems an intricate maze. What we should like to picture to ourselves is young and old reading these stories together, and the elder students selecting for their own benefit, and for the benefit of the younger, a few stanzas here and there from "The Faerie Queene" by way of illustration. Of course we do not make this humble suggestion to the initiated, but to those—and their name is Legion—who at present know nothing or next to nothing of what is certainly one of the masterpieces of English literature.

JOHN W. HALES.

CONTENTS

The Red Cross Knight

"Right faithful true he was in deed and word"

The Court of the Queen

ONCE upon a time, in the days when there were still such things as giants and dragons, there lived a great Queen. She reigned over a rich and beautiful country, and because she was good and noble every one loved her, and tried also to be good. Her court was the most splendid one in the world, for all her knights were brave and gallant, and each one thought only of what heroic things he could do, and how best he could serve his royal lady.

The name of the Queen was Gloriana, and each of her twelve chief knights was known as the Champion of some virtue. Thus Sir Guyon was the representative of *Temperance*, Sir Artegall of *Justice*, Sir Calidore of *Courtesy*, and others took up the cause of *Friendship*, *Constancy*, and so on.

Every year the Queen held a great feast, which lasted twelve days. Once, on the first day of the feast, a stranger in poor clothes came to the court, and, falling before the Queen, begged a favour of her. It was always the custom at these feasts that the Queen should refuse nothing that was asked, so she bade the stranger say what it was he wished. Then he besought that, if any cause arose which called for knightly aid, the adventure might be entrusted to him.

When the Queen had given her promise he stood quietly on one side, and did not try to mix with the other guests who were feasting at the splendid tables. Although he was so brave, he was very gentle and modest, and he had never yet proved his valour in fight, therefore he did not think himself worthy of a place among the knights who had already won for themselves honour and renown.

Soon after this there rode into the city a fair lady on a white ass. Behind her came her servant, a dwarf, leading a warlike horse that bore the armour of a knight. The face of the lady was lovely, but it was very sorrowful.

Making her way to the palace, she fell before Queen Gloriana, and implored her help. She said that her name was Una; she was the daughter of a king and queen who formerly ruled over a mighty country; but, many years ago, a huge dragon came and wasted all the land, and shut the king and queen up in a brazen castle, from which they might never come out. The Lady Una therefore besought Queen Gloriana to grant her one of her knights to fight and kill this terrible dragon.

Then the stranger sprang forward, and reminded the Queen of the promise she had given. At first she was unwilling to consent, for the Knight was young, and, moreover, he had no armour of his own to fight with.

Then said the Lady Una to him, "Will you wear the armour that I bring you, for unless you do you will never succeed in the enterprise, nor kill the horrible monster of Evil? The armour is not new, it is scratched and dinted with many a hard-fought battle, but if you wear it rightly no armour that ever was made will serve you so well."

Then the stranger bade them bring the armour and put it on him, and Una said, "Stand, therefore, having your loins girt about with truth, and having on the breastplate of righteousness, and your feet shod with the preparation of the gospel of peace; above all taking the shield of faith, wherewith ye shall be able to quench all the fiery darts of the wicked, and take the helmet of salvation and the sword of the SPIRIT, which is the word of GOD."

And when the stranger had put off his own rough clothes and was clad in this armour, straightway he seemed the goodliest man in all that company, and the Lady Una was well pleased with her champion; and, because of the red cross which he wore on his breastplate and on his silver shield, henceforth he was known always as "the Red Cross

Knight." But his real name was *Holiness*, and the name of the lady for whom he was to do battle was *Truth*.

So these two rode forth into the world together, while a little way behind followed their faithful attendant, *Prudence*. And now you shall hear some of the adventures that befell the Red Cross Knight and his two companions.

The Wood of Error

The first adventure happened in this way. Scarcely had the Red Cross Knight and the Lady Una started on their journey when the sky suddenly became overcast, and a great storm of rain beat down upon the earth. Looking about for shelter, they saw, not far away, a shady grove, which seemed just what they wanted. The trees here had great spreading branches, which grew so thickly overhead that no light could pierce the covering of leaves. Through this wood wide paths and alleys, well trodden, led in all directions. It seemed a truly pleasant place, and a safe shelter against the tempest, so they entered in at once.

At first, as they roamed along the winding paths they found nothing but pleasure. Deeper and deeper into the heart of the wood they went, hearing with joy the sweet singing of the birds, and filled with wonder to see so many different kinds of beautiful trees clustered in one spot. But by-and-by, when the storm was over and they wished to go forward on their journey, they found, to their sorrow, that they had lost their way. It was impossible to remember by which path they had come; every way now seemed strange and unknown. Here and there they wandered, backwards and forwards; there were so many turnings to be seen, so many paths, they knew not which to take to lead them out of the wood.

In this perplexity, at last they determined to go straight forward until they found some end, either in or out of the wood. Choosing for this purpose one of the broadest and most trodden paths, they came presently, in the thickest part of the wood, to a hollow cave. Then the Red Cross Knight dismounted from his steed, and gave his spear to the dwarf to hold.

"Take heed," said the Lady Una, "lest you too rashly provoke mischief. This is a wild and unknown place, and peril is often without show. Hold back, therefore, till you know further if there is any danger hidden there."

"Ah, lady," said the Knight, "it were shame to go backward for fear of a hidden danger. Virtue herself gives light to lead through any darkness."

"Yes," said Una; "but I know better than you the peril of this place, though now it is too late to bid you go back like a coward. Yet wisdom warns you to stay your steps, before you are forced to retreat. This is the Wandering Wood, and that is the den of Error, a horrible monster, hated of all. Therefore, I advise you to be cautious."

"Fly, fly! this is no place for living men!" cried timid Prudence.

But the young Knight was full of eagerness and fiery courage, and nothing could stop him. Forth to the darksome hole he went, and looked in. His glittering armour made a little light, by which he could plainly see the ugly monster. Such a great, horrible thing it was, something like a snake, with a long tail twisted in knots, with stings all over it. And near this wicked big creature, whose other name was *Falsehood*, there were a thousand little ones, varying in shape, but every one bad and ugly; for you may be quite sure that wherever one of this horrible race is found, there will always be many others of the same family lurking near.

When the light shone into the cave all the little creatures fled to hide themselves, and the big parent Falsehood rushed out of her den in terror. But when she saw the shining armour of the Knight she tried to turn back, for she hated light as her deadliest foe, and she was always accustomed to live in darkness, where she could neither see plainly nor be seen.

When the Knight saw that she was trying to escape, he sprang after her as fierce as a lion, and then the great fight began. Though he strove

valiantly, yet he was in sore peril, for suddenly the cunning creature flung her huge tail round and round him, so that he could stir neither hand nor foot.

Then the Lady Una cried out, to encourage him, "Now, now, Sir Knight, show what you are! Add faith unto your force, and be not faint! Kill her, or else she will surely kill you."

With that, fresh strength and courage came to the Knight. Gathering all his force, he got one hand free, and gripped the creature by the throat with so much pain that she was soon compelled to loosen her wicked hold. Then, seeing that she could not hope to conquer in this way, she suddenly tried to stifle the Knight by flinging over him a flood of poison. This made the Knight retreat a moment; then she called to her aid all the horrid little creeping and crawling monsters that he had seen before, and many others of the same kind, or worse. These came swarming and buzzing round the Knight like a cloud of teasing gnats, and tormented and confused him with their feeble stings. Enraged at this fresh attack, he made up his mind to end the matter one way or another, and, rushing at his foe, he killed her with one stroke of his sword.

Then Lady Una, who, from a distance, had watched all that passed, came near in haste to greet his victory.

"Fair Knight," she said, "born under happy star! You are well worthy of that armour in which this day you have won great glory, and proved your strength against a strong enemy. This is your first battle. I pray that you will win many others in like manner."

The Knight deceived by the Magician

After his victory over Falsehood, the Red Cross Knight again mounted his steed, and he and the Lady Una went on their way. Keeping carefully to one path, and turning neither to the right hand nor the left, at last they found themselves safely out of the Wood of Error.

But now they were to fall into the power of a more dangerous and treacherous foe than even the hateful monster, Falsehood.

They had travelled a long way, and met with no fresh adventure, when at last they chanced to meet in the road an old man. He looked very wise and good. He was dressed in a long black gown, like a hermit, and had bare feet and a grey beard; he had a book hanging from his belt, as was the custom with scholars in those days. He seemed very quiet and sad, and kept his eyes fixed on the ground, and all the time, as he went along, he seemed to be saying prayers, and lamenting over his own wickedness.

When he saw the travellers he made a very humble salute to them. The Red Cross Knight returned the greeting with all courtesy, and asked him if he knew of any strange adventures that were then taking place.

"Ah, my dear son!" said the hermit, "how should a simple old man, who lives in a lonely cell, and does nothing all day but sorrow for his own faults-how should such a man know any tidings of war or worldly trouble? It is not fitting for me to meddle with such matters. But, if indeed you desire to hear about danger and evil near at hand, I can tell you about a strange man who wastes all the surrounding country."

"That," said the Knight, "is what I chiefly ask about, and I will reward you well if you will guide me to the place where he dwells. For it is a disgrace to knighthood that such a creature should be allowed to live so long."

"His dwelling is far away from here, in the midst of a barren wilderness," answered the old man. "No living person may ever pass it without great danger and difficulty."

"Now," said the Lady Una, "night is drawing near, and I know well that you are wearied with your former fight. Therefore, take rest, and with the new day begin new work."

"You have been well advised, Sir Knight," said the old man. "Day is now spent; therefore take up your abode with me for this night."

The travellers were well content to do this, so they went with the apparently good old man to his home.

It was a little lowly hermitage, down in a dale by the side of a forest, far from the beaten track of travellers. A small chapel was built near, and close by a crystal stream gently welled forth from a never-failing fountain. Arrived at the house, they neither expected nor found any entertainment; but rest was what they chiefly needed, and they were well satisfied, for the noblest mind is always the best contented. The old man had a good store of pleasing words, and knew well how to fit his talk to suit his visitors. The evening passed pleasantly, and then the hermit conducted his guests to the lodgings where they were to spend the night.

But when they were safely asleep a horrid change came over the old man, for in reality he was not good at all, although he pretended to be so. His heart was full of hatred, malice, and deceit. He called himself Archimago, which means a "Great Magician," but his real name was *Hypocrisy*. He knew that as long as Holiness and Truth kept together, no great harm could come to either of them; so he determined to do everything in his power to separate them. For this purpose he got out all his books of magic, and set to work to devise cunning schemes and spells. He was so clever and wily that he could deceive people much better and wiser than himself. He also had at his bidding many bad little spirits, who ran about and did his messages; these he used to help his friends and frighten his enemies, and he had the power of making them take any shape he wished.

Choosing out two of the worst of these, he sent one on a message to King Morpheus, who rules over the Land of Sleep. He bade him bring back with him a bad, false dream, which Archimago then carried to the sleeping Knight. So cunningly did he contrive the matter, that when the Knight awoke the next morning he never knew that it had only been a dream, but believed that all the things he had seen in his sleep had really happened.

In the meanwhile, Archimago dressed up the other bad spirit to look like Una, so that at a little distance it was impossible to tell any difference in the two figures. He knew that the only way to part Holiness and Truth was to make Holiness believe by some means that Truth was not as good as she appeared to be. He knew also that the Red Cross Knight would believe nothing against the Lady Una except what he saw with his own eyes. Therefore he laid his plans with the greatest care and guile.

Now we shall see how he succeeded in his wicked endeavour.

The Knight forsakes Una

The next morning at daybreak the Knight awoke, sad and unrested after the unpleasant dreams that had come to him in the night. He did not know he had been asleep; he thought the things that troubled him had really happened.

It was scarcely dawn when Archimago rushed up to him in a state of pretended sorrow and indignation.

"The Lady Una has left you," said this wicked mail. "She is not good as she pretends to be. She cares nothing at all for you, nor for the noble work on which you are bound, and she does not mean to go any farther with you on your toilsome journey."

The Red Cross Knight started up in anger. This was like his dream, and he knew not what was true nor what was false.

"Come," said Archimago, "see for yourself."

He pointed to a figure in the distance whom the Knight took to be Una. Then, indeed, he was forced to believe what the wicked magician

told him. He now took for granted that Una had been deceiving him all along, and had seized this moment to escape.

He forgot all her real sweetness and goodness and beauty; he only thought how false and unkind she was. He was filled with anger, and he never paused a moment to reflect if there could be any possibility of mistake. Calling his servant, he bade him bring his horse at once, and then these two immediately set forth again on their journey.

Here the Red Cross Knight was wrong, and we shall see presently into what perils and misfortunes he fell because of his hasty want of faith. If he had had a little patience he would soon have discovered that the figure he saw was only a dressed-up imitation. The real Lady Una all this time was sleeping quietly in her own bower.

When she awoke and found that her two companions had fled in the night and left her alone behind, she was filled with grief and dismay. She could not understand why they should do such a thing. Mounting her white ass, she rode after them with all the speed she could, but the Knight had urged on his steed so fast it was almost useless to try to follow. Yet she never stayed to rest her weary limbs, but went on seeking them over hill and dale, and through wood and plain, sorely grieved in her tender heart that the one she loved best should leave her with such ungentle discourtesy.

When the wicked Archimago saw that his cunning schemes had succeeded so well he was greatly pleased, and set to work to devise fresh mischief. It was Una whom he chiefly hated, and he took great pleasure in her many troubles, for hypocrisy always hates real goodness. He had the power of turning himself into any shape he chose—sometimes he would be a fowl, sometimes a fish, now like a fox, now like a dragon. On the present occasion, to suit his evil purpose, it seemed best to him to put on the appearance of the good knight whom he had so cruelly beguiled.

Therefore, Hypocrisy dressed himself up in imitation armour with a silver shield and everything exactly like the Red Cross Knight. When he sat upon his fiery charger he looked such a splendid warrior you would have thought it was St. George himself.

Holiness fights Faithless, and makes Friends with False Religion

The true St. George, meanwhile, had wandered far away. Now that he had left the Lady Una, he bad nothing but his own will to guide him, and he no longer followed any fixed purpose.

Presently he saw coming to meet him another warrior, fully armed. He was a great, rough fellow, who cared nothing for GOD or man; across his shield, in gay letters, was written "Sans Foy," which means *Faithless*.

He had with him a companion, a handsome lady, dressed all in scarlet, trimmed with gold and rich pearls. She rode a beautiful palfrey, with gay trappings, and little gold bells tinkled on her bridle. The two came along laughing and talking, but when the lady saw the Red Cross Knight, she left off her mirth at once, and bade her companion attack him.

Then the two knights levelled their spears, and rushed at each other. But when Faithless saw the red cross graven on the breastplate of the other, he knew that he could never prevail against that safeguard. However, he fought with great fury, and the Red Cross Knight had a hard battle before he overcame him. At last he managed to kill him, and he told his servant to carry away the shield of Faithless in token of victory.

When the lady saw her champion fall, she fled in terror; but the Red Cross Knight hurried after her, and bade her stay, telling her that she had nothing now to fear. His brave and gentle heart was full of pity to see her in so great distress, and he asked her to tell him who she was, and who was the man that had been with her.

Melting into tears, she then told him the following sad story:—She said that she was the daughter of an emperor, and had been engaged to marry a wise and good prince. Before the wedding-day, however, the prince fell into the hands of his foes, and was cruelly slain. She went

out to look for his dead body, and in the course of her wandering met the Saracen knight, who took her captive. "Sans Foy" was one of three bad brothers. The names of the others were "Sans Loy," which means *Lawless*, and "Sans Joy," which means *Joyless*. She further said that her own name was "Fidessa," or *True Religion*, and she besought the Knight to have compassion on her, because she was so friendless and unhappy.

"Fair lady," said the Knight, "a heart of flint would grieve to hear of your sorrows. But henceforth rest safely assured that you have found a new friend to help you, and lost an old foe to hurt you. A new friend is better than an old foe."

Then the seemingly simple maiden pretended to look comforted, and the two rode on happily together.

But what the lady had told about herself was quite untrue. Her name was not "Fidessa" at all, but "Duessa," which means *False Religion*. If Una had still been with the Knight, he would never have been led astray; but when he parted from her he had nothing but his own feelings to guide him. He still meant to do right, but he was deceived by his false companion, who brought him into much trouble and danger.

Una and the Lion

All this while the Lady Una, lonely and forsaken, was roaming in search of her lost Knight. How sad was her fate! She, a King's daughter, so beautiful, so faithful, so true, who had done no wrong either in word or deed, was left sorrowful and deserted because of the cunning wiles of a wicked enchanter. Fearing nothing, she sought the Red Cross Knight through woods and lonely wilderness, but no tidings of him ever came to her.

One day, being weary, she alighted from her steed, and lay down on the grass to rest. It was in the midst of a thicket, far from the sight of any traveller. She lifted her veil, and put aside the black cloak which always covered her dress.

"Her angel's face,
As the great eye of Heaven shinèd bright,
And made a sunshine in the shady place."

Suddenly, out of the wood there rushed a fierce lion, who, seeing Una, sprang at her to devour her; but, when he came nearer, he was amazed at the sight of her loveliness, and all his rage turned to pity. Instead of tearing her to pieces, he kissed her weary feet and licked her lily hand as if he knew how innocent and wronged she was.*

When Una saw the gentleness of this kingly creature, she could not help weeping.

Sad to see her sorrow, he stood gazing at her; all his angry mood changed to compassion, till at last Una mounted her snowy palfrey and once more set out to seek her lost companion.

The lion would not leave her desolate, but went with her as a strong guard and as a faithful companion. When she slept he kept watch, and when she waked he waited diligently, ready to help her in any way he could. He always knew from her looks what she wanted.

Long she travelled thus through lonely places, where she thought her wandering Knight might pass, yet never found trace of living man.

*The figure of the lion may be taken as the emblem of *Honour*, which always pays respect to *Truth*.

At length she came to the foot of a steep mountain, where the trodden grass showed that there was a path for people to go. This path she followed till at last she saw, slowly walking in the front of her, a damsel carrying a jar of water.

The Lady Una called to her to ask if there were any dwelling-place near, but the rough-looking girl made no answer; she seemed not able to speak, nor hear, nor understand. But when she saw the lion standing beside her, she threw down her pitcher with sudden fear and fled away. Never before in that land had she seen the face of a fair lady, and the sight of the lion filled her with terror. Fast away she fled, and never looked behind till she came at last to her home, where her blind mother sat all day in darkness. Too frightened to speak, she caught hold of her mother with trembling hands, while the poor old woman, full of fear, ran to shut the door of their house.

By this time the weary Lady Una had arrived, and asked if she might come in; but, when no answer came to her request, the lion, with his strong claws, tore open the wicket-door and let her into the little hut. There she found the mother and daughter crouched up in a dark corner, nearly dead with fear.

The name of the poor old blind woman was *Superstition*. She tried to be good in a very mistaken way. She hid herself in her dark corner, and was quite content never to come out of it. When the beautiful Lady Una, who was all light and truth, came to the hut, the mother and daughter, instead of making her welcome, hated her, and would gladly have thrust her out.

Trying to soothe their needless dread, Una spoke gently to them, and begged that she might rest that night in their small cottage. To this they unwillingly agreed, and Una lay down with the faithful lion at her feet to keep watch. All night, instead of sleeping, she wept, still sorrowing for her lost Knight and longing for the morning.

In the middle of the night, when all the inmates of the little cottage were asleep, there came a furious knocking at the door. This was a wicked thief, called "Kirkrapine," or *Church-robber*, whose custom it was to go about stealing ornaments from churches, and clothes from clergymen, and robbing the alms-boxes of the poor. He used to share his spoils with the: daughter of the blind woman, and to-night he had come with a great sackful of stolen goods.

When he received no answer to his knocking, he got very angry indeed, and made a loud clamour at the door; but the women in the hut were too much afraid of the lion to rise and let him in. At last he burst open the door in a great rage and tried to enter, but the lion sprang upon him and tore him to pieces before he could even call for help. His terrified friends scarcely dared to weep or move in case they should share his fate.

When daylight came, Una rose and started again on her journey with the lion to seek the wandering Knight. As soon as they had left, the two frightened women came forth, and, finding Church-robber slain outside the cottage, they began to wail and lament; then they ran after Una, railing at her for being the cause of all their ill; they called after her evil wishes that mischief and misery might fall on her and follow her all the way, and that she might ever wander in endless error.

When they saw that their bad words were of no avail, they turned back, and there in the road they met a knight, clad in armour; but, though he looked such a grand warrior, it was really only the wicked enchanter, Hypocrisy, who was seeking Una, in order to work her fresh trouble. When he saw the old woman, Superstition, he asked if she could give him any tidings of the lady. Therewith her passion broke out anew; she told him what had just happened, blaming Una as the cause of all her distress. Archimago pretended to condole with her, and then, finding out the direction in which Una had gone, he followed as quickly as possible.

Before long he came up to where Una was slowly travelling; but seeing the noble lion at her side, he was afraid to go too near, and turned

away to a hill at a little distance. When Una saw him, she thought, from his shield and armour, that it was her own true knight, and she rode up to him, and spoke meekly, half-frightened.

"Ah, my lord," she said, "where have you been so long out of my sight? I feared that you hated me, or that I had done something to displease you, and that made everything seem dark and cheerless. But welcome now, welcome!"

"My dearest lady," said false Hypocrisy, "you must not think I could so shame knighthood as to desert you. But the truth is, the reason why I left you so long was to seek adventure in a strange place, where Archimago said there was a mighty robber, who worked much mischief to many people. Now he will trouble no one further. This is the good reason why I left you. Pray believe it, and accept my faithful service, for I have vowed to defend you by land and sea. Let your grief be over."

When Una heard these sweet words it seemed to her that she was fully rewarded for all the trials she had gone through. One loving hour can make up for many years of sorrow. She forgot all that she had suffered; she spoke no more of the past. True love never looks back, but always forward. Before her stood her Knight, for whom she had toiled so sorely, and Una's heart was filled with joy.

In the Hands of the Enemy

Una and the Magician (who was disguised as the Red Cross Knight) had not gone far when they saw some one riding swiftly towards them. The new-comer was on a fleet horse, and was fully armed; his look was stern, cruel, and revengeful. On his shield in bold letters was traced the name "Sans Loy," which means *Lawless*. He was one of the brothers of "Sans Foy," or Faithless, whom the real Red Cross Knight had slain, and he had made up his mind to avenge his brother's death.

When he saw the red cross graven on the shield which Hypocrisy carried, he thought that he had found the foe of whom he was in search, and, levelling his spear, he prepared for battle. Hypocrisy, who was a mean coward, and had never fought in his life, was nearly fainting with fear; but the Lady Una spoke such cheering words that he be-

gan to feel more hopeful. Lawless, however, rushed at him with such fury that he drove his lance right through the other's shield, and bore him to the ground. Leaping from his horse, he ran towards him, meaning to kill him, and exclaiming, "Lo, this is the worthy reward of him that slew Faithless!"

Una begged the cruel knight to have pity on his fallen foe, but her words were of no avail. Tearing off his helmet, Lawless would have slain him at once, but he stopped in astonishment when, instead of the Red Cross Knight, he saw the face of Archimago. He knew well that crafty Hypocrisy was skilled in all forms of deceit, but that he took care to shun fighting and brave deeds. Now, indeed, had Hypocrisy's guile met with a just punishment.

"Why, luckless Archimago, what is this?" cried Lawless. "What evil chance brought you here? Is it your fault, or my mistake, that I have wounded my friend instead of my foe?"

But the old Magician answered nothing; he lay still as if he were dying. So Lawless spent no more time over him, but went over to where Una waited, lost in amazement and sorely perplexed.

Her companion, whom she had imagined was her own true Knight, turned out to be nothing but an impostor, and she herself had fallen into the hands of a cruel enemy. When the brave lion saw Lawless go up to Una and try to drag her roughly from her palfrey, full of kingly rage he rushed to protect her. He flew at Lawless and almost tore his shield to pieces with his sharp claws. But, alas! he could not overcome the warrior, for Lawless was one of the strongest men that ever wielded spear, and was well skilled in feats of arms. With his sharp sword he struck the lion, and the noble creature fell dead at his feet.

Poor Una, what was to become of her now? Her faithful guardian was gone, and she found herself the captive of a cruel foe. Lawless paid no heed to her tears and entreaties. Placing her on his own horse, he rode off with her; while her snow-white ass, not willing to forsake her, followed meekly at a distance.

The House of Pride

Now the Red Cross Knight, because of his lack of loyalty to Una, fell into much danger and difficulty. His first fault was in believing evil of her so readily, and leaving her forlorn; after that he was too easily beguiled by the pretended goodness and beauty of Duessa. All who fight in a good cause must beware of errors such as these. If matters do not go exactly as we wish, we must not lose heart and get impatient; even if we cannot understand what is happening, we must trust that all will be well. We must keep steadily to the one true aim set before us, or else, like the Red Cross Knight, we may be led astray by false things that are only pleasant in appearance, and have no real goodness.

Duessa and the Knight travelled for a long way, till at last they saw in front of them a grand and beautiful building. It seemed as if it were the house of some mighty Prince; a broad highway led up to it, all trodden bare by the feet of those who flocked thither. Great troops of people of all sorts and condition journeyed here, both by day and night.

But few returned, unless they managed to escape, beggared and disgraced, when, ever afterwards, they lived a life of misery.

To this place Duessa guided the Red Cross Knight, for she was tired with the toilsome journey, and the day was nearly over.

It was a stately palace, built of smooth bricks, cunningly laid together without mortar. The walls were high, but neither strong nor thick, and they were covered with dazzling gold-foil. There were many lofty towers and picturesque galleries, with bright windows and delightful bowers; and on the top there was a dial to tell the time.

It was lovely to look at, and did much credit to the workman that designed it; but it was a great pity that so fair a building rested on so frail a foundation. For it was mounted high up on a sandy hill that kept shifting and falling away. Every breath of heaven made it shake; and all the back parts, that no one could see, were old and ruinous, though cunningly painted over.

Arrived here, Duessa and the Red Cross Knight passed in at once, for the gates stood wide open to all. They were in charge of a porter, called "Ill-come," who never denied entrance to any one. The hall inside was hung with costly tapestry and rich curtains. Numbers of people, rich and poor, were waiting here, in order to gain sight of the Lady of this wonderful place.

Duessa and the Knight passed through this crowd, who all gazed at them, and entered the Presence Chamber of the Queen.

What a dazzling sight met. their eyes! Such a scene of splendour had never been known in the court of any living prince. A noble company of lords and ladies stood on every side, and made the place more beautiful with their presence.

High above all there was a cloth of state, and a rich throne as bright as' the sun. On the throne, clad in royal robes, sat the Queen. Her garments were all glittering with gold and precious jewels; but so great was her beauty that it dimmed even the brightness of her throne. She sat there in princely state, shining like the sun. She hated and despised all lowly things of earth. Under her scornful feet lay a dreadful dragon, with a hideous tall. In her hand she held a mirror in which she often looked at her face; she took great delight in her own appearance, for she was fairer than any living woman.

"Lo! underneath her scornful feet was layne
A dreadful dragon with an hideous trayne;
And in her hand she held a mirrhour bright,
Wherein her face she often viewed fayne,
And in her self-loved semblance took delight."

She was the daughter of grisly Pluto, King of Hades, and men called her proud Lucifera. She had crowned herself a queen, but she had no rightful kingdom at all, nor any possessions. The power which she had obtained she had usurped by wrong and tyranny. She ruled her realm not by laws, but by craft, and according to the advice of six old wizards, who with their bad counsels upheld her kingdom.

As soon as the Knight and Duessa came into the presence-chamber, an usher, by name *Vanity*, made room and prepared a passage for them, and brought them to the lowest stair of the high throne. Here they made a humble salute, and declared that they had come to see the Queen's royal state, and to prove if the wide report of her great splendour were true.

With scornful eyes, half unwilling to look so low, she thanked them disdainfully, and did not show them any courtesy worthy of a queen, scarcely even bidding them arise. The lords and ladies of the court, however, were all eager to appear well in the eyes of the strangers. They shook out their ruffles, and fluffed up their curls, and arranged their gay attire more trimly; and each one was jealous and spiteful of the others.

They did their best to entertain the Knight, and would gladly have made him one of their company. To Duessa, also, they were most polite and gracious, for formerly she had been well known in that court. But to the knightly eyes of the warrior all the glitter of the crowd seemed vain and worthless, and he thought that it was unbefitting so great a queen to treat a strange knight with such scant courtesy.

Suddenly, Queen Lucifera rose from her throne, and called for her coach. Then all was bustle and confusion, every one rushing violently forth. Blazing with brightness she paced down the hall, like the sun dawning in the east. All the people thronging the hall thrust and pushed each other aside to gaze upon her. Her glorious appearance amazed the eyes of all men.

Her coach was adorned with gold and gay garlands, and was one of the most splendid carriages ever seen, but it was drawn by an ugly and ill-matched team. On every animal rode one of her evil Councillors, who was much like in nature to the creature that carried him.

The first of these, who guided all the rest, was *Idleness*, the nurse of

". . . This was drawne of six unequall beasts
On which her six sage Counsellours did ryde."

Sin. He chose to ride a slothful ass; he looked always as if he were half asleep, and as if he did not know whether it were night or day. He shut himself away from all care, and shunned manly exercise, but if there were any mischief to be done he joined in it readily. The Queen was indeed badly served who had Idleness for her leading Councillor.

Next to him came *Gluttony*, riding on a pig; then *Self-indulgence* on a goat, *Avarice* on a camel, *Envy* on a wolf, and *Wrath* on a lion. Each in his own way was equally hideous and hateful.

As they went along, crowds of people came round, shouting for joy; always before them a foggy mist sprang up, covering all the land, and under their feet lay the dead bones of men who had wandered from the right path.

So forth they went in this goodly array to enjoy the fresh air, and to sport in the flowery meadows. Among the rest, next to the chariot, rode the false Duessa, but the good Knight kept far apart, not joining in the noisy mirth which seemed unbefitting a true warrior.

Having enjoyed themselves awhile in the pleasant fields, they returned to the stately palace. Here they found that a wandering knight had just arrived. On his shield, in red letters, was written the name "Sans Joy," which means *Joyless*, and he was the brother of *Faithless*, whom the Red Cross Knight had slain, and of *Lawless*, who had taken Una captive. He looked sullen and revengeful, as if he had in his mind bitter and angry thoughts.

When he saw the shield of his slain brother, Faithless, in the hands of the Red Cross Knight's page, he sprang at him and snatched it away. But the Knight had no mind to lose the trophy which he had won in battle, and, attacking him fiercely, he again got possession of it.

Thereupon they hastily began to prepare for battle, clashing their shields and shaking their swords in the air. But the Queen, on pain of her severe displeasure, commanded them to restrain their fury, saying that if either had a right to the shield, they should fight it out fairly the next day.

That night was passed in joy and gaiety, feasting and making merry in bower and hall. The steward of the court was *Gluttony*, who poured forth lavishly of his abundance to all; and then the chamberlain, *Sloth*, summoned them to rest.

The Battle for the Shield

That night, when every one slept, Duessa stole secretly to the lodgings of the pagan knight Joyless. She found him wide awake, restless, and troubled, busily devising how he might annoy his foe. To him she spoke many untrue words.

"Dear joyless," she said, "I am so glad that you have come. I have passed many sad hours for the sake of Faithless, whom this traitor slew. He has treated me very cruelly, keeping me shut up in a dark cave; but now I will take shelter with you from his disdainful spite. To you belongs the inheritance of your brother, Faithless. Let him not be unavenged."

"Fair lady, grieve no more for past sorrows," said Joyless; "neither be afraid of present peril, for needless fear never profited any one, nor is it any good to lament over misfortunes that cannot be helped. Faithless is dead, his troubles are over; but I live, and I will avenge him."

"Oh, but I fear what may happen," she answered, "and the advantage is on his side."

"Why, lady, what advantage can there be when both fight alike?" asked Joyless.

"Yes, but he bears a charmed shield," said Duessa, "and also enchanted armour that no one can pierce. None can wound the man that wears them."

"Charmed or enchanted, I care not at all," said Joyless fiercely, "nor need you tell me anything more about them. But, fair lady, go back whence you came and test awhile. To-morrow I shall subdue the Red Cross Knight, and give you the heritage of dead Faithless."

"Wherever I am, my secret aid shall follow you," she answered, and then she left him.

At the first gleam of dawn the Red Cross Knight sprang up and dressed himself for battle in his sun-bright armour. Forth he stepped into the hall, where there were many waiting to gaze at him, curious to know what fate was in store for the stranger knight. Many minstrels were there, making melody to drive away sadness; many singers that

could tune their voices skilfully to harp and viol; many chroniclers that could tell old stories of love and war.

Soon after, came the pagan knight, Joyless, warily armed in woven mail. He looked sternly at the Red Cross Knight, who cared not at all how any living creature looked at him. Cups of wine were brought to the warriors, with dainty Eastern spices, and they both swore a solemn oath to observe faithfully the laws of just and fair fighting.

At last, with royal pomp, came the Queen. She was led to a railed-in space of the green field, and placed under a stately canopy. On the other side, full in all men's view, sat Duessa, and on a tree near was hung the shield of Faithless. Both Duessa and the shield were to be given to the victor.

A shrill trumpet bade them prepare for battle. The pagan knight was stout and strong, and his blows fell like great iron hammers. He fought for cruelty and vengeance. The Red Cross Knight was fierce, and full of youthful courage; he fought for praise and honour. So furious was their onslaught that sparks of fire flew from their shields, and deep marks were hewn in their helmets.

Thus they fought, the one for wrong, the other for right, and each tried to put his foe to shame. At last Joyless chanced to look at his brother's shield which was hanging near. The sight of this doubled his anger, and he struck at his foe with such fury that the Knight reeled twice, and seemed likely to fall. To those who looked on, the end of the battle appeared doubtful, and false Duessa began to call loudly to Joyless,—

"Thine the shield, and I, and all!"

Directly the Red Cross Knight heard her voice he woke out of the faintness that had overcome him; his faith, which had grown weak, suddenly became strong, and he shook off the deadly cold that was creeping over him.

This time he attacked joyless with such vigour that he brought him down upon his knees. Lifting his sword, he would have slain him, when suddenly a dark cloud fell between them. Joyless was seen no more; he had vanished! The Knight called aloud to him, but received no answer: his foe was completely hidden by the darkness.

Duessa rose hastily from her place, and ran to the Red Cross Knight, saving,—

"O noblest Knight, be angry no longer! Some evil power has covered your enemy with the cloud of night, and borne him away to the regions of darkness. The conquest is yours, I am yours, the shield and the glory are yours."

Then the trumpets sounded, and running heralds made humble homage, and the shield, the cause of all the enmity, was brought to the Red Cross Knight. He went to the Queen, and, kneeling before her, offered her his service, which she accepted with thanks and much satisfaction, greatly praising his chivalry.

So they marched home, the Knight next the Queen, while all the people followed with great glee, shouting and clapping their hands. When they got to the palace the Knight was given gentle attendants and skilled doctors, for he had been badly hurt in the fight. His wounds were washed with wine, and oil, and healing herbs, and all the while lovely music was played round his bed to beguile him from grief and pain.

While this was happening, Duessa secretly left the palace, and stole away to the Kingdom of Darkness, which is ruled over by the Queen of Night. This queen was a friend of her own, and was always ready to help in any bad deeds. Duessa told her of what had befallen the pagan knight, joyless, and persuaded her to carry him away to her own dominions. Here he was placed under the care of a wonderful doctor, who was able to cure people by magic, and Duessa hastened back to the House of Pride.

When she got there she was dismayed to find that the Red Cross Knight had already left, although he was not nearly healed from the wounds which he had received in battle.

The reason why he left was this. One day his servant, whose name you may remember was Prudence, came and told him that he had discovered in the palace a huge, deep dungeon, full of miserable prisoners. Hundreds of men and women were there, wailing and lamenting-grand lords and beautiful ladies, who, from foolish behaviour or love of idle pomp, had wasted their wealth and fallen into the power of the wicked Queen of Pride. When the good Red Cross Knight heard this, he determined to stay no longer in such a place of peril.

Rising before dawn, he left by a small side door, for he knew that if he were seen he would be at once put to death. To him the place no more seemed beautiful; it filled him with horror and disgust. Riding under the castle wall, the way was strewn with hundreds of dead bodies of those who had perished miserably. Such was the dreadful sight of the House of Pride.

Una and the Woodland Knight

We left Una in a piteous plight, in the hands of a cruel enemy, the pagan knight Lawless.

Paying no heed to her tears and entreaties, he placed her on his horse, and rode off with her till he came to a great forest.

Una was almost in despair, for there seemed no hope of any rescue. But suddenly there came a wonderful way of deliverance.

In the midst of the thick wood Lawless halted to rest. This forest was inhabited by numbers of strange wild creatures, quite untaught, almost savages. Hearing Una's cries for help, they came flocking up to see what was the matter. Their fierce, rough appearance so frightened Lawless that he jumped on to his horse and rode away as fast as he could.

When the wild wood-folk came up they found Una sitting desolate and alone. They were amazed at such a strange sight, and pitied her sad condition. They all stood astonished at her loveliness, and could not imagine how she had come there.

Una, for her part, was greatly terrified, not knowing whether some fresh danger awaited her. Half in fear, half in hope, she sat still in amazement. Seeing that she looked so sorrowful, the savages tried to show that they meant to be friendly. They smiled, and came forward gently, and kissed her feet. Then she guessed that their hearts were kind, and she arose fearlessly and went with them, no longer afraid of any evil.

Full of gladness, they led her along, shouting and singing and dancing round her, and strewing all the ground with green branches, as if she had been a queen. Thus they brought her to their chief, old Sylvanus.

When Sylvanus saw her., like the rest he was astonished at her beauty, for he had never seen anything so fair. Her fame spread through the forest, and all the other dwellers in it came to look at her. The Hamadryads, who live in the trees, and the Naiades, who live in the flowing fountains, all came flocking to see her lovely face. As for the woodlanders, henceforth they thought no one on earth fair but Una.

Glad at such good fortune, Una was quite contented to please the simple folk. She stayed a long while with them, to gather strength after her many troubles. During this time she did her best to teach them, but the poor things were so ignorant, it was almost impossible to make them understand the difference between right and wrong.

It chanced one day that a noble knight came to the forest to seek his kindred who dwelt there. He had won much glory in wars abroad, and distant lands were filled with his fame. He was honest, faithful, and true, though not very polished in manner, nor accustomed to a courtly life. His name was Sir Satyrane. He had been born and brought up in the forest, and his father had taught him nothing but to be utterly fearless. When he grew up, and could master everything in the forest, he went abroad to fight foreign foes, and his fame was soon carried through all lands. It was always his custom, after some time spent in labour and adventure, to return for a while to his native woods, and so it happened on this occasion that he came across Una.

The first time he saw her she was surrounded by the savages, whom she was trying to teach good and holy things. Sir Satyrane wondered at the wisdom which fell from her sweet lips, and when, later on, he saw her gentle and kindly deeds, he began to admire and love her. Although noble at heart, he had never had any one to teach him, but now he began to learn from Una faith and true religion.

The False Pilgrim

Una's thoughts were still fixed on the Red Cross Knight, and she was sorry to think of his perilous wandering. She was always sad at heart, and spent her time planning how to escape. At last she told her wish to Sir Satyrane, who, glad to please her in any way, began to devise how he could help her to get free from the savage folk. One day, when Una was left alone, all the woodlanders having gone to pay court to their chief, old Sylvanus, she and Sir Satyrane rode away together, They went so fast and so carefully that no one could overtake them, and thus at last they came to the end of the forest, and out into the open plain.

Towards evening, after they had journeyed a long distance, they met a traveller. He seemed as if he were a poor, simple pilgrim; his clothes were dusty and travel-worn; his face brown and scorched with the sun; he leant upon a staff, and carried all his necessaries in a scrip, or little bag, hanging behind.

Sir Satyrane asked if there were any tidings of new adventures, but the stranger had heard of none. Then Una began to ask if he knew anything about a knight who wore on his shield a red cross.

"Alas! dear lady," he replied, "I may well grieve to tell you the sad news! I have seen that knight with my own eyes, both alive and also dead."

When Una heard these cruel words she was filled with sorrow and dismay, and begged the pilgrim to tell her everything he knew.

Then he related how on that very morning he had seen two knights preparing for battle. One was a pagan, the other was the Red Cross Knight. They fought with great fury, and in the end the Red Cross Knight was slain.

This story was altogether false. The pretended pilgrim was no other than the wicked enchanter Archimago, or *Hypocrisy*, in a fresh disguise. But Sir Satyrane and Una believed everything he told them.

"Where is this pagan now? asked Satyrane.

"Not far from here," replied the pilgrim; "I left him resting beside a fountain."

Thereupon Sir Satyrane hastily marched off, and soon came to the place where he guessed that the other would be found. This pagan knight turned out to be Lawless, from whom, you may remember, Una had escaped in the forest, before she was found by the woodlanders. Sir Satyrane challenged Lawless to fight, and they were soon engaged in a fierce battle. Poor Una was so terrified at this new peril, and in such dread of Lawless, that she did not wait to see what the end would be, but fled far away as fast as she could.

Archimago had been watching everything from a secret hiding-place. Now, when he saw Una escaping. he quickly followed, for he hoped to be able to work her some further mischief.

" The Knight, approaching nigh, of him inquired
Tidings of warre, and of adventures new."

Giant Pride

When Duessa found that the Red Cross Knight had left the palace of Queen Lucifera, she immediately set out in search of him. It was not long before she found him where he sat wearily by the side of a fountain to rest himself. He had taken off all his armour, and his steed was cropping the grass close by. It was pleasant in the cool shade, and the soft wind blew refreshingly upon his forehead, while, in the trees above, numbers of singing birds delighted him with their sweet music.

Duessa at first pretended to be angry with the Knight for leaving her so unkindly, but they were soon good friends again. They stayed for some time beside the fountain, where the green boughs sheltered them from the scorching heat.

But although it looked so lovely and tempting, the fountain near which they sat was an enchanted one. Whoever tasted its waters grew faint and feeble.

The Knight, not knowing this, stooped down to drink of the stream, which was as clear as crystal. Then all his strength turned to weakness, his courage melted away, and a deadly chill crept over him.

At first he scarcely noticed the change, for he had grown careless both of himself and of his fame. But suddenly he heard a dreadful sound—a loud bellowing which echoed through the wood. The earth seemed to shake with terror, and all the trees trembled. The Knight, astounded, started up, and tried to seize his weapons. But before he could put on his armour, or get his shield, his monstrous enemy came stalking into sight.

It was a hideous Giant, great and horrible. The ground groaned under him. He was taller than three of the tallest men put together. His name was Orgoglio, or *Pride*, and his father's name was *Ignorance*. He was puffed up with arrogance and conceit, and because he was so big and strong he despised every one else. He leant upon a gnarled oak, which he had torn up by its roots from the earth; it also served him as a weapon to dismay his foemen.

When he saw the Knight he advanced to him with dreadful fury.

The latter, quite helpless, all in vain tried to prepare for battle. Disarmed, disgraced, inwardly dismayed, and faint in every limb, he could scarcely wield even his useless blade. The Giant aimed such a merciless stroke at him, that if it had touched him it would have crushed him to powder. But the Knight leapt lightly to one side, and thus escaped the blow. So great, however, was the wind that the club made in whirling through the air that the Knight was overthrown, and lay on the ground stunned.

When Giant Pride saw his enemy lying helpless, he lifted up his club to kill him, but Duessa called to him to stay his hand.

"O great Orgoglio," she cried, "spare him for my sake, and do not kill him. Now that he is vanquished make him your bond-slave, and, if you like, I will be your wife!"

Giant Pride was quite pleased with this arrangement, and, taking up the Red Cross Knight before he could awake from his swoon, he carried him hastily to his castle, and flung him, without pity, into a deep dungeon.

As for Duessa, from that day forth she was treated with the greatest honour. She was given gold and purple to wear, and a triple crown was placed upon her head, and every one had to obey her as if she were a queen. To make her more dreaded, Orgoglio gave her a hideous dragon to ride. This dragon had seven heads, with gleaming eyes, and its body seemed made of iron and brass. Everything good that came within its reach it swept away with a great long tail, and then trampled under foot.

All the people's hearts were filled with terror when they saw Duessa riding on her dragon.

Prince Arthur

When the Red Cross Knight was made captive by Giant Pride and carried away, Prudence, his servant, who had seen his master's fall, sorrowfully collected his forsaken possessions-his mighty armour, missing when most needed, his silver shield, now idle and masterless, so his sharp spear that had done good service in many a fray. With these he departed to tell his sad tale.

He had not gone far when he met Una, flying from the scene of battle, while Sir Satyrane hindered Lawless from pursuing her. When she saw Prudence carrying the armour of the Red Cross Knight, she guessed something terrible had happened, and fell to the ground as if she were dying of sorrow.

Unhappy Prudence would gladly have died himself, but he did his best to restore Una to life. When she had recovered she implored him to tell. her what had occurred.

Then the dwarf told her everything that had taken place since they parted. How the crafty Archimago had deceived the Red Cross Knight by his wiles, and made him believe that Una had left him; how the Knight had slain Faithless and had taken pity on Duessa because of the false tales she told. Prudence also told Una all about the House of Pride and its perils; he described the fight which the Knight had with Joyless, and lastly, he told about the luckless conflict with the great Giant Pride, when the Knight was made captive, whether living or dead he knew not.

Una listened patiently, and bravely tried to master her sorrow, which almost broke her heart, for she dearly loved the Red Cross Knight, for whose sake she had borne so many troubles. At last she rose, quite resolved to find him, alive or dead. The dwarf pointed out the way by which Giant Pride had carried his prisoner, and Una started on her quest. Long she wandered, through woods and across valleys, high over hills, and low among the dales, tossed by storms and beaten by the wind, but still keeping steadfast to her purpose.

At last she chanced by good fortune to meet a knight, marching with his squire. This knight was the most glorious she had ever seen. His glittering armour shone far off, like the glancing light of the brightest ray of sunshine; it covered him from top to toe, and left no place unguarded. Across his breast he wore: a splendid belt, covered with jewels that sparkled like stars. Among the jewels was one of great value, which shone with such brilliancy that it amazed all who beheld it. Close to this jewel hung the knight's sword, in an ivory sheath, carved with curious devices. The hilt was of burnished gold, the handle of mother-of-pearl, and it was buckled on with a golden clasp.

The helmet of this knight was also of gold, and for crest it had a golden dragon with wings. On the top of all was a waving plume, decked with sprinkled pearls, which shook and danced in every little breath of wind.

The shield of the warrior was closely covered, and might never be seen by mortal eye. It was not made of steel nor of brass, but of one perfect and entire diamond. This had been hewn out of the adamant rock with mighty engines; no point of spear could ever pierce it, nor dint of sword break it asunder.

This shield the knight never showed to mortals, unless he wished to dismay some huge monster or to frighten large armies that fought unfairly against him. No magic arts nor enchanter's spell had any power against it. Everything that was not exactly what it seemed to be faded before it and fell to ruin.

The maker of the shield was supposed to be Merlin, a mighty magician; he made it with the sword and armour for this young prince when the latter first took to arms.

The name of the knight was Prince Arthur, type of all Virtue and Magnificence, and pattern of all true Knighthood.

His squire bore after him his spear of ebony wood; he was a gallant and noble youth, who managed his fiery steed with much skill and courage.

When Prince Arthur came near Una, he greeted her with much courtesy. By her unwilling answers he guessed that some secret sorrow was troubling her, and he hoped that his gentle and kindly words would persuade her to tell him the cause of her grief.

"What good will it do to speak of it?" said Una.

When I think of my sorrow it seems to me better to keep it hidden than to make it worse by speaking of it. Nothing in the world can lighten my misfortunes. My last comfort is to be left alone to weep for them."

"Ah, dear lady," said the gentle Knight, "I know well that your grief is great, for it makes me sad even to hear you speak of it. But let me entreat you to tell me what is troubling you. Misfortunes may be overcome by good advice, and wise counsel will lessen the worst injury. He who never tells of his hurts will never find help."

His words were so kind and reasonable that Una was soon persuaded to tell him her whole story. She began with the time when she had gone to the Court of Queen Gloriana to seek a champion to release her parents from the horrible dragon, and ended with the account of how the Red Cross Knight had fallen a prey to Giant Pride, who now held him captive in a dark dungeon.

"Truly, lady, you have much cause to grieve," said Prince Arthur when the story was finished. "But be of good cheer, and take comfort. Rest assured I will never forsake you until I have set free your captive Knight."

His cheerful words revived Una's drooping heart, and so they set forth on their journey, Prudence guiding them in the right way.

The Wondrous Bugle and the Mighty Shield

Badly indeed would it now have fared with the Red Cross Knight had it not been for the Lady Una. Even good people daily fall into sin and temptation, but as often as their own foolish pride or weakness leads them astray, so often will Divine love and care rescue them, if only they repent of their misdoings. Thus we see how Holiness, in the guise of the Red Cross Knight, was for a while cast down and defeated; yet in the end, because he truly repented, help was given him to fight again and conquer.

Prince Arthur and the Lady Una travelled till they came to a castle which was built very strong and high.

"Lo," cried the dwarf, "yonder is the place where my unhappy master is held captive by that cruel tyrant!"

The Prince at once dismounted, and bade Una stay to see what would happen. He marched with his squire to the castle walls, where he found the gates shut fast. There was no warder to guard them, nor to answer to the call of any who came.

Then the squire took a small bugle which hung at his side with twisted gold and gay tassels. Wonderful stories were told about that bugle; every one trembled with dread at its shrill sound. It could easily be heard three miles off, and whenever it was blown it echoed three times. No false enchantment or deceitful snare could stand before the terror of that blast. No gate was so strong, no lock so firm and fast, but at that piercing noise it flew open or burst.

This was the bugle which Prince Arthur's squire blew before the gate of Giant Pride. Then the whole castle quaked, and every door flew open. The Giant himself, dismayed at the sound, came rushing forth in haste from an inner bower, to see what was the reason of this sudden uproar, and to discover who had dared to brave his power. After him came Duessa, riding on her dragon with the seven heads; every head had a crown on it, and a fiery tongue of flame.

When Prince Arthur saw Giant Pride, he took his mighty shield and flew at him fiercely; the Giant lifted up his club to smite him, but the Prince leaped to one side, and the weapon, missing him, buried itself with such force in the ground, that the Giant could not quickly pull it out again. Then with his sharp sword Prince Arthur struck at the Giant, and wounded him severely.

Duessa, seeing her companion's danger, urged forward her dragon to help him, but the brave squire sprang in between it and the Prince, and with his drawn sword drove it back. Then the angry Duessa took a golden cup, which she always carried, and which was full of a secret poison. Those who drank of that cup either died, or else felt despair seize them. She lightly sprinkled the squire with the contents of this cup, and immediately his courage faded away, and he was filled with sudden dread. He fell down before the cruel dragon, who seized him with its claws, and nearly crushed the life out of him. He had no power nor will to stir.

When Prince Arthur saw what had happened, he left Giant Pride and turned against the dragon, for he was deeply grieved to see his beloved squire in such peril. He soon drove back the horrible creature, but now once again the Giant rushed at him with his club. This time the blow struck the Prince with such force, that it bore him to the ground. In the fall, his shield, that had been covered, lost by chance its veil, and flew open.

Then through the air flashed such a blazing brightness, that no eye could bear to look upon it. Giant Pride let fall the weapon with which he was just going to slay the Prince, and the dragon was struck blind, and tumbled on the ground.

"Oh, help, Orgoglio, help, or we all perish!" cried Duessa.

Gladly would Giant Pride have helped her, but all was in vain; when that light shone he had no power to hurt others, nor to defend himself; so Prince Arthur soon killed him.

When he was dead, his great body, that had seemed so big and strong, suddenly melted away, and nothing was left but what looked like the shrivelled skin of a broken balloon; for, after all, there was no real substance in him, but he was simply puffed out with emptiness and conceit, and his grand appearance was nothing but a sham.

So that was the end of Giant Pride.

When false Duessa saw the fall of Giant Pride she flung down her golden cup, and threw aside her crown, and fled away. But the squire followed, and soon took her prisoner. Telling him to keep safe guard on her, Prince Arthur boldly entered the Giant's Castle. Not a living creature could he spy; he called loudly, but no one answered; a solemn silence reigned everywhere, not a voice was to be heard, not a person seen, in bower or hall.

At last an old, old man, with beard as white as snow, came creeping along; he guided his feeble steps with a staff, for long ago his sight had failed. On his arm he bore a bunch of keys, all covered with rust. They were the keys of all the doors inside the castle; they were never used, but he still kept possession of them.

It was curious to see the way in which this old man walked, for always, as he went forward, he kept his wrinkled face turned back, as if he were trying to look behind. He was the keeper of the place, and the father of the dead Giant Pride; his name was *Ignorance*.

Prince Arthur, as was fitting, honoured his grey hair and gravity, and gently asked him where all the people were who used to live in that stately building. The old man softly answered him that he could not tell. Again the Prince asked where was the Knight whom the Giant had taken captive?

"I cannot tell," said the old man.

Then the Prince asked which was the way into the castle, and again he got the same answer, "I cannot tell."

At first he thought the man was mocking him, and began to be much displeased. But presently, seeing that the poor old thing could not help his foolishness, he wisely calmed his anger. Going up to him he took the keys from his arm, and made an entrance for himself. He opened each door without the least difficulty; there was no one to challenge him, nor any bars to hinder his passage.

Inside the castle he found the whole place fitted up in the most splendid manner, decked with royal tapestry, and shining with gold, fit for the presence of the greatest prince. But all the floors were dirty, and strewn with ashes, for it was here that the wicked Giant Pride used to slay his unhappy victims.

Prince Arthur sought through every room, but nowhere could he find the Red Cross Knight. At last he came to an iron door, which was

"Whome when his Lady saw, to him she ran
With hasty joy: to see him made her glad,
And sad to view his visage pale and wan."

fast locked, but he found no key among the bunch to open it. In the, door, however, there was a little grating, and through this the Prince called as loudly as be could, to know if there were any living person shut up there whom he could set free.

Then there came a hollow voice in answer. "Oh, who is that who brings to me the happy choice of death? Here I lie, dying every hour, yet still compelled to live, bound in horrible darkness. Three months have come and gone since I beheld the light of day. Oh, welcome, you who bring true tidings of death."

When Prince Arthur heard these words his heart was so filled with pity and horror at any noble knight being thus shamefully treated, that, in his strength and indignation, he rent open the iron door. But entering, he found no floor; there was a deep descent, as dark as a pit, from which came up a horrible deadly smell.

Neither darkness, however, nor dirt, nor poisonous smell could turn the Prince from his purpose, and he went forward courageously. With great trouble and difficulty he found means to raise the captive, whose own limbs were too feeble to bear him, and then he carried him out of the castle.

What a mournful picture was now the Red Cross Knight! His dull, sunken eyes could not bear the unaccustomed light of the sun; his cheeks were thin and gaunt; his mighty arms, that had fought so often and so bravely, were nothing now but bones; all his strength was gone, and all his flesh shrunk up like a withered flower.

When Una saw Prince Arthur carrying the Red Cross Knight out of the castle she ran to them joyfully; it made her glad even to see the Knight, but she was full of sorrow at the sight of his pale, wan face, which had formerly been radiant with the glory of youth.

"My dearest lord," she cried, "what evil star has frowned on you and changed you thus? But welcome now, in weal or woe, my dear lord whom I have lost too long! Fate, who has been our foe so long, will injure us no further, but shall pay penance with threefold good for all these wrongs."

The unhappy man, dazed with misery, had no desire to speak of his troubles; his long-endured famine needed more relief.

"Fair lady," then said the victorious Prince,

things that were grievous to do or to bear it brings no pleasure to recall. The only good that comes from past danger is to make us wiser and more careful for the future. This day's example has deeply written this lesson on my heart-perfect happiness can never be lasting while we still live on earth.

"Henceforth, Sir Knight," he continued, "take to yourself your old strength, and master these mishaps by patience. Look where your foe lies vanquished, and the wicked woman, Duessa, the cause of all your misery, stands in your power, to let her live or die."

"To kill her would be to act unworthily," said Una, "and it would be a shame to avenge one's self on such a weak enemy. But take off her scarlet robe and let her fly!"

So they did as Una bade them. They took from Duessa all her finery—her royal robe, and purple cloak, and all the rich ornaments with which she was decked. And when this disguise was taken from her, they saw her as she really was—old, and ugly, and bad. She would no longer be able to deceive people by her pretended goodness, and youth, and beauty, for every one who saw her shrunk away in horror.

"Such," said Una, "is the face of Falsehood when its borrowed light is laid aside, and all its deceitfulness is made known."

Thus, having taken from Duessa her power to work evil, they set her free to go where she pleased. She fled to a barren wilderness, where she lurked unseen in rocks and caves, for she always hated the light.

But Prince Arthur, and the Red Cross Knight, and fair Una stayed for awhile in the castle of Giant Pride, to rest themselves and to recover their strength. And here they found a goodly store of all that was dainty and rare.

The Knight with the Hempen Rope

When the two Knights and the Lady Una had rested awhile in the castle of Giant Pride, they set out again on their journey. Before they parted, Prince Arthur and the Red Cross Knight gave each other beautiful gifts—tokens of love and friendship. Prince Arthur gave a box of adamant, embossed with gold, and richly ornamented; in it were enclosed a few drops of a precious liquid of wonderful power, which would immediately heal any wound. In return the Red Cross Knight gave the Prince a Bible, all written with golden letters, rich and beautiful.

Thus they parted, Prince Arthur to go about his own work, and the Knight to fight the terrible Dragon that was laying waste the kingdom that belonged to Una's father and mother. But she, seeing how thin and ill her champion looked, and knowing that he was still weak and weary, would not hasten forward, nor let him run the chance of any further fighting, until he had recovered his former strength.

As they travelled, they presently saw an armed knight galloping towards them. It seemed as though he were flying from a dreaded foe, or some other grisly thing. As he fled, his eyes kept looking backwards as if the object of his terror were pursuing him, and his horse flew as if it had wings to its feet.

When he came nearer they saw that his head was bare, his hair almost standing on end with fright, and his face very pale. Round his neck was a hempen rope, suiting ill with his glittering armour.

The Red Cross Knight rode up to him, but could scarcely prevail upon him to stop.

"Sir Knight," he said, "pray tell us who hath arrayed you like this, and from whom you are flying, for never saw I warrior in so unseemly a plight."

The stranger seemed dazed with fear, and at first answered nothing; but after the gentle Knight had spoken to him several times, at last he replied with faltering tongue, and trembling in every limb: "I beseech you, Sir Knight, do not stop me, for lo! he comes—he comes fast after me!"

With that he again tried to run away, but the Red Cross Knight prevented him, and tried to persuade him to say what was the matter.

"Am I really safe from him who would have forced me to die?" said the stranger. "May I tell my luckless story?"

"Fear nothing," said the Knight; "no danger is near now.

Then the stranger told how he and another knight had lately been companions. The name of his friend was Sir Terwin. He was bold and brave, but because everything did not go exactly as he wished, he was

"So as they traveild, lo! they gan espy
An armed knight towards them gallop fast,
That seemed from some feared foe to fly,
Or other griesly thing that him aghast."

not happy. One day when they were feeling very sad and comfortless, they met a man whose name was *Despair*. Greeting them in a friendly fashion, Despair soon contrived to find out from them what they were feeling, and then he went on to make the worst of everything. He told them there was no hope that things would get any better, and tried to persuade them to put an end to all further trouble by killing themselves. To Sir Terwin he lent a rusty knife, and to the other knight a rope. Sir Terwin, who was really very unhappy, killed himself at once; but Sir Trevisan, dismayed at the sight, fled fast away, with the rope still round his neck, half dead with fear.

"May you never hear the tempting speeches of Despair," he ended.

"How could idle talking persuade a man to put an end to his life?" said the Red Cross Knight. He was ready to despise the danger, and he trusted in his own strength to withstand it.

"*I* know," said the stranger, "for trial has lately taught me; nor would I go through the like again for the world's wealth. His cunning, like sweetest honey, drops into the heart, and all else is forgotten. Before one knows it, all power is secretly stolen, and only weakness remains. Oh, sir, do not wish ever to meet with Despair."

"Truly," said the Red. Cross Knight, "I shall never rest till I have heard what the traitor has to say for himself. And, Sir Knight, I beg of you, as a favour, to guide me to his cabin."

"To do you a favour, I will ride back with you against my will," said Sir Trevisan; "but not for gold, nor for anything else will I remain with you when you arrive at the place. I would rather die than see his deadly face again."

In the Cave of Despair

Sir Trevisan and the Red Cross Knight soon came to the place where Despair had his dwelling. It was in a hollow cave, far underneath a craggy cliff, dark and dreary. On the top always perched a melancholy owl, shrieking his dismal note, which drove all cheerful birds far away. All around were dead and withered trees, on which no fruit nor leaf ever grew.

When they arrived, Sir Trevisan would have fled in terror, not daring to go near, but the Red Cross Knight forced him to stay, and soothed his fears.

They entered the gloomy cave, where they found a miserable man sitting on the ground, musing sullenly. He had greasy, unkempt locks, and dull and hollow eyes, and his cheeks were thin and shrunken, as if he never got enough to eat. His garment was nothing but rags, all patched, and pinned together with thorns. At his side lay the dead body of Sir Terwin, just as Sir Trevisan had told.

When the Red Cross Knight saw this sad sight, all his courage blazed up in the desire to avenge him, and he said to Despair, "Wretched man! you are the cause of this man's death. It is only just that you should pay the price of his life with your own."

"Why do you speak so rashly?" said Despair. "Does not justice teach that he should die who does not deserve to live? This man killed himself by his own wish. Is it unjust to give to each man his due? Or to let him die who hates to live longer? Or to let him die in peace who lives here in trouble? If a man travels by a weary, wandering way, and comes to a great flood between him and his wished—for home, is it not a gracious act to help him to pass over it? Foolish man! would you riot help him to gain rest, who has long dwelt here in woe?"

Thus spoke Despair, and he said many beautiful and persuasive words concerning Death. And as the Red Cross Knight listened, all his courage and all his anger melted away, and it seemed to him that there would be no sweeter thing in the whole world than to lie down and be at rest.

"What is the good of living?" said Despair. "The longer you live the more sins you commit. All those great battles that you are so proud of winning, all this strife and bloodshed and revenge, which are praised now, hereafter you will be sorry for. Has not your evil life lasted long enough? He that hath once missed the right way, the farther he goes, the farther he goes wrong. Go no farther, then—stray no farther. Lie down here and take your rest. What has life to make men love it so? Fear, sickness, age, loss, labour, sorrow, strife, pain, hunger, cold, and fickle fortune, all these, and a thousand more ills make life to be hated rather than loved. Wretched man! you indeed have the greatest need of death if you will truly judge your own conduct. Never did knight who dared warlike deeds meet with more luckless adventures. Think of the deep dungeon, wherein you were lately shut up; how often then did you wish for death! Though by good luck you escaped from there, yet death would prevent any further mischance into which you may happen to fall."

Then Despair went on to speak to the Red Cross Knight of all his sins. He pointed out the many wrong things he had done, and said that he had been so faithless and wicked that there was no hope for him of any mercy or forgiveness. Rather than live longer and add to his sins, it would be better for him to die at once, and put an end to all.

The Knight was greatly moved by this speech, which pierced his heart like a sword. Too well he knew that it was all true. There came to his conscience such a vivid memory of all his wrongdoings that all his strength melted away, as if a spell had bewitched him. When Despair saw him waver and grow weak, and that his soul was deeply troubled, he tried all the harder to drive him to utter misery.

"Think of all your sins," he said. "God is very angry with you. You are not worthy to live. It is only just that you should die. Better kill yourself at once."

"Then Despair went and fetched a dagger, sharp and keen, and gave it to the Red Cross Knight. Trembling like an aspen-leaf, the Knight took it, and lifted up his hand to slay himself.

When Una saw this, she grew cold with horror, but, starting forward, she snatched the knife from his hand, and threw it to the ground, greatly enraged.

"Fie, fie, faint-hearted Knight!" she cried. "What is the meaning of this shameful strife? Is *this* the battle which you boasted you would fight with the horrible fiery Dragon? Come, come away, feeble and faithless man! Let no vain words deceive your manly heart, nor wicked thoughts dismay your brave spirit. Have you not a share in heavenly mercy? Why should you then despair who have been chosen to fight the good fight? If there is Justice, there is also Forgiveness, which soothes the anguish of remorse and blots out the record of sin. Arise, Sir Knight, arise and leave this evil place."

So up he rose, and straightway left the cave. When Despair saw this,

"Ere long they come where that same wicked wight
His dwelling has, low in a hollow cave,
For underneath a craggy cliff ypight,
Dark, doleful, dreary, like a greedy grave,
That still for carrion carcases doth crave."

and that his guest would safely depart in spite of all his beguiling words, he took a rope and tried to hang himself. But though he had tried to kill himself a thousand times, he could never do so, until the last day comes when all evil things shall perish for ever.

How the Red Cross Knight came to the House of Holiness

The bravest man who boasts of bodily strength may often find his moral courage fail in the hour of temptation. If he gain the victory, let him not ascribe it to his own skill, but rather to the grace of God.

From what had happened in the Cave of Despair, Una saw that her Knight had grown faint and feeble; his long imprisonment had wasted away all his strength, and he was still quite unfit to fight. Therefore she determined to bring him to a place where he might refresh himself, and recover from his late sad plight.

There was an ancient house not far away, renowned through all the world for its goodness and holy learning, so well was it guided and governed by a wise matron. Her only joy was to comfort those in trouble and to help the helpless poor. She was called Dame Celia—the "Heavenly Lady"—and she had three beautiful daughters, Fidelia (*Faith*), Speranza (*Hope*), and Charissa (*Love*).

Arrived at the House of Holiness, they found the door fast locked, for it was warily watched, night and day, for fear of many foes. But when they knocked, the porter straightway opened to them. He was an aged man, with grey hair and slow footsteps; his name was *Humility*. They passed in, stooping low, for the way he showed them was strait and narrow, even as all good things are hardest at the beginning. But when they had entered they saw a spacious court, very pleasant to walk in. Here they were met by a frank, honest-looking man, called *Zeal*, who gladly acted as their guide till they came to the hall.

The squire of the household received them, and made them welcome; his name was *Reverence*. He was very gentle, modest, and sincere, always treating every one with the greatest kindness and courtesy, not from any pretended politeness, but because of his own good and sweet disposition.

He conducted them to the lady of the house, who was busied as usual in some good works. Directly Dame Celia saw Una, she knew who she was; her heart filled with joy, and she put her arms round her and kissed her.

"Oh, happy earth," she cried, "whereon your innocent feet still tread! What good fortune has brought you this way, or did you wander here unknowingly? It is strange to see a knight-errant in this place, or any other man, for there are few who choose the narrow path or seek the right."

Una replied that they had come to rest their weary limbs, and to see the lady herself, whose fame and praise had reached them.

Then Dame Celia entertained them with every courtesy she could think of, and nothing was lacking to show her generosity and wisdom. Whilst they were talking, two beautiful maidens came in; they were Faith and Hope, the daughters of the lady. Faith was arrayed all in lily-white, and her face shone like the light of the sun; in one hand she held a book. Her younger sister, Hope, was clad all in blue, and carried a silver anchor; her face was not as cheerful as Faith's, but it was very noble and steadfast.

Presently a servant, called *Obedience*, came and conducted the guests to their rooms, in order that they might rest awhile. Afterwards Una asked Faith if she would allow the Red Cross Knight to enter her school house, in order that he might share in her heavenly learning, and hear the divine wisdom of her words.

So the Knight went to school to learn of Faith, and many were the wondrous things she taught him. Now he saw in its true light all the error of his ways, and he began truly to repent of all his wrongdoings. The thought of them was so bitter, that he felt he was no longer worthy to live.

Then came Hope with sweet comfort, and bade him trust steadily and not lose heart. And Dame Celia, seeing how unhappy he was, sent to him a wonderful doctor, called *Patience*. Thanks to his skill and wisdom, and to the careful nursing of his attendant, *Repentance*, the Red Cross Knight presently recovered, and grew well and strong again.

After this Una took him one day to visit the third daughter, whose name was Love. She was so wonderfully beautiful and good that there were few on earth to compare with her. They found her in the midst of a group of happy children; she wore a yellow robe, and sat in an ivory chair, and at her side were two turtle-doves.

Una besought Love to let the Red Cross Knight learn of her whatever she could teach, and to this request Love gladly agreed. Then she began to instruct the Knight in all good things. She spoke to him of love and righteousness, and how to do well, and bade him shun all wrath and hatred, which are displeasing to GOD. And when she: had well taught him this, she went on to show him the path to heaven.

The better to guide his weak and wandering steps, she called an ancient matron, named *Mercy*, well known for her gracious and tender ways. Into her careful charge Love gave the Knight, to lead in the right path, so that he should never fall in all his journeying through the wide world, but come to the end in safety.

Then Mercy, taking the Knight by the hand, led him away by a narrow path; it was scattered with bushy thorns and ragged briars, but these she always cleared away before him, so that nothing might hinder his ready passage. And whenever his footsteps were cumbered, or began to falter and stray, she held him fast, and bore him up, so that he never fell.

The City of the Great King

Soon after leaving the House of Holiness, the Red Cross Knight and his guide, Mercy, came to a hospital by the wayside. Some bedesmen lived here, who had vowed all their life to the service of the King of Heaven, and who spent their days in doing good. Their gates were always open to weary travellers, and one of the brothers sat waiting to call in all poor and needy passers-by. Each of the brothers had a separate duty to perform. The first had to entertain travellers; the second, to give food to the needy; the third, clothing to those who had none; the fourth, to relieve prisoners and to redeem captives; the fifth, to comfort the sick and the dying; the sixth, to take charge of those who

"The Knight and Una entering fayre her greet,
And bid her joy of that her happy brood;
Who them requites with court'sies seeming meet,
And entertaynes with friendly cheerefull mood."

were dead, and to deck them with dainty flowers; the seventh had to look after widows and orphans. Mercy was a great friend of theirs, and Love was the founder of their order.

They stayed at the hospital for some time, while the Knight was taught all kinds of good works. He was very quick at learning, and soon became so perfect that no cause of blame or rebuke could be found in him.

Leaving the hospital, he next came with his guide to a steep and high hill, on the top of which was a church, with a little hermitage close by. Here there dwelt an old man, called *Contemplation*. He spent all his days in prayer and meditation, never thinking of worldly business, but only of God and goodness. When he saw the travellers approaching, at first he felt vexed, for he thought they would distract his thoughts to earthly matters. But recognizing Mercy, whom he loved and respected, he greeted them civilly, and asked why they had climbed that tedious height.

"For that same purpose which every living person should make his aim—the wish to go to Heaven," replied Mercy. "Does not the path lead straight from here to that most glorious place which shines with ever-living light? The keys were given into your hands by Faith, who requires that you show the lovely city to this knight in accordance with his desire."

Then Contemplation took the Red Cross Knight, and, after the latter had fasted awhile and prayed, he led him to the highest part of the hill.

From there he showed him a little path, steep and long, which led to a goodly city. The walls and towers were built very high and strong, of pearl and precious stones, more beautiful than tongue can tell. It was called "The City of the Great King," and in it dwelt eternal peace and happiness.

As the Knight stood gazing, he could see the blessed angels descending to and fro, and walking in the streets of the city, as friend walks with friend. At this he much wondered, and he began to ask what was the stately building that lifted its lofty towers so near the starry sky, and what unknown nation dwelt there.

"Fair Knight," said his companion, "that is Jerusalem—the New

"From thence, far off he unto him did shew
A little path that was both steepe and long,
Which to a goodly Citty led his vew,
Whose wals and towres were builded high and strong
Of perle and precious stone that earthly tong
Cannot describe, nor wit of man can tell."

Jerusalem, which God has built for those to dwell in that are His chosen people, cleansed from sinful guilt by Christ, who died for the sins of the whole world. Now they are saints together in that city."

"Until now," said the Knight, "I thought that the city of Queen Gloriana, whence I come, was the fairest that might ever be seen. But now I know otherwise, for that great city yonder far surpasses it."

"Most true," said the holy man. "Yet for an earthly place the kingdom of Queen Gloriana is the fairest that eye can behold. And you, Sir Knight, have done good service by aiding a desolate and oppressed maiden. But when you have won a famous victory, and high amongst all knights have hung your shield, follow no more the pursuit of earthly conquest, for bloodshed and war bring sin and sorrow. Seek this path which I point out to you, for it will in the end bring you to Heaven. Go peaceably on your pilgrimage to the City of the Great King. A blessed end is ordained for you. Amongst the saints you shall be a saint, the friend and patron of your own nation. Saint George you shall be called—'Saint George for merry England, the sign of Victory.'"

"O holy Sire!" said the Knight, "how can I requite you for all that you have done for me?"

H is eyes were dazzled by the brightness of the glory at which he had been gazing, so that he could scarcely see the ground by which to return; so dark are earthly things compared with divine.

Thanking and rewarding the good man for all his trouble, the Red Cross Knight returned to Una, who was anxiously awaiting him. She received him with joy, and after he had rested a little, she bade him be mindful of the task still before him. So they took leave of Dame Celia and her three daughters, and once more set out on their journey.

The Last Fight

At last Una and the Knight came to Una's kingdom, where her parents were held captive, and all the land lay wasted by the terrible dragon. As they drew near their journey's end, Una began to cheer her companion with brave words.

"Dear Knight," she said, "who for my sake have suffered all these sorrows, may Heaven reward you for your weary toll! Now we have come to my own country, and the place where all our perils dwell. This is the haunt of the horrible monster, therefore be well on your guard and ready for the foe. Call up all your courage, and do better than you have ever done before, so that hereafter you shall be renowned. above all knights on earth."

At this moment they heard a hideous roaring sound, which filled the air, and almost shook the solid ground. Soon they saw the dreadful dragon where he lay stretched on the sunny side of a great hill. Directly he caught sight of the glittering armour of the Knight, he quickly roused himself, and hastened towards them.

The Red Cross Knight bade Una go to a hill at some distance, from where she might behold the battle and be safe from danger. She had scarcely done so when the huge beast drew near, half flying, and half running in his haste.

He was a dreadful creature to look at, very big, covered with brazen scales like a coat of steel, which he clashed loudly as he came. He had two immense wings with which he could fly, and at the point of his great, knotted tail were two stings, sharper than the sharpest steel. Worse even than these, however, were his cruel claws, which tore to pieces everything that came within their clutches. He had three rows of iron teeth, and his eyes, blazing with wrath, sparkled like living fire.

Such was the terrible monster with whom the Red Cross Knight had now to do battle.

All day they fought; and when evening came, the Knight was quite worn out and almost defeated. As it chanced, however, close by was a spring, the waters of which possessed a wonderful gift of healing. The Knight was driven backwards and fell into this well. The dragon clapped his wings in triumph, for he thought he had gained the victory. But so great was the power of the water in this well that although the Knight's own strength was utterly exhausted, yet he rose out of it refreshed and vigorous. The dawn of the next day found him stronger than ever, and ready for battle.

The name of the spring was called the Well of Life.

All through the second day the battle lasted, and again, when evening came, the Knight was almost defeated. But this night he rested

"And to the Knight his daughter deare he tyde
With sacred rites and vowes for ever to abyde.

* * * * * * *

His owne two hands the holy knotts did knitt,
That none but death for ever can divide."

under a beautiful tree laden with goodly fruit; the name of the tree was the Tree of Life. From it flowed, as from a well, a trickling stream of balm, a perfect cure for all ills, and whoever ate of its fruit attained to everlasting life.

The strength of the Red Cross Knight alone would never have been sufficient to overcome the terrible Dragon of Sin, but the water of the Well of Life, and the balm from the Tree of Life, gave him a power that nothing could resist.

On the morning of the third day he slew the dragon.

"Ease after War"

The sun had scarcely risen on the third day, when the watchman on the walls of the brazen tower saw the death of the dragon. He hastily called to the captive King and Queen, who, coming forth, ordered the tidings of peace and joy to be proclaimed through the whole land.

Then all the trumpets sounded for victory, and the people came flocking as to a great feast, rejoicing at the fall of the cruel enemy, from whose bondage they were now free.

Forth from the castle came the King and Queen, attended by a noble company. In front marched a goodly band of brave young men, all able to wield arms, but who now bore laurel branches in sign of victory and peace. These they threw at the feet of the Red Cross Knight, and hailed him conqueror.

Then came beautiful maidens with garlands of flowers and timbrels; troops of merry children ran in front, dancing and singing to the sound of sweet music. When they reached the spot where Una stood, they bowed before her, and crowned her with a garland, so that she looked—as indeed she was—a queen.

The King gave goodly gifts of gold and ivory to his brave champion, and thanked him a thousand times for all that he had done. Then the Red Cross Knight and Una were brought in triumph to the palace; the trumpets and the clarions sounded, and all the people sang for joy, and strewed their garments in the way. At the palace everything was splendid and beautiful, as befitted a prince's court, and here a great feast was held.

The King and Queen made their guest tell them all the strange adventures and perils that had befallen him. They listened with much interest and pity to his story. Then said the King:—

"Dear son, great are the evils which you have borne, so that I know not whether most to praise or to pity you. Never has living man passed through a sea of more deadly dangers. But since you have arrived safely at the shore, now let us think of ease and everlasting rest."

"Ah! dearest sovereign," replied the brave Knight, "I may not yet think of ease or rest. For by the vow which I made when I first took up arms, I plighted myself to return to Queen Gloriana, and to serve her in warlike ways for six years."

The King, when he heard this, was very sorry, but he knew that the vow must be kept.

"As soon as the six years are over," said he, "you shall return here and marry my daughter, the Lady Una. I proclaimed through the world that whoever killed the dragon should have my only daughter to be his wife, and should be made heir of my kingdom. Since you have won the reward by noble chivalry, lo! here I yield to you my daughter and my kingdom."

Then Una stepped forward, radiant as the morning star and fair as the flowers in May. She wore a garment of lily-white, that looked as if it were woven of silk and silver. The blazing brightness of her beauty and the glorious light of her sunshiny face can scarcely be told. Even her dear Knight, who had been with her every day, wondered at the sight.

So the Red Cross Knight and Una were betrothed. Every one, young and old, rejoiced, and a solemn feast was held through all the land. Now, indeed, the Knight thought himself happy. Whenever his eye beheld Una, his heart melted with joy; no wickedness nor envy could ever again harm their love.

Yet even in the midst of his happiness he remembered the vow he had made to return to Queen Gloriana. His work was not yet done, and at last the day came when he had to leave Una, and set forth again on his travels.

We know, however, that whatever new perils Jay before him, he would be able to overcome them all by the help of his heavenly armour, and that in the end he would be restored to Una, to dwell happily with her for ever.

"The Good Sir Guyon"

Sir Guyon meets the Magician

ARCHIMAGO, the wicked magician, who had worked such mischief to Una and the Red Cross Knight, was very angry when he found that in the end all his evil wiles were defeated, and that the Knight and the lady were happily betrothed. He would willingly have brought more trouble on them, but he was powerless to do any harm to Una, for she was now safely restored to her own kingdom, and living in the care of her father and mother. He therefore directed all his spite against the Knight, who had once more to set forth on his adventures, as he had promised Queen Gloriana to serve her faithfully for six years. At the end of that time he hoped to return and marry Una, and the King, her father, had made him heir to the throne.

Archimago, whose other name you may remember was *Hypocrisy*,

"Upon the way him fortuned to meete,
Faire marching underneath a shadie hill,
A goodly Knight, all armed in harnesse meete."

set all his wits to work to see what harm he could do the Knight, for he knew that, after all the troubles he had fallen into, he would be more than usually careful. He kept laying snares for him, and placed spies wherever he went, but the Knight had now become so wise and wary that he always found out and shunned the danger. Archimago, however, still kept on hoping he should find some way to hurt him, and at last his opportunity came.

It happened, one day, that the enchanter saw marching to meet him a noble knight. The stranger was clad in shining armour and rode a splendid war-horse; his bearing was very stately, and his face, although calm and beautiful, was so stern and noble that all his friends loved him and his foes feared him. He was one of the chief knights of Queen Gloriana's court, a man of great honour and power in his native land. His name was Sir Guyon.

As the Red Cross Knight was known as the Champion of *Holiness*, so Sir Guyon was known as the Knight of *Temperance*.

With him now there was an aged palmer or pilgrim, clad in black; his hair was grey and he leant on a staff. To judge by his look he was a wise and grave old man, and he seemed to be acting as guide to the Knight, who carefully checked his prancing horse to keep pace with his slow footsteps.

The name of the black palmer was *Conscience*, and he went with Sir Guyon as his companion and adviser, somewhat in the same fashion as *Prudence* had gone as servant with the Red Cross Knight.

When Archimago saw Sir Guyon, he immediately stopped him, just as on a former occasion he had stopped the Red Cross Knight.

This time he had a fresh story to tell, which, of course, was perfectly false. He implored Sir Guyon to come to the help of a beautiful maiden, cruelly ill-treated by a rough knight, who had cut off her golden locks, and threatened to kill her with his sharp sword.

"What!" cried Sir Guyon, his gentle nature roused to indignation, "is the man still alive who could do such a deed?"

"He is alive, and boasts of it," said wicked Hypocrisy. "Nor has any other knight yet punished him for it."

"Take me to him at once," said Sir Guyon.

"That I can easily do," said Archimago. "I will show you where he is," and he hurried off in high glee, because he thought that at last he had found a way of revenging himself on the Red Cross Knight.

Friend or Foe?

Archimago and Sir Guyon came presently to a place where a beautiful lady sat alone, with torn clothes and ruffled hair; she was weeping bitterly and wringing her hands, and when Sir Guyon asked her the cause of her grief, she said it was because she had been most cruelly treated by a rough knight.

This lady who seemed so good and gentle was, in reality, no other than Duessa (or *Falsehood*), who had formerly led the Red Cross Knight into such trouble. Her old companion, Archimago, had found her wandering forlorn in the desert whither she had been banished by Prince Arthur, and had again decked her out in fine clothes and ornaments, so that she might help him in his wicked schemes.

Her cunning quite deceived Sir Guyon, who believed everything she told him.

"Be comforted, fair lady," he said, "and tell me who did this, so that I can punish him at once."

"I do not know his name," she replied, "but he rode a dappled grey steed, and on his silver shield there was a red cross."

When Sir Guyon heard this he was amazed.

"I cannot think how that knight could have done such a deed," he said, "for I can say boldly he is a right good knight. I was present when he first took arms and started out to help the Lady Una, since when he has won great glory, as I have heard tell. Nevertheless, he shall be made to explain this, and if he cannot clear himself of all blame, be sure he shall be well punished."

Duessa was greatly pleased when she heard this, for now she hoped there would be a quarrel between the two knights.

Archimago then led Sir Guyon by an unknown way through woods and across mountains, till they came at last to a pleasant dale which lay between two hills. A little river ran through this valley, and

by it sat a knight with his helmet unlaced, refreshing himself with the cool water after his long journey and hard work.

"Yonder is the man!" cried Archimago. "He has come here thinking to hide himself, but in vain, for you will soon make him repent of his cruelty. All success to you! We will stay here, and watch from a distance."

Archimago and Duessa left Sir Guyon, who immediately rushed forward to the attack. The stranger, seeing a knight hurrying so fiercely towards him, seized his own weapons, prepared for battle, and sprang to meet him. Vie two had almost met when Sir Guyon suddenly lowered his spear.

"Mercy, Sir Knight! Mercy!" he cried. "Pardon my rashness, that had almost led me to disgrace my honour by raising my weapon against the sacred badge on your shield."

When the Red Cross Knight, for he indeed it was, heard the other's voice, he knew him at once,

"Ah! dear Sir Guyon," he said, bowing courteously, "it is I rather who should be blamed. In my reckless haste I almost did violence to the image of Queen Gloriana which I now see inscribed on your shield. The fault is mine!"

So the two knights made friends, and talked very happily together, and Sir Guyon explained how he had been cheated by Archimago and Duessa, who had both now fled away. Then up came Guyon's guide, Conscience, and as soon as his eye fell on the Red Cross Knight, he knew him, for he had seen him at the court of Queen Gloriana.

"Joy be with you, and everlasting fame, for the great deeds you have done!" he cried. "Your glorious name is enrolled in the heavenly register, where you have won a seat among the saints. But we luckless mortals are only now beginning to run the race in which you have gained such renown." Then to his master he said, "God grant you, Guyon, to end your work well, and bring your weary bark safely to the wished-for haven."

"Palmer," said the Red Cross Knight, "give the praise to God, to whom all honour is due, and who made my hand the organ of His might. Attribute nothing to me except a willing heart; for all that I did, I only did as I ought. But as for you, fair sir, whose turn it is now," he added to Guyon, "may you prosper as well as you can wish, and may we hear thrice happy tidings of you; for you are indeed worthy, both in courage and gentle manners."

Then the two Knights took leave of each other with much courtesy and goodwill. Sir Guyon went forward on his journey, still guided by the Black Palmer, who led him over hill and dale, pointing out the way with his staff, and by his wise judgment guarding his master from all dangers into which his own hasty nature might have made him fall.

The Story of the Knight and the Lady

After leaving the Red Cross Knight, Guyon and the Black Palmer (or *Conscience*) travelled for some distance, fighting and winning many battles as they went, which brought much honour to the Knight.

But the chief adventure in Sir Guyon's life began in this way:

One day, passing through a forest, they heard sounds of bitter weeping and lamentation.

"If I cannot be revenged for all my misery," cried a voice, "at least nothing can prevent my dying, Come then, come soon, come, sweetest death! But, thou, my babe, who hast seen thy father's fall, long mayest thou live, and thrive better than thy unhappy parents. Live to bear witness that thy mother died for no fault of her own."

When Sir Guyon heard these piteous words, he dismounted, and rushed into the thicket, where he found a beautiful lady dying on the ground. In her arms there was a lovely baby, and the dead body of an armed knight lay close beside them.

Horrified at the sight, Sir Guyon did all he could to restore the lady to life, but she begged him to leave her alone to die in peace; her sorrows, she said, were more than she could bear, and therefore she had tried to kill herself.

"Dear lady," said Sir Guyon, "all that I wish is to comfort you, and to bring you some relief, therefore tell me the cause of your misfortune."

"Listen, then," she answered. "This dead man, the gentlest, bravest knight that ever lived, was my husband, the good Sir Mordant. One day he rode forth, as is the custom of knights, to seek adventures, and it chanced most unhappily he came to the place where the wicked Acrasia lives-Acrasia, the false enchantress, who has brought ruin on so many knights. Her dwelling is within a wandering island, in Perilous Gulf. Fair sir, if ever you travel there, shun the hateful place! I will tell you the name—it is called the *Bower of Bliss*. Acrasia's one aim in life is *Pleasure*. In the Bower of Bliss nothing is thought of but eating and

drinking, and every kind of luxury and extravagance. All those who come within it forget everything good and noble, and care for nothing but to amuse themselves. When my dear knight never returned to me, I set forth in search of him, and here I found him, a captive to the spells of Acrasia. At first he did not even know me; but by-and-by, with great care, I brought him back to a better state of mind, and persuaded him to leave the Bower of Bliss. But the wicked enchantress, angry at losing one of her victims, gave him a parting cup of poison, and stooping to drink at this well, he suddenly fell dead. When I saw this—"Here the lady's own words failed, and, lying down as if to sleep, quiet death put an end to all her sorrow.

Sir Guyon felt such grief at what had happened that he could scarcely keep from weeping. Turning to the Palmer, he said: "Behold here this image of human life, when raging passion like a fierce tyrant robs reason of its proper sway. The strong it weakens, and the weak it fills with fury; the strong (like this Knight) fall soonest through excess of pleasure; the weak (like this Lady) through excess of grief. But Temperance with a golden rule can measure out a medium between the two, neither to be overcome by pleasure, nor to give way to despair. Thrice happy man who can tread evenly between them! But, since this wretched lady did wrong through grief, and not from wickedness, it is not for us to judge her. Let us give her an honourable burial. Death comes to all, the good and the bad alike, and, after death, each must answer for his own deeds. But both alike should have a fitting burial."

So Sir Guyon and the Black Palmer dug a grave under the cypress-trees, and here they tenderly placed the dead bodies of the Knight and the Lady, and bade them sleep in everlasting peace. And before they left the spot, Sir Guyon swore a solemn vow that he would avenge the hapless little orphan child for the death of his parents.

The Three Sisters

After the burial of the Knight and the Lady, Sir Guyon gave the little baby into the care of the Palmer, and, lading himself with the heavy armour of the dead Sir Mordant, the two started again on their journey. But when they came to the place where Sir Guyon had left his steed, with its golden saddle and costly trappings, they found, to their surprise and vexation, that it had quite disappeared. They were obliged, therefore, to go forward on foot.

By-and-by they came to a famous old Castle, built on a rock near the sea. In this castle lived three sisters, who were so different in character that they could never agree. The eldest and the youngest were always quarrelling, and they were both as disagreeable as possible to the middle sister. Elissa, the eldest, was very harsh and stern; she always looked discontented, and she despised every kind of pleasure or merriment. It was useless ever to attempt to make her smile; she was always frowning and scolding in a way not at all becoming to any gentle lady.

Perissa, the youngest sister, was just as bad in the other direction;

". . . At last they to a Castle came,
Built on a rocke adjoyning to the seas."

she cared for nothing but amusement, and was so full of laughter and play that she forgot all rules of right and reason, and became quite thoughtless and silly. She spent all her time in eating, and drinking, and dressing herself up in fine clothes.

These two sisters showed the evil of two extremes but the middle sister, Medina, or "*Golden Mean*," as she was sometimes called, was the type of moderation, and all that was right and proper. She was sweet, and gracious, and womanly; not harsh and stern, like Elissa, nor yet heedless and silly, like Perissa. She dressed richly, but quietly, and her clothes suited her well: they were different alike from Elissa's stinginess and Perissa's extravagance.

When Medina saw Sir Guyon approaching the castle, she met him on the threshold, and led him in like an honoured guest. But her sisters were very angry when they heard of his arrival. There were two other visitors at the castle just then, and they also were very angry. Sir Hudibras was a friend of the eldest sister. He was very savage and sullen, slowwitted, but big and strong. Sans-loy, or *Lawless*, was the friend of the youngest sister. He was the same Lawless who had been so cruel to poor Una, and he was just as bold and unruly now as he had been then, and he never cared what wrong he did to any one.

These two hated each other, and were always quarrelling, but when they heard of the coming of the stranger knight, they both flew to attack him. On the way, however, they began fighting with each other, and, hearing the noise, Sir Guyon ran to try to stop them, whereupon they both turned upon him. The two sisters stood by, and encouraged them to go on fighting; but Medina ran in amongst them, and entreated them to stop. Her gentle words at last appeased their anger, and they laid down their weapons, and consented to make friends.

Then Medina invited them all to a feast, which she had prepared in honour of Sir Guyon. Elissa and Perissa came very unwillingly, though they attempted to hide their grudging and envy under a pretence of cheerfulness. One sister thought the entertainment provided far too much, and the other sister thought it far too little. Elissa would scarcely speak or eat anything, while Perissa chattered and ate far more than was right or proper.

After the feast, Medina begged Sir Guyon to tell them the story of his adventures, and to say on what quest he was now bound.

Then Sir Guyon told them all about the court of the Faerie Queene, Gloriana, and how he had sworn service to her, and promised to go out into the world to fight every kind of evil. The task he had now in hand was to find out the wicked enchantress, Acrasia, and to destroy her dwelling, for she had done more bad deeds than could be told, and, among them, had brought about the deaths of the father and mother of the poor little baby he had taken under his care.

By the time Sir Guyon's tale was finished the night was far spent, and all the guests in the castle betook themselves to rest.

Braggadochio

As soon as it was dawn, Sir Guyon arose, and, mindful of his appointed work, armed himself again for the journey.

The little baby whom he had rescued he entrusted to the tender care of Medina, entreating her to train him up as befitted his noble birth. Then, since his good steed had been stolen from him, he and the Palmer fared forward on foot.

It will be remembered that when Sir Guyon heard the cries for help of the Lady Amavia, he dismounted, and ran into the thicket, leaving his horse outside. While he was absent, there wandered that way an idle, worthless fellow, called Braggadochio. This was a man who never did anything great or good, but who was extremely vain and boastful, and always trying to make out that he was somebody grand. When he saw the beautiful horse with its golden saddle and rich trappings, and Sir Guyon's spear, he immediately took possession of them, and hurried away. He was so puffed up with self-conceit that he felt now as if he were really some noble knight, and he hoped that every one else would think the same of him. He determined to go first to court, where he thought such a gallant show would at once attract notice and gain him favour.

Braggadochio had never been trained in chivalry; he rode very badly, and could not manage Sir Guyon's splendid high-spirited horse in the least. He managed, however, to stick on somehow, and presently, seeing a man sitting on a bank by the roadside, and wishing to show off, he rode at him, pretending to aim at him with his spear. The silly fellow fell flat down with fear, crying out for mercy. Braggadochio was very proud and delighted at this, and shouted at him in a loud voice, "Die, or yield thyself my captive!" The man was so terrified that he promised at once to become Braggadochio's servant. So the two went on together. They were excellently well suited, for both were vain, and

false, and cowardly, while Braggadochio tried to get his own way, by bluster, and his companion by cunning.

Trompart (or *Deceit*), for that was the man's name, speedily discovered the folly of his master. He was very wily-witted and well accustomed to every form of cunning trickery, and, to suit his own purpose, he flattered tip Braggadochio, and did all he could to encourage his idle vanity.

Presently, as the two went along, they met the wicked magician, Archimago (or *Hypocrisy*), who was now just as angry with Sir Guyon as he had been before with the Red Cross Knight. When he saw Braggadochio, he thought he had found a good opportunity to be revenged on both the knights, and, going up to him, he asked if he would be willing to fight them.

Braggadochio immediately pretended to fall into a great rage against them, and said he would slay them both. Then Archimago, seeing that he had no sword, warned him that he must arm himself with the very best weapons, for they were two of the mightiest warriors living.

"Silly old man said!" Braggadochio boastfully. "Stop giving advice. Isn't one brave man enough, without sword or shield, to make an army quail? You little know what this right hand can do. Once, when I killed seven knights with one sword, I swore thenceforward never to wear a sword in battle again, unless it could be the one that the noblest knight on earth wears."

"Good!" said the magician quickly; "that sword you shall have very shortly. For now the best and noblest knight alive is Prince Arthur, who lives in the land of the Faerie Queene. He has a sword that is like a flaming brand. I will undertake that, by my devices, this sword is found to-morrow at your side."

At these words the boaster began to quake, for he could not think who it was that spoke like this. Then Archimago suddenly vanished, for the north wind, at his command, carried him away, lifting him high into the air.

Braggadochio and Deceit looked all about, but could find no trace of him. Nearly dead with fright, they both fled, never turning to look round till, at last, they came to a green forest where they hid themselves. Even here fear followed them, and every trembling leaf and rustle of the wind made their hair stand on end.

Fury's Captive

As Sir Guyon and his guide, the Black Palmer, went on their way, they presently saw at some distance what seemed to be a great uproar and commotion. Hurrying near, they found a big savage man dragging along and beating a handsome youth. An ugly old woman followed them, shouting and railing, and urging the man not to let go the youth, but to treat him worse and worse.

The name of the bad man was *Fury*; the old woman was his mother, and was called *Occasion*. The youth was a young squire, named Phaon.

Fury had Phaon completely in his power, but in his blind and senseless rage he scarcely knew what he was about, and spent half his force in vain. He often struck wide of the mark, and frequently hurt himself unawares, like a bull rushing at random, not knowing where he hits and not caring whom he hurts.

When Sir Guyon saw the sad plight of the young squire, he ran to help him; but Fury grappled with the Knight and flung him to the ground. Sir Guyon sprang to his feet, and drew his sword, but, seeing this, the Palmer cried, "Not so, O Guyon; never think the monster can be mastered or destroyed in that fashion. He is not a foe to be wounded by steel or overthrown by strength. This cruel wretch is Fury, who works much woe and shame to knighthood. That old hag, his mother, is the cause of all his wrath and spite. Whoever will conquer Fury, must first get hold of Occasion and master her. When she is got rid of, or strongly withstood, Fury himself is easily managed. But she is very difficult to catch, for her hair hangs so thickly over her eyes, it is often impossible to know her, and when she has once slipped past, you can never overtake her."

When Sir Guyon heard this, he left Fury and went to catch Occasion. All happened as the Palmer said. Directly the wicked old woman was captured, and her angry tongue silenced, her son turned to fly. Sir Guyon followed, and soon made him prisoner; but even when bound in iron chains, Fury kept grinding and gnashing his teeth, shaking his copper-coloured locks, and threatening revenge.

"A mad man, or that feigned mad to bee,
Drew by the haire along upon the grownd
A handsom stripling with great crueltee,
Whom sore he bett."

Then Sir Guyon turned to the young squire, and asked him how he had fallen into the power of such a wretch.

Phaon said all his misfortunes arose from his giving way to wrath and jealousy. He had a dear friend, about whom malicious stories were told, and without waiting to find out whether or not they were true, he killed this friend in sudden anger. When he discovered that he had been misled, and that his friend was innocent, he was filled with grief, and swore to be revenged on the two people who had deceived him. To one he gave a deadly draught of poison, and the other he was pursuing with a drawn sword, when' he himself was overtaken by Fury, who completely mastered him.

"As long as I live," he ended, "I shall never get over the agony caused me by Grief and Fury."

"Squire," said Sir Guyon, "you have suffered much, but all your ills may be softened if you do not give way to such violence."

Then said the Palmer, "Wretched is the man who never learns to govern his passions. At first they. are feeble and can be easily managed, but through lack of control they lead to fearful results. Fight against them while they are young, for when they get strong they do their best to overcome all the good in you. Ungoverned wrath, jealousy, and grief have, been the cause of this squire's downfall."

"Unlucky Phaon," said Sir Guyon; "since you have fallen into trouble through your hot, impatient disposition, henceforth take heed, and govern your ways carefully, less a worse evil come upon you."

While Sir Guyon spoke, they saw far off a man running towards them, whose flying feet went so fast that he was almost hidden in a cloud of dust.

The Anger of Fire

The man soon reached Sir Guyon and the Palmer, hot, panting, and breathless. He was a bold-looking fellow, not in the least abashed by Sir Guyon, but casting scornful glances at him.

Behind his back he bore a brazen shield, which looked as if it belonged to some famous knight. On it was drawn the picture of a flaming fire, round which were the words "*Burnt, I do burn.*" In his hand the man carried two sharp and slender darts, tipped with poison.

When he came near, he said boldly to Guyon, "Sir Knight—if you be a knight—I advise you to leave this place at once, in case of further harm. If you choose to stay, you do so at your own peril!"

Sir Guyon wondered at the fellow's boldness, though he scorned his idle vanity. He asked him mildly why any harm should come to him if he remained.

"Because," replied the man, "there is now coming, and close at hand, a knight of wondrous power, who never yet met an enemy without doing him deadly harm, or frightening him dreadfully. You need not hope for any better fate, if you choose to stay."

"What is his name?" said Sir Guyon, "and where does he come from?"

"His name is Pyrocles, which means *the Anger of Fire*," was the answer, "and he is called so from his hot and cruel temper. He is the brother of Cymocles, which means *the Anger of the Sea-Waves*, for Cymocles is wild and revengeful. They are the sons of *Malice* and *Intemperance*. I am *Strife*, the servant of Pyrocles, and I find work for him to do and stir him up to mischief. Fly, therefore, from this dreadful place, or your foolhardiness may bring you into danger."

"Never mind about that," said Sir Guyon, "but tell me whither you are now bound. For it must be some great reason that makes you in such a hurry."

"My master has sent me to seek out Occasion," said Strife. "He is furious to fight, and woe betide the man who first falls in his way."

"You must be mad," said the Palmer, "to seek out Occasion and cause for strife. She comes unsought, and follows even when shunned. Happy the man who can keep away from her."

"Look," said Sir Guyon, "yonder she sits, bound. Take that message to your master."

At this Strife grew very angry, and seizing one of his darts, he hurled it at Sir Guyon. The Knight caught it on his shield, whereupon Strife fled away, and was soon lost to sight.

Not long after, Sir Guyon saw a fierce-looking knight riding swiftly towards him. His armour sparkled like fire, and his horse was bright red, and champed and chafed at his bit as his master spurred him roughly forward. This was Pyrocles.

Not waiting to speak, he furiously attacked Sir Guyon, but after a sharp battle he was utterly defeated, and obliged to beg for mercy.

This Sir Guyon courteously granted, and asked the reason why Pyrocles had attacked him so fiercely.

The knight replied it was because he heard that Sir Guyon had taken captive a poor old woman, and chained her up. He demanded that she and her son Fury should be set free.

"And is that all that has so sorely displeased you?" said Sir Guyon, smiling. "There they are; I hand them over to you."

Pyrocles, delighted, rushed to set free the captives, but they were scarcely untied before their rage and spite burst forth with double fury. They did everything they could to make Pyrocles and Sir Guyon fight again. They not only railed against Sir Guyon for being the conqueror, but also against Pyrocles for allowing himself to be conquered.

Sir Guyon stood apart and refused to be drawn into the quarrel; but Pyrocles could not help getting enraged, and he and Fury were soon in the midst of a terrible fight.

Seeing that Pyrocles was getting the worst Of it, Sir Guyon would have gone to his help, but the Palmer held him back, and refused to let him interfere.

"No," he said firmly, "it is idle for you to pity him. He has brought this trouble upon himself by his own folly and wilfulness, and he must now bear the punishment."

So, as there was nothing more to be done, Sir Guyon and the Palmer started again on their journey.

The Idle Lake

In the course of their journey, Sir Guyon and the Palmer came at last to the shores of a great lake. The water of this lake was thick and sluggish, unmoved by any wind or tide. In the midst of it floated an island, a lovely plot of fertile land, set like a little nest among the wide waves. The island was full of dainty herbs and flowers, beautiful trees

"He boldly spake, 'Sir Knight, if knight thou bee,
Abandon this forestalled place at erst,
For fear of further harme, I counsell thee,
Or bide the chaunce at thine owne jeopardie.'"

with spreading branches, and with birds singing sweetly on every branch. But everything there—the flowers, the trees, and the singing birds—only served to tempt weak-minded people to be slothful and lazy. Lying on the soft grass in some shady dell, they forgot there was any such thing as work or duty, and cared for nothing but to sleep away the time in idle dreams.

Up to the present, Sir Guyon had only had to face adventures of a stern and painful kind, but now he was to be put to quite a different test. Would he fall a prey to the sloth and luxury of this island, or would he remain faithful to his knightly duty?

When Sir Guyon and his companion, Conscience, came to the shore of the lake, they saw, floating near, a little gondola, all decked with boughs. In the gondola sat a beautiful lady, amusing herself by singing and laughing loudly. She came at once when Guyon called, and offered to ferry him across the lake; but when the Knight was in the boat, she refused to let the Palmer get in, and neither money nor entreaties would induce her to take the old man with them. Sir Guyon was very unwilling to leave his guide behind, but he could not go back, for the boat, obeying the lady's wish, shot away more swiftly than a swallow flies. It needed no oar nor pilot to guide it, nor any sails to carry it with the wind; it knew how to go exactly where its owner wanted, and could save itself both from rocks and shoals.

The name of the lady in the gondola was Phædria; she was one of the servants of the wicked enchantress, Acrasia, whom Sir Guyon was now on his way to attack. She hoped that the beautiful island would entrap the Knight, and make him delay his journey and forget his purpose.

On the way, as was her custom, she began joking and laughing loudly, thinking this would amuse her guest. Sir Guyon was so kind and courteous that he was quite ready to join in any real merriment; but when he saw his companion grow noisier and sillier every moment, he began to despise her and did not care to share her foolish attempts at fun. But she went on still in the same manner till at last they reached the island.

When Sir Guyon saw this land, he knew he was out of his way, and was very angry.

"But whenas Guyon of that land had sight,
He wist himselfe amisse, and angry said;
'Ah, Dame! perdy ye have not doen me right,
Thus to mislead mee, whiles I you obaid:
Mee litle needed from my right way to have straid.'"

"Lady," he said, "you have not done right to me, to mislead me like this, when I trusted you. There was no need for me to have strayed from my right way."

"Fair sir," she said, "do not be angry. He who travels on the sea cannot command his way, nor order wind and weather at his pleasure. The sea is wide, and it is easy to stray on it; the wind is uncertain. But here you may rest awhile in safety, till the season serves to attempt a new passage. Better be safe in port than on a rough sea," she ended laughingly.

Sir Guyon was not at all pleased, but he checked his anger and stepped on shore. Phædria at once began to show off all the delights of the island, which grew in beauty wherever she went. The flowers sprang freshly, the trees burst into bud and early blossom, and a whole chorus of birds broke into song. And the lady, more sweetly than any bird on bough, would often sing with them, surpassing, as she easily could, their native music with her skilful art. She strove, by every device in her power, so to charm Sir Guyon that he would forget all deeds of daring and his knightly duty.

But Sir Guyon was wise, and took care not to be carried away by these delights, though he would not seem so rude as to despise anything that a gentle lady did to give him pleasure. He spoke many times of his desire to leave, but she kept on making excuses to delay his journey.

Now it happened that Phædria had already allured to the island another knight. This was Cymocles, whose name means *the Anger of the Sea*. He was the brother of Pyrocles (*the Anger of the Fire*), whom you may remember Sir Guyon had already fought and conquered. Cymocles had been sunk in a heavy sleep when Sir Guyon arrived, but when he woke up and discovered the new-comer, he flew at once into a furious rage, and rushed to attack him.

Sir Guyon, of course, was quite ready to defend himself, and Cymocles soon found that he had never before met such a powerful foe. The fight between them was so terrible that Phædria, overcome with pity and dismay, rushed forward, and implored them, for her sake, to stop. She blamed herself as the cause of all the mischief, and entreated them not to disgrace the name of knighthood by strife and cruelty, but to make peace and be friends.

So great is the power of gentle words to a brave and generous heart, that at her speech their rage began to relent. When all was over, Sir Guyon again begged the lady to let him depart, and to give him passage to the opposite shore. She was now quite as glad as he was for him to go, for she saw that all her folly and vain delights were powerless to tempt him from his duty, and she did not want her selfish ease and pleasure to be troubled with terror and the clash of arms. So she bade him get into the little boat again, and soon conveyed him swiftly to the farther strand.

The Realm of Pluto

Sir Guyon having lost his trusty guide, who was left behind on the shore of the Idle Lake, had now to go on his way alone. At last he came to a gloomy glade, where the thick branches and shrubs shut away the daylight. There, lurking in the shade, he found a rude, savage man, very ugly and unpleasant-looking. His face was tanned with smoke, his eyes dull, his head and beard streaked with soot, his hands were coal-black, as if burnt at a smith's forge, and his nails were like claws.

His iron coat, all overgrown with rust, was lined with gold, which, though now darkened with dirt, seemed as if it had been formerly a work of rich and curious design. In his lap he counted over a mass of coin, feasting his eyes and his covetous wishes with the sight of his huge treasury. Round about on every side lay great heaps of gold, which could never be spent: some were the rough ore, others were beaten into great ingots and square wedges; some were round plates, without mark of any kind, but most were stamped, and bore the ancient and curious inscription of some king or emperor.

As soon as the man saw Sir Guyon, he rose, in great haste and fright, to hide his mounds of treasure, and began with trembling hands to pour them through a wide hole into the earth. But Sir Guyon, though he was himself dismayed at the sight, sprang lightly forward to stop him.

"Who are you that live here in the desert, and hide away from people's sight, and from their proper use, all these rich heaps of wealth?" he asked.

Looking at him with great disdain, the man replied, "You are very rash and heedless of yourself, Sir Knight, to come here to trouble me, and my heaps of treasure. I call myself 'King of this world and worldlings'—Great Mammon—the greatest power on earth. Riches, renown, honour, estate, and all the goods of this world, for which men incessantly toll and moil, flow forth from me in abundance. If you will deign to serve and follow me, all these mountains of gold shall be at your command, and, if these will not suffice, you shall have ten times as much."

"Mammon," said the Knight, "your boast of kingship is in vain, and your bribe of golden wages is useless. Offer your gifts to those who covet such dazzling gain. It would ill befit me, who spend my days in deeds of daring and pursuit of honour, to pay any attention to the tempting baits with which you bewitch weak men. Any desire for worldly dross mixes badly with, and debases the true heroic spirit which joys in fighting for crowns and kingdoms. Fair shields, gay steeds, bright armour are my delight. These are the riches fit for a venturous knight."

Mammon went on trying to tempt the Knight with all sorts of alluring promises, but Sir Guyon stood firm. He pointed out the evils that had come through riches, which he considered the root of all unquietness—first got with guile—then kept with dread, afterwards spent with pride and lavishness, and leaving behind them grief and heaviness. They were the cause of infinite mischief, strife and debate, bloodshed and bitterness, wrong-doing and covetousness, which noble hearts despise as dishonour. Innocent people were murdered, kings slain, great cities sacked and burnt, and other evils, too many to mention, were caused by riches.

"Son," said Mammon at last, "let be your scorn, and leave the wrongs done in the old days to those who lived in them. You who live in these later times must work for wealth, and risk your life for gold. If you choose to use what I offer you, take what you please of all this

abundance; if you don't choose, you are free to refuse it, but do not afterwards blame the thing you have refused."

"I do not choose to receive anything," replied the Knight, "until I am sure that it has been well come by. How do I know but what you have got these goods by force or fraud from their rightful owners?"

"No eye has ever yet seen, nor tongue counted, nor hand handled them," said Mammon. "I keep them safe hidden in a secret place. Come and see."

"Then Mammon lei Sir Guyon through the thick covert, and

found a dark way which no man could spy, that went deep down into the ground, and was compassed round with dread and horror. At length they came into a larger space, that stretched into a wide plain; a broad beaten highway ran across this, leading straight to the grisly realm of Pluto, ruler of the Lower Regions.

It was indeed a horrible road. By the wayside sat fiendish Vengeance and turbulent Strife, one brandishing an iron whip, the other a knife, and both gnashing their teeth and threatening the lives of those who went by. On the other side, in one group, sat cruel Revenge and rancorous Spite, disloyal Treason and heart-burning Hate; but gnawing jealousy sat alone out of their sight, biting his lips; and trembling Fear ran to and fro, finding no place where he might safely shroud himself. Lamenting Sorrow Jay in the darkness, and Shame hid his ugly face from living eye. Over them always fluttered grim Horror, beating his iron wings, and after him flew owls and night-ravens, messengers of evil tidings, while a Harpy—a hideous bird of ill omen—sitting on a cliff near, sang a song of bitter sorrow that would have broken a heart of flint, and when it was ended flew swiftly after Horror.

All these lay before the gates of Pluto, and passing by, Sir Guyon and Mammon said nothing to them, but all the way wonder fed the eyes and filled the thoughts of Sir Guyon.

At last Mammon brought him to a little door that was next adjoining to the wide-open gate of Hades, and nothing parted them; there was only a little stride between them, dividing the House of Riches from the mouth of the Lower Regions.

Before the door sat self-consuming Care, keeping watch and ward, day and night, for fear lest Force or Fraud should break in, and steal the treasure he was guarding. Nor would he allow Sleep once to come near, although his drowsy den was next.

Directly Mammon arrived, the door opened, and gave passage to him. Sir Guyon still kept following, for neither darkness nor danger could dismay him.

The Cave of Mammon

As soon as Mammon and Sir Guyon entered the House of Riches, the door immediately shut of itself, and from behind it leapt forth an ugly fiend, who followed them wherever they went. He kept an eager watch on Guyon, hoping that before long the Knight would lay a covetous hand on some of the treasures, in which case he was ready to tear him to pieces with his claws.

The form of the house inside was rude and strong, like a huge cave hewn out of the cliff; from cracks in the rough vault hung lumps of gold, and every rift was laden with rich metal, so that they seemed ready to fall in pieces, while high above all the spider spun her crafty web, smothered in smoke and clouds blacker than jet. The roof, and floor, and walls were all of gold, but covered with dust and hid in darkness, so that no one could see the colour of it; for the cheerful daylight never came inside that house, only a faint shadow of uncertain light, like a dying lamp. Nothing was to be seen but great iron chests and strong coffers, all barred with double bands of metal, so that no one could force them open by violence; but all the ground was strewn with the bones of dead men, who had lost their lives in that place, and were now left there unburied.

They passed on, and Guyon spoke not a word till they came to an iron door, which opened to them of its own accord, and showed them such a store of riches as the eye of man had never seen before.

Then Mammon, turning to the warrior, said, "Behold here the world's happiness! Behold here the end at which all men aim, to be made rich! Such favour—to be happy—is now laid before you."

"I will not have your offered favour," said the Knight, "nor do I intend to be happy in that way. Before my eyes I place another happiness, another end. To those that take pleasure in them, I resign these base things. But I prefer to spend my fleeting hours in fighting and brave deeds, and would rather be lord over those who have riches than have them myself, and be their slave."

At that the fiend gnashed his teeth, and was angry because he was kept so long from his prey, for he thought that so glorious a bait would surely have tempted his guest. Had it done so, he would have snatched him away lighter than a dove in a falcon's claws.

But, when Mammon saw he had missed his object, he thought of another way to entrap the Knight unawares. He led him away into another room where there were a hundred furnaces burning fiercely. By every furnace were many evil spirits horrible to see, busily engaged in tending the fires, or working with the molten metal. When they saw Guyon they all stood stock still to wonder at him, for they had never seen such a mortal before; he was almost afraid of their staring eyes and hideous figures.

"Behold what living eye has never seen before," said Mammon. "Here is the fountain of the world's good. If, therefore, you will be rich, be well advised and change your wilful mood, lest hereafter you may wish and not be able to have."

"Let it suffice that I refuse all your idle offers," said Guyon. "All that I need I have. Why should I covet more than I can use? Keep such vain show for your worldlings, but give me leave to follow my quest."

Mammon was much displeased, but he led him forward, to entice him further. He brought him through a dark and narrow way to a broad gate, built of beaten gold. The gate was open, but there stood in front of it a sturdy fellow, very bold and defiant-looking. In his right hand he held an iron club, but he himself seemed as if he were made of gold. His name was Disdain. When he saw Guyon he brandished his club, but Mammon bade him be still, and led his guest past him.

He took him into a large place, like some solemn temple; great golden pillars upheld the massive roof, and every pillar was decked with crowns and diadems, such as princes wore while reigning on earth. A crowd of people of every sort and nation were there assembled, all pressing with a great uproar to the upper part, where was placed a high throne. On it sat a woman, clad in gorgeous robes of royalty. Her face seemed marvellously fair; her beauty threw such brightness round that all men could see it; it was not all her own, however, but was partly made up by art.

As she sat there, glittering, she held a great gold chain, the upper end of which reached high into heaven, and the other end deep down

"Behold thou Faeries sonne, with mortall eye,
That living eye before did never see:
* * * * * *
Here is the fountaine of the worldes good:
Now, therefore, if thou wilt enriched bee,
Avise thee well, and chaunge thy wilfull mood."

into the lower regions; and all the crowd around her pressed to catch hold of that chain, to climb aloft by it, and excel others.

The name of the chain was *Ambition*, and every link was a step of dignity. Some thought to raise themselves to a high place by riches, some by pushing. some by flattery, some by friends—and all by wrong ways, for those that were up themselves kept others low, and those that were low held tight hold of others, not letting them rise, while every one strove to throw down his companions.

When Guyon saw this he began to ask what all the crowd meant, and who was the lady that sat on the throne.

"That goodly person, round whom every one flocks, is my dear daughter," said Mammon. "From her alone come honour and dignity, and this world's happiness, for which all men struggle, but which few get. She is called Philotime, *the Love of Honour*, and she is the fairest lady in the world. Since you have found favour with me, I will make her your wife, if you like, that she may advance you, because of your work and just merits."

"I thank you much, Mammon," said the gentle Knight, "for offering me such favour, but I am only a mortal, and, I know well, an unworthy match for such a wife. And, if I were not, yet is my troth plighted and my love declared to another lady, and to change one I s love without cause is a disgrace to a knight."

Mammon was inwardly enraged, but, hiding his feelings, he led him away, through the grisly shadows, by a beaten path, into a garden well furnished with herbs and fruits of an unknown kind. They were not such as men gather from the fertile earth, sweet and of good taste, but deadly black, both leaf and flower. Here grew cypress and ebony, poppy and deadly nightshade, hemlock, and many other poisonous plants. The place was called the Garden of Proserpine. In the midst was a silver seat, under a thick arbour, and near by grew a great tree with spreading branches, laden with golden apples.

Mammon showed the Knight many wonders in the Garden of Proserpine, and tried to tempt him to sit in the silver seat, or to eat of the golden apples. If Guyon had done so, the horrible monster who waited behind would have pounced on him and torn him to pieces; but he was wary and took care not to yield to temptation, so the beguiler was cheated of his prey, But now he began to feel weak and ill for want of food and sleep, for three days had passed since he entered the cave. So he begged Mammon to guide him back to the surface of the earth by the way they had come. Mammon, though very unwilling, was forced to obey; but the change was too much for Guyon in his feeble state, and as soon as he came into the light, and began to breathe the fresh air, he fainted away.

The Champion of Chivalry

During the time that Guyon stayed in the house of Mammon, the Palmer, whom the maid of the Idle Lake had refused to take in her boat, had found a passage in some other way. On his journey he came near the place where Guyon lay in a trance, and suddenly he heard a voice calling loud and clear, "Come hither, hither! Oh, come quickly!"

He hurried in the direction of the cry, which led him to the shady dell where Mammon had formerly counted his wealth. Here he found Guyon senseless on the ground, but watched over by a beautiful angel.

At first he was dismayed, but the angel bade him not be frightened, for that life and renewed vigour would soon come back to the Knight. He now handed him over to the charge of the Palmer, and bade him watch with care, for fresh evil was at hand.

Thus saving, the angel vanished, and the Palmer, turning to look at Guyon, was rejoiced to find a feeble glimmer of life in him, which he cherished tenderly.

At last there came that way two Pagan knights in shining armour, led by an old man, and with a light-footed page far in front, scattering mischief and enmity wherever he went. These were the two bad brothers, Pyrocles and Cymocles, the sons of Anger, guided by the false Archimago, while their servant, Atin (or *Strife*) stirred them up to quarrelling and vengeance.

When they came to the place where the Palmer sat watching over the sleeping body of the Knight, they knew the latter at once, for they had both lately fought with him. They reviled the Palmer, and began heaping abuse on Sir Guyon, whom they thought dead, and declared

that they would strip him of his armour, which was much too good for such a worthless creature. The Palmer implored them not to do such a shameful and dishonourable deed, but his entreaties were in vain; one brother laid his hand on the shield, the other on the helmet, both fiercely eager to possess themselves of the spoil.

At this moment they saw coming towards them an armed knight of bold and lofty grace, whose squire bore after him an ebony spear and a covered shield. Well did the magician know him by his arms and bearing when he saw his prancing Libyan steed, and he cried to the brothers, "Rise quickly, and prepare yourselves for battle, for yonder comes the mightiest knight alive—Prince Arthur, the flower of grace and chivalry."

The brothers were so impressed that they started up and greedily prepared for battle. Pyrocles, who had lost his own weapons in the fight with Fury, snatched a sword from Archimago, although the latter warned him it was a magic sword, and would do no harm to Prince Arthur, for whom it had been made long ago, and who was its rightful owner. Pyrocles only laughed at the magician's warning, and having bound Guyon's shield to his wrist, he was ready for the fray.

By that time the stranger Knight had come near, and greeted them courteously. They returned no answer, but looked very disdainful, and then, turning to the Palmer, Prince Arthur noticed that at his feet lay an armed man, in whose dead face he read great nobility.

"Reverend sir," he said, "what great misfortune has befallen this Knight? Did he die a natural death, or did he fall by treason or by fight?"

"Not by one or the other," said the Palmer; "but his senses are drowned in sleep, and these cruel foes have taken advantage of it to revenge their spite and rob him of his armour; but you, fair sir, whose honourable look promises hope of help, may I beseech you to take pity on his sad plight, and by your power protect him?"

"Palmer," he said, "there is no knight so rude, I trust, as to do outrage to a sleeping spirit. Maybe, better reason will soften their rash revenge. Well, chosen words have a secret power in appeasing anger. If not, leave to me your Knight's last defence."

Then, turning to the brothers, he first tried what persuasion would do. He took for granted that their wrath was provoked by wrongs they had suffered, and did not challenge the right or justice of their actions; but, on behalf of the sleeping man, he entreated pardon for anything he might have done amiss.

To this gentle speech the brothers made rude and insulting answers, and Pyrocles, not waiting to set the Prince on guard, lifted high the magic sword, thinking to kill him. The faithful steel refused to harm its master, and swerved from the mark, but the blow was so furious it made man and horse reel. Prince Arthur was such a splendid rider that he did not fall from the saddle; but, full of anger, he cried fiercely—

"False traitor! you have broken the law of arms by striking a foe unchallenged, but you shall soon right bitterly taste the fruit of your treason, and feel the law which you have disgraced."

With that he levelled his spear at Pyrocles, and the two were soon engaged in a fiery battle. Cymocles rushed to his brother's aid, and they both fell on the Prince with terrific fury, so that he had hard work to defend himself. So mighty was his power that neither of his foes could stand against it; but whenever he smote at Pyrocles, the latter threw in front of him Guyon's shield, on which was portrayed the face of the Faerie Queene, and when he saw this, the Prince's hand relented, and he stayed the stroke, because of the love and loyalty he bore the picture. This often saved the Pagan knight from deadly harm, but at last Prince Arthur overcame and killed both him and his brother, while false Archimago and Strife fled fast away.

By this time Sir Guyon had awakened from his trance, and was much grieved when he found that his shield and sword had disappeared; but when he saw beside him his faithful companion, whom he had lost some days before, he was very glad. The Palmer was delighted to see him rise looking so well, and told him not to trouble about the loss of his weapons, for they would soon be restored to him. Then he told Guyon all that had happened, and how the strange Knight had fought for him with the two wicked brothers.

When he heard this, Sir Guyon was deeply touched, and felt all his heart fill with affection. Bowing to Prince Arthur with due reverence, as to the defender of his life, he said, "My lord, my liege, by whose most gracious aid I live this day and see my foes subdued, what reward would be sufficient to repay you for your great goodness, unless to be ever bound—"

But the Prince interrupted. "Fair sir, what need is there to reckon a good turn as a debt to be paid? Are not' all knights bound by oath to withstand the power of the oppressor? It is sufficient that I have done my duty properly."

So they both found that a good deed is made gracious by kindness and courtesy.

The House of Temperance

After the Pagan brothers were conquered, and Prince Arthur had recovered his stolen sword and Guyon his lost shield, the two went on their way together, talking pleasantly as they journeyed along. When the sun was near setting they saw in the distance a goodly castle, placed near a river, in a pleasant valley. Thinking this place would do to spend the night in, they marched thither, but when they came near, and dismounted from their tired steeds, they found the gates barred and every fastening locked, as though for fear of foes. They thought this was done as an insult to them, to prevent their entrance, till the Squire blew his horn under the castle wall, which shook with the sound as if it would fall. Then a watchman quickly looked forth from the highest tower, and called loudly to the knights to ask what they required so rudely. They gently answered that they . wished to enter.

"Fly, fly, good knights!" he said; "fly fast away if you love your lives, as it is right you should. Fly fast, and save yourselves from instant death. You may not enter here, though we would most willingly let you in if only we could. But a thousand enemies rage round us, who have held the castle in siege for seven years, and many good knights who have sought to save us have been slain."

As he spoke, a thousand villains, with horrible outcry, swarmed around them from the adjoining rocks and caves—vile wretches, ragged, rude, and hideous, all threatening death, and all armed in a curious manner, some with unwieldy clubs, some with long spears, some with rusty knives, some with staves heated in the fire. They looked like wild bulls, staring with hollow eyes, and with stiff hair standing on end.

They assailed the Knights fiercely, and made them recoil, but when Prince Arthur and Sir Guyon charged again their strength began to fail, and they were unable to withstand them, for the champions broke on them with such might that they were forced to fly like scattered sheep before the rush of a lion and a tiger. The Knights with their shining blades soon broke their rude ranks, and drove them into confusion, hewing and slashing at them; and now, when faced boldly, they found that they were nothing but idle shadows, for, though they seemed bodies, they had really no substance.

When they had dispersed this troublesome rabble, Prince Arthur and Guyon came again to the castle gate, and begged entrance, where they had been refused before. The report of their danger and conflict having reached the ears of the lady who dwelt there, she came out with a goodly train of squires and ladies to bid them welcome.

The lady's name was Alma. She was as beautiful as it was possible to be, in the very flower of her youth, yet full of goodness and modesty. She was clad in a robe of lily-white, reaching from her shoulders to the ground; the long, loose train, embroidered with gold and pearls, was carried by two fair damsels. Her yellow-golden hair was trimly arranged, and she wore no head-dress except a garland of sweet roses.

She entertained the Knights nobly, and, when they had rested a little, they begged her, as a great favour, to show them over her castle. This she consented to do.

First she led them up to the castle wall, which was so high that no foe could climb it, and yet was both beautiful and fit for defence. It was not built of brick, nor yet of stone, sand, nor mortar, but of clay. The pity was that such goodly workmanship could not last longer, for it must soon turn back to earth.

Two gates were placed in this building, the one (*mouth*) by which all passed in far excelling the other in workmanship. When it was locked, no one could pass through, and when it was opened no man could shut it. Within the barbican sat a porter (the *tongue*), day and night keeping watch and ward; nobody could go in or out of the gate without strict scrutiny. Utterers of secrets he debarred, babblers of folly, and those who told tales of wrong-doing; when cause required it, his alarm-bell might be heard far and wide, but never without occasion.

Round the porch on each side sat sixteen warders (the *teeth*), all in bright array; tall yeomen they seemed, of great strength, and were ranged ready for fight.

Alma then took the Knights over the rest of the castle, and showed them so many curious and beautiful things that their minds were filled

"But soone the knights with their bright-burning blades
Broke their rude troupes, and orders did confound,
Hewing and slashing at their idle shades;
For though they bodies seem, yet substaunce from them fades."

with wonder, for they had never before seen so strange a sight. Presently she brought them back into a beautiful parlour (the *heart*), hung with rich tapestry, where sat a bevy of fair ladies (the *feelings*, *tastes*, &c.), amusing themselves in different ways. Some sang, some laughed, some played with straws, some sat idly at ease; but others could not bear to play—all amusement was annoyance to them. This one frowned, that one yawned, a third blushed for shame, another seemed envious or shy, while another gnawed a rush and looked sullen.

After that, Alma took her guests up to a stately turret (the *head*), in which two beacons (the *eyes*) gave light, and flamed continually, for they were most marvellously made of living fire, and set in silver sockets, covered with lids that could easily open and shut.

In this turret there were many rooms and places, but three chief ones, in which dwelt three honourable sages, who counselled fair Alma how to govern well. The first of these could foresee things to come; the second could best advise of things present; the third kept things past in memory, so that no time or occasion could arise which one or other of them could not deal with.

The first sat in the front of the house, so that nothing should hinder his coming to a conclusion quickly; he made up his mind in advance, without listening to reason; he had a keen foresight, and an active brain that was never idle and never rested. His room held a collection of the oddest and queerest things ever seen or imagined. It was filled, too, with flies, that buzzed all about, confusing men's eyes and ears, with a sound like a swarm of bees. These were idle thoughts and fancies, dreams, visions, soothsayings, prophecies, &c., and all kinds of false tales and lies.

The second counsellor was a much older man. He spent all his time meditating over things that had really happened, and in studying law, art, science and philosophy, so that he had grown very wise indeed.

The third counsellor was a very, very aged man. His chamber seemed very ruinous and old, and was therefore at the back of the house, but the walls that upheld it were quite firm and strong. He was half blind, and looked feeble in body, but his mind was still vigorous. All things that had happened, however ancient they were, he faithfully recorded, so that nothing might be forgotten.

The names of Alma's three counsellors were Imagination, Judgment, and Memory.

The Rock of Reproach and the Wandering Islands

The next morning, before it was light, Sir Guyon, clad in his bright armour, and accompanied by the Palmer in his black dress, started once more on his journey to find the wicked enchantress, Acrasia, and the Bower of Bliss. At the river ford, they found a ferryman, whom Alma had commanded to be there with his well-rigged boat. They went on board, and he immediately launched his bark, and Lady Alma's country was soon left far behind.

For two days they sailed without even seeing land; but on the morning of the third day, they heard, far away, a hideous roaring that filled them with terror, and they saw the surges rage so high, they feared to be drowned.

Then said the boatman, "Palmer, steer aright, and keep an even course, for we must needs pass yonder way. That is the Gulf of Greediness, which swallows up all it can devour, and is in a constant turmoil."

On the other side, stood a hideous rock of mighty magnet stone, whose craggy cliffs were dreadful to behold. Great jagged reefs ran out into the water, and threatened, death to all who came near. Yet passers-by were unable to keep away, for trying to escape the devouring jaws of the Gulf of Greediness, they were dashed to pieces on the rock.

As they drew near this dreadful spot, the ferryman had to put forth all his strength and skill to row them past. On the one hand, they saw the horrible gulf, that looked as if it were sucking down all the sea into itself; and on the other hand, they saw the perilous rock, on whose sharp cliffs lay the ribs of many shattered vessels, together with the dead bodies of those who had recklessly flung themselves to destruction.

The name of the rock was the "Rock of Reproach." It was a dangerous and hateful place, to which no fish nor fowl ever came, but only screaming sea-gulls and cormorants, who sat waiting on the cliff to

"Said then the Boteman, 'Palmer, stere aright,
And keepe an even course; for yonder way
We needes must pas (God doe us well acquight).'"

prey on the unhappy wretches whose extravagant and thriftless living had brought them to ruin.

Sir Guyon and his companions passed by this dangerous spot in safety, and the ferryman rowed them briskly over the dancing billows.

At last, far off, they spied many islands floating on every side among the waves. Then said the Knight, "Lo, I see the land, so, Sir Palmer, direct your course to it."

"Not so," said the ferryman, "lest we unknowingly run into danger; for those same islands, which now and then appear, are not firm land, nor have they any certain abiding-place; they are straggling plots, which run to and fro in the wide waters, wherefore they are called the 'Wandering Islands,' and are to be shunned, for they have drawn many a traveller into danger and distress. Yet from far off, they seem very pleasant, both fair and fruitful, the ground spread with soft, green grass, and the tall trees covered with leaves, and decked with white and red blossoms that might well allure passers-by. But whoever once sets his foot on those islands can never recover it, but evermore wanders, uncertain and unsure."

Sir Guyon and the Palmer listened to their pilot, as seemed fitting, and they passed on their way.

"Now," said the cautious boatman, when they had left behind them the Wandering Islands (or, *listless idleness*), "we must be careful to take good heed of our safety here, for a perilous passage lies before us. There is a great quicksand, and a whirlpool of hidden danger; therefore, Sir Palmer, keep a steady hand, for the narrow way lies between them."

Scarcely had he spoken, when near at hand they spied the quicksand; it was almost covered with water, but they knew it at once by the waves round it and the discoloured sea. It was called the Quicksand of Unthriftiness.

Passing by, they saw a goodly ship, laden from far with precious merchandise, and well fitted as a ship could be, which through misadventure or carelessness had run herself into danger. The mariners and merchants, with much toil, laboured in vain to recover their prize and to save the rich wares from destruction, but neither toll nor trouble served to free her from the quicksand.

On the other side, they saw the dangerous pool that was called the Whirlpool of Decay, in which many had haplessly sunk, of whom no memory remained. The circling waters whirled round, like a restless wheel, eager to draw the boat into the outer limit of the labyrinth, and to drown the travellers. But the heedful ferryman rowed with all his might, so that they passed by in safety and left the dreaded danger behind.

Suddenly they saw in the midst of the ocean, the surging waters rise like a mountain, and the great sea puffed up, as though threatening to devour everything. The waves came rolling along, and the billows roared in fury, though there was not a breath of wind. At this, Sir Guyon, the Palmer, and the ferryman were greatly afraid, for they knew not what strange horror was approaching.

Sea-Monsters and Land-Monsters

Presently they saw a hideous crowd of huge sea-monsters, such as terrified any one to behold; every shape of ugliness and horror was there—water-snakes, and whales, and sword-fish, and hippopotamuses, and sharks, and every kind of sea-monster, and they came along in thousands, with a dreadful noise and a hollow, rumbling roar. No wonder the Knight was appalled, for, compared with these, all that we hold dreadful on earth were but a trifle.

"Fear nothing," then said the Palmer, "for these creatures that look like monsters are not so in reality; they are only disguised into these fearful shapes by the wicked enchantress to terrify us, and to prevent our continuing our journey."

Then, lifting up his magic staff, he smote the sea, which immediately became calm, and all the make-believe monsters fled to the bottom of the ocean.

Free from that danger, the travellers kept on their way, and as they went, they heard a pitiful cry, as of some one wailing and weeping. At last, on an island, they saw a beautiful maiden, who seemed in great sorrow, and who kept calling to them for help. Directly Guyon heard her, he bade the Palmer steer straight to her rescue; but the latter, knowing better, said, "Fair sir, do not be displeased if I disobey you, for it would be a bad thing to listen to her, for really there is nothing the matter; it is only a trick to entrap you."

The Knight was guided by his advice, and the ferryman held steadily straight on his course.

The next temptation they had to face was of a different kind. They came to a lovely bay, sheltered on the one side by a steep hill, and on the other by a high rock, so that between them was a still and pleasant haven. In this bay lived five mermaids, who could sing in the sweetest manner possible, but the only use they made of their skill in melody was to allure travellers, whom, when they had got hold of, they killed. So now to Guyon as he passed, they began to sing their sweetest tunes, greeting him as the mightiest knight that had ever fought in battle, and bidding him to turn his rudder into the quiet bay, where his storm-beaten vessel might safely ride.

"This is the port of rest from troublous toll," they sang; "the world's sweet inn from pain and wearisome turmoil."

The rolling sea and the waves breaking on the rock mingled with their singing, and the wind whistled in harmony. The sound so delighted Guyon that he bade the boatman row slowly, to let him listen to their melody. But the Palmer wisely counselled him not to do this, and so they got safely past the danger, and soon after they saw, in the distance, the land to which they were directing their course.

Then suddenly a thick fog came down upon them, hiding the cheerful daylight, and making the whole world seem a confused mass. They were much dismayed at this, not knowing which way to steer in the darkness, and fearing that they would fall into some hidden danger. To add to their confusion, they were attacked by a flock of horrible birds, which flew screaming round them, beating at them with their wicked wings—owls, and ravens, and bats, and screech-owls. Yet the travellers would not stay because of these, but went straight forward, the ferryman rowing, while the Palmer kept a firm hand on the rudder, till at last the weather began to clear, and the land showed plainly. Then the Palmer warned Sir Guyon to have his armour in readiness, for peril would soon assail him.

The Knight obeyed, and when the boat reached the shore, he and the Palmer stepped out, fully armed, and carefully prepared against every danger.

They had not gone far, before they heard a hideous bellowing, and a pack of wild beasts rushed forward as if to devour them. But when they came near, the Palmer lifted up his wonderful staff, and immediately they were quelled, and shrank back trembling.

Passing these, Sir Guyon and the Palmer soon came to the place the Knight was seeking—the object of his long and toilsome quest-the home of the wicked enchantress—the "Bower of Bliss."

The Bower of Bliss

It was a lovely spot, a place adorned in the most perfect way by which art could imitate nature; everything sweet and pleasing, or that the daintiest fancy could devise, was gathered here in lavish profusion. A light fence enclosed it, and a rich ivory gate, wonderfully carven, stood open to all those that came thither.

In the porch sat a tall, handsome porter, whose looks were so pleasant that he seemed to entice travellers to him, but it was only to deceive them to their own ruin. He was the keeper of the garden, and his name was *Pleasure*. He was decked with flowers, and by his side was set a great bowl of wine, with which he pleased all new-comers. He offered it to Sir Guyon, but the latter refused his idle courtesy, and overthrew the bowl.

Passing through the gate, they beheld a large and spacious plain, strewn on every side with delights. The ground was covered with green grass, and made beautiful with all kinds of lovely flowers; the skies were always bright, and the air soft and balmy; no storm or frost ever came to harm the tender blossoms; neither scorching heat nor piercing cold to hurt those who dwelt therein.

Guyon wondered much at the loveliness of that sweet place, yet would not suffer any of its delights to allure him, but passed straight through, and still looked forward. Presently he came to a beautiful arbour, fashioned out of interlacing boughs and branches. This was arched over with a clustering vine, richly laden with bunches of lus-

"Ere long they heard an hideous bellowing
Of many beasts, that roared outrageously.
* * * * * * *
But soone as they approcht with deadly threat,
The Palmer over them his staffe upheld."

cious grapes—some were deep purple like the hyacinth—some like rubies, laughing red—some like emeralds, not yet well ripened, and there were others of burnished gold. They almost broke down the branches with their weight, and seemed to offer themselves to be freely gathered by the passers-by.

In the arbour sat a finely dressed lady; she held in her left hand a golden cup, and with her right hand she gathered the ripe fruit, and squeezed the juice of the grapes into the cup. It was her custom to give a draught of this wine to every stranger that passed, but when she offered it to Guyon to taste, he took the cup out of her hand, and flung it to the ground, so that it was broken and all the wine spilt. *Excess*, for that was the lady's name, was very angry at this, but she could not withstand the Knight, and was obliged to let him pass, and he went on, heedless of her displeasure.

Then before his eyes appeared a most lovely paradise, abounding in every sort of pleasure: rainbow-coloured flowers, lofty trees, shady dells, breezy mountains, rustling groves, crystal streams—it was impossible to tell which was art and which nature, they were so cunningly mingled; both combined made greater the beauty of the other, and adorned this garden with an endless variety.

In the midst of all, stood a fountain made of the most precious materials on earth, so pure and bright that one could see the silver flood running through every channel. It was wrought all over with curious carving, and above all was spread a trail of ivy of the purest gold, coloured like nature, so that any one who saw it would surely think it was real ivy. Numberless little streams continually welled out of this fountain, and formed a little lake, through the shallow water of which one could see the bottom, all paved with shining jasper.

Then at last Sir Guyon and the Palmer drew near to the "Bower of Bliss," so called by the foolish favourites of the wicked enchantress.

"Now, sir, consider well," said the Palmer, "for here is the end of all our travel. Here dwells Acrasia, whom we must surprise, or else she will slip away, and laugh at our attempt."

Soon they heard the most lovely melody, such as might never be heard on mortal ground. It was almost impossible to say what kind of music it was, for all that is pleasing to the ear there joined in harmony—the joyous singing of birds, angelic voices, silver-sounding instruments, murmuring waters, and the whispering wind; and through it all they heard the singing of one voice, sweeter than all the others.

But in spite of the lovely music heard on every side, Sir Guyon and the Palmer never left their path; they kept on through many groves and thickets, till at last they came in sight of the wicked enchantress herself. She lay, half-sleeping, on a bed of roses, clad in a veil of silk and silver, all round were many fair ladies and boys singing sweetly. Not far off was her last victim, a gallant-looking youth, over whom she had cast an evil spell. His brave sword and armour hung idly on a tree, and he lay sunk in a heavy slumber, forgetful of all the noble deeds in which he had once delighted.

Sir Guyon and the Palmer cautiously drew near, then suddenly rushed forward, and flung over Acrasia a net which the skilful Palmer had made for the occasion. All her attendants immediately fled in terror. Acrasia tried all her arts and crafty wiles to set herself free, but in vain; the net was so cunningly woven, neither guile nor force could disentangle her.

Then Sir Guyon broke down without pity all the pleasant bowers, and the stately palace, and trampled down the gardens, and burnt the banqueting-hall, so that nothing was left of the beautiful place to tempt other people to ruin.

As for Acrasia, they led her away captive, bound with adamantine chains, for nothing else would keep her safe; and when they came back to the place where they had met the wild beasts, these again flew fiercely at them, as if they would rescue their mistress. But the Palmer soon pacified them.

Then Guyon asked what was the meaning of these beasts that lived there.

"These seeming beasts are really men whom the enchantress has thus transformed," replied the Palmer. "Now they are turned into these hideous figures, in accordance with their bad and ugly minds."

"A sad end of an ignoble life, and a mournful result of excess in pleasure," said the Knight. "But, Palmer, if it may so please you, let them be returned to their former state."

So the Palmer struck them with his staff, and immediately they

were turned into men. Very queer and ill at ease they looked. Some were inwardly ashamed, and some were angry to see the Lady Acrasia captive. But one in particular, who had lately been a hog, Grill by name, loudly lamented, and abused the Knight for bringing him back from the shape of a hog into that of a man.

Then said Guyon, "See how low a man can sink, to forget so soon the excellence in which he was created, and to choose rather to he a beast without intelligence!"

"Worthless men delight in base things," said the Palmer. "Let Grill be Grill, and have his hoggish mind. But let us depart hence, while wind and weather serve."

So Sir Guyon, having overthrown the power of the wicked enchantress, went back to the house of Alma, where he had left Prince Arthur. The captive Acrasia he sent under a strong guard to the court of the Faerie Queene, to be presented to Queen Gloriana as a proof that he had accomplished his hard task; but he himself travelled forth with Prince Arthur, to make further trial of his strength and to seek fresh adventures.

The Legend of Britomart

How Sir Guyon met a Champion mightier than himself

AFTER the capture of the wicked enchantress Acrasia, Prince Arthur and Sir Guyon travelled long and far together in all sorts of dangerous places. They met with many perilous adventures, which won them great glory and honour, for their aim was always to relieve the weak and oppressed, and to recover right for those who had suffered wrong.

At last one day, as they rode across an open plain, they saw a Knight spurring towards them. An aged squire rode beside him, and on the Knight's shield was emblazoned a lion on a golden field.

When they saw him, Sir Guyon begged Prince Arthur to let him be the one to face the attack, and the Prince agreeing, Guyon levelled his spear and galloped towards the Knight. They met with such fury that the stranger reeled in his saddle, and Guyon himself, before he was aware, was hurled from his horse.

His fall filled him with shame and sorrow, for never yet since he bore arms had such a disgrace happened to him. He need not, however, have been so grieved, for it was no fault of his own that he was dismounted. The spear that brought him to the ground was enchanted, and no one could resist it.

But Guyon would have felt far more sorry and ashamed had he known that the Knight who overthrew him was in reality a maiden. The stranger was no other than the famous Princess Britomart, daughter of Ryence, King of South Wales. She was roaming the world in search of Artegall, the champion Knight of justice, whose image she had once beheld in a magic mirror given by the magician Merlin to her father. So grand and noble was the image of this splendid Knight that Britomart felt she could never rest until she had seen him in reality. She dressed herself in the armour of a knight, and her old nurse, Glaucé, disguised herself as her squire, and together the two left the court of King Ryence and wandered through the world in search of Sir Artegall.

Sir Guyon, full of anger at his fall, and eager to revenge himself, rose hastily, drew his sword, and rushed at the foe; but his attendant, the Black Palmer, who had been his faithful companion and guide in all his former adventures, implored his master not to run into fresh danger. By his great wisdom he could tell that Britomart's spear was enchanted, and that no mortal power could withstand it.

Prince Arthur joined his entreaties to the Palmer's, and they both spoke so wisely that Guyon's anger melted away. Britomart and he became reconciled, and swore a firm friendship. In those days, when knights fought together, it was often not at all in malice, but only to test their strength and manliness. The one who conquered won much renown, but the vanquished felt no spite nor envy. It is a great thing to be able to lose with a good grace, without becoming sulky and dis-

"But Guyon selfe, ere well he was aware,
Nigh a speares length behind his crouper fell."

agreeable. Later ages might do well in this respect to learn a lesson from the days of chivalry.

So Britomart, Prince Arthur, and Sir Guyon then travelled on together in the most friendly fashion, seeking further adventures. For some time nothing happened, but at length they came to a wide forest, which seemed very horrible and dreary. They rode a long way through this, but found no track of living creature, except bears, and lions, and bulls, which roamed all around. Suddenly, out of the thickest part of the wood, something rushed past them.

How Britomart fought with Six Knights

The creature that rushed from the wood, across the path of Britomart, Sir Guyon, and Prince Arthur, was a milk-white pony. On its back was a lovely lady, whose face shone as clear as crystal, though it was now white with fear. Her garments were all worked with beaten gold, and the trappings of her steed were covered with glittering embroidery. The pony fled so fast that nothing could hold it, and they could scarcely see the lady. She kept casting backward glances, as if she feared some evil that closely pursued her, and her bright yellow hair flew out far behind in the wind like the trail of a blazing comet.

The name of the lady was Florimell.

As the Knights stood gazing after her, there rushed from the same thicket a rough, clownish woodman, fiercely urging on his tired horse through thick and thin, over bank and bush, hoping by some means to get hold of Florimell. He was a huge, cruel-looking fellow, and in his hand he carried a sharp boar-spear.

Directly Prince Arthur and Sir Guyon saw this they stayed not a moment to see which would be first, but both spurred after as fast as they could to rescue the lady from the villain.

Britomart waited some time to see if they would return, but finding they did not come back she again set forward on her journey with steadfast courage. She intended no evil, nor did she fear any.

At last, when she had nearly reached the edge of the wood, she spied far away a stately Castle, to which she immediately directed her steps.

This castle was a fine building, and placed for pleasure near the edge of the forest, but in front of the gate stretched a wide, green plain.

On this plain Britomart saw six knights, who were all engaged in cruel battle against one Knight. They attacked him with great violence all at the same time, and sorely beset him on every side, so that he was nearly breathless; but nothing could dismay him, and he never yielded a foot of ground, although he was sorely wounded. He dealt his blows stoutly, and whichever way he turned he made his enemies recoil, so that not one of all the six dared face him alone. They were like cowardly curs having some savage creature at bay, who run about here and there to snatch a bite at their prey whenever his back is turned.

When Britomart saw this gallant Knight in such distress and danger, she ran quickly to his rescue, and called to the six others to cease their attack on a single enemy. They paid no attention, but rather increased their spiteful fury, till Britomart, rushing through the thickest crowd, broke up their band, and compelled them, by force, to listen to peace. Then she began mildly to inquire the cause of their dispute and outrageous anger.

Thereupon the single Knight answered, "These six tried by force to make me give up my own dear lady, and love another. I would rather die than do such a thing. For I love one lady, the truest one on earth, and I have no desire to change. For her dear sake I have endured many a bitter peril and met with many a wound."

"Then, certainly, you six are to blame," said Britomart, "for it would be a great shame for a knight to leave his faithful lady—it would be better to die. Neither can you compel love by force."

Then spoke one of the six. "There dwells within this Castle a fair lady whose beauty has no living rival. She has ordained this law, which we approve—that every knight who comes this way, and has no lady of his own, shall enter her service, never to leave it. But if he has already a lady whom he loves, then he must give her up, or else fight with us to prove that she is fairer than our lady."

"Truly," said Britomart, "the choice is hard. But, suppose the knight overcame, what reward would he get?"

"Then he would be advanced to high honour, and win the hand of our lady," was the answer. "Therefore, sir, if you love any one—"

"But faire before the gate a spatious playne
Mantled with greene, it selfe did spredden wyde,
On which she saw six knights, that did darrayne
Fiers battail against one with cruel might and mayne."

"I certainly will not give up my love, nor will I do service to your lady," replied Britomart. "But I will revenge the wrong you have done to this Knight."

Then she rode at the six with her enchanted spear, and overthrew three of them before they were well aware of it. The fourth was dismayed by the Knight to whose rescue she had come, and the two others gave in before she touched them.

"Too well we see our own weakness and your matchless power," they said. "Henceforth, fair sir, according to her own law, the lady is yours, and we plight our loyalty to you as liegemen."

So they threw their swords under Britomart's feet, and afterwards besought her to enter into the castle, and reap the reward of her victory.

Britomart consenting, they all went in together.

How it fared with Britomart in Castle Joyous

The stately mansion into which Britomart and the rescued Knight now entered was called "Castle Joyous," and the owner of it was known to her retainers by the name of "the Lady of Delight." It would be impossible to tell all the wonderful richness and beauty of this building, which was adorned fit for the palace of a prince.

Passing through a lofty and spacious chamber, every pillar of which was pure gold, set with pearls and precious stones, the knights came to an inner room, hung with the most costly tapestry. The place was filled with the sweetest music and the singing of birds, but the wasteful luxury they saw on every side did not please Britomart nor the Knight, and they looked with a scornful eye on such lavish profusion.

Then they came into the presence of the Lady of the Castle. They found her seated on a splendid couch, glittering with gold and embroidery. She seemed very generous and of rare beauty, but she was neither gentle nor modest, and she never hesitated to gratify her own desires at any cost.

When she saw Britomart, who, in her armour, appeared to be a young and handsome knight, she took a great liking to her, and

"But one of these sixe knights, Gardanté hight,
Drew out a deadly bow and arrow keene,
Which forth he sent, with felonous despight
And fell intent, against the virgin sheene."

thought how nice it would be if she would enter into her service, and stay altogether at the Castle. All through the splendid supper which was presently served, she tried to make herself as agreeable as ever she could, hoping that Britomart would be tempted to remain. After supper, she begged her to lay aside her armour, and enjoy some sport; but this the maiden refused to do, for she wore it as a disguise. Britomart would not be so discourteous as to repulse the kindly spoken offers of goodwill, but she in her heart thought that such a sudden affection for a wandering guest could not be worth very much.

When the supper-tables were cleared away, all the knights, and squires, and dames began to make merry. There was dancing and gambling, and every kind of revelry; but through it all Malecasta (which was the real name of the Lady of Delight) was plotting in her own mind how she could get hold of Britomart. If the gallant young Knight (as she thought him) would not consent to stay of his own free will, she determined to detain him by guile.

So that night, when Britomart had taken off her armour and was fast asleep, Malecasta went to her room. Britomart sprang up in a great fright, and ran to seize her weapon; but Malecasta shrieked for her six knights, and they all came rushing in, armed and half-armed. When they saw Britomart, with her sword drawn, they were afraid to go near her; but, one of them drew a deadly bow, and shot a keen arrow at her, which wounded her in the side. But the noise had also wakened the other Knight, who now ran to her help, and, fighting together side by side, they soon defeated their foes.

When they were all put to shameful flight, Britomart arrayed herself again in her armour, for she would stay no longer in a place where such things were done by those who were apparently noble knights and ladies. Quite early, therefore, while the dawn was still grey, she and her companion-knight took their steeds and went forth upon their journey.

How Britomart looked into the Magic Mirror

As Britomart and the Knight journeyed away from Castle Joyous, it came into the Knight's mind to ask the Princess what had brought her into that part of the country, and why she disguised herself thus: for she seemed a beautiful lady when she was dressed as one, but the handsomest knight alive when she was clad in armour.

"Fair sir," replied Britomart, "I would have you know that from the hour when I left my nurse's arms, I have been trained up in warlike ways, to toss spear and shield, and to meet and overthrow warrior knights. I loathe to lead the lazy life of pleasure that most ladies do, fingering fine needle and fancy thread; I would rather die at the point of the foeman's spear. All my delight is set on deeds of arms, to hunt out perils and adventures wherever they may be met by sea or land, not for riches nor for reward, but only for glory and honour. For this reason, I came into these parts, far from my native country, without map or compass, to seek for praise and fame.

"For report has blazed forth that here, in the land of the Faerie Queene, many famous knights and ladies dwell, and many strange adventures can be found, out of which much glory may be won; and to prove this, I have begun this voyage. But may I ask of you, courteous Knight, tidings of one who has behaved very badly to me, and con whom I am seeking to revenge myself; he is called Artegall."

Britomart did not mean what she said of Artegall; she only spoke like this to conceal her real feelings. As soon as the words were uttered she repented, and would have recalled them, but her companion answered almost before she had finished speaking. He said she was very wrong to upbraid so scornfully a gentle Knight, for of all who ever rode at tilt or tourney, the noble Artegall was the most renowned. It would be very strange, therefore, if any shameful thought ever entered his mind, or if he did any deed deserving of blame, for noble courage does nothing unworthy of itself.

Britomart grew wonderfully glad to hear her love thus highly praised, and rejoiced that she had given her heart to one so gallant; but in order to lead the Knight to speak further in the same style, she still pretended to find fault with Artegall, and asked where he might be found, because she wanted to fight with him.

"Ah, if only reason could persuade you to soften your anger!" said the Knight. "It is a bold thing to imagine you can bind a man like this down to hard conditions, or to hope to match in equal fight one whose prowess has no living rival. Besides, it is not at all easy to tell where or how he can be found, for he never dwells in any settled spot, but roams all over the world, always doing noble deeds, defending the rightful cause of women and orphans, whenever he hears they are oppressed by might or tyranny. Thus he wins the highest honour."

These words sank into Britomart's heart, and filled her with rapture; but still she would not let her companion see it.

"Since it is so difficult to find Sir Artegall," she said, "tell me some marks by which he may be known, in case I happen to meet him by chance. What is he like? What is his shield—his arms—his steed—and anything else that may distinguish him?"

The Knight set himself to point out all these, and described Sir Artegall in every particular.

But Britomart knew already exactly what Sir Artegall was like; and this is how she came to know it.

Long ago in Britain she had seen his image plainly revealed in a magic mirror, and ever since then she had loved no one else.

For in the days when her father, King Ryence, reigned over South Wales, Merlin, the great magician, had by his spells devised a wonderful looking-glass, the fame of which soon went through all the world.

For this mirror had the power of showing perfectly whatever thing the world contained, between heaven and earth, provided it had to do with the person who looked into it. Whatever a foe had done, or a friend had feigned, was revealed in this mirror, and it was impossible to keep anything secret from it.

The mirror was round and hollow, and seemed like a great globe of glass. Merlin gave it to King Ryence as a safeguard, so that if foes ever invaded his kingdom he would always know it at home before he heard tidings, and thus be able to prevent them. A present which could thus detect treason and overthrow enemies, was a famous one for a prince.

One day Britomart happened to go into her father's private room. Nothing was kept hidden from her, for she was his only daughter, and his heir. When she spied the mirror, she first looked in to see herself, but in vain. Then, remembering the strange power it was said to possess, she tried to think of some interesting thing that concerned herself, and thus she wondered what husband fortune would allot to her.

Immediately there was presented to her eyes the picture of a gallant

Knight, clad in complete armour. His face, under the uplifted visor of the helmet, showed forth like the sun, to terrify his foes and make glad his friends. His heroic grace and noble bearing added to the grandeur of his figure.

His crest was a crouching hound, and all his armour seemed of an antique fashion, but was wonderfully massive and stout, and fretted all round with gold; written on it in ancient lettering were the words—

"Achilles arms, which Artegall did win."

On his shield he bore the device of a little crowned ermine on an azure field.

Britomart looked well at the figure of this Knight, and liked it well, and then went on her way, never dreaming that her future fate lay hidden at the bottom of this globe of glass.

How Britomart went to the Cave of the Magician Merlin

After Britomart had seen the figure of Sir Artegall in the magic mirror, a strange thing happened. She grew pale and ill, and lost all her merry spirits, and she no longer cared to do any of the things in which she had formerly delighted. At night, instead of sleeping, she tossed about, and sighed and wept; or if she did close her eyes for a few minutes, it was only to dream of dreadful things, and to start awake again suddenly, with cries of terror.

Her old nurse, Glaucé, was much distressed to see such a sad change in her dear young mistress, and one night when Britomart had been more restless than usual, she begged her to say what was troubling her, and if she were secretly fretting over anything.

Then Britomart told Glaucé of the splendid Knight she had seen in the magic mirror, and how she longed to see him again. If it were some living person, there might have been some hope for her, but now there was none, for it was only the shade or semblance of a knight. So grand and noble was the appearance of Artegall that Britomart's heart ached with sorrow to think she should never see him in real life.

Glaucé tried to comfort her, and spoke cheerfully, but at first Britomart would not be consoled, for she did not see how things could ever be better for her. It was very foolish of her, she owned, to love only a shadow, but she knew the remembrance of Sir Artegall would never fade as long as life lasted, and she felt that death only could put an end to her grief.

"Well," said the faithful old nurse, "if it is a choice between death and seeing him again, I swear to you by right or wrong to discover that Knight."

Her cheerful words quite soothed Britomart's sad heart, and she lay down again in bed, and actually got a little sleep; as for Glaucé, she turned the lamp low, and sat by the bedside to watch and weep over her dear young lady.

After that, Glaucé tried every way she could think of to cure Britomart's grief; but neither medicine, nor charms, nor good advice did her any good, and the nurse began to fear the King would be very angry with her when he heard what had happened to his dear daughter.

At last she thought that he who made the mirror in which Britomart had seen the strange vision of the Knight, would surely be able to tell where the real man could be found. Disguising themselves, therefore, in poor clothes, so that no one would know who they were, she and Britomart took their way to the place where the great magician, Merlin, had his dwelling, low underneath the ground, in a deep dell, far from the light of day. It was a hideous, hollow cave, under a rock that lay near a swift river foaming down the woody hills.

Arrived here, Glaucé and Britomart at first loitered about outside, afraid to go into the cave, and beginning to doubt whether they had done well to come. The brave maiden, with love to befriend her, was the first to enter, and there she found the magician deep in some work of wonder, busily writing strange characters on the ground.

Merlin was not in the least surprised at their bold visit, for he knew quite well beforehand of their coming; but he bade them unfold their business,—as though anything in the world were hidden from him!

Then Glaucé told him that for the last three months some strange malady had taken hold of the young maiden; what it was, or whence it sprang, she knew not, but this she knew, that if a remedy were not found, she would soon see her dead. Merlin began to smile softly at Glaucé's smooth speeches, for he knew quite well she was not telling him the whole truth, and he said, "By what you say, your young lady has more need of a doctor than of my skill. He who can get help elsewhere, seeks in vain wonders from magic."

Glaucé was rather taken aback at hearing these words, and vet she was unwilling to let her purpose appear plainly.

"If any doctor's skill could have cured my dear daughter," she said, "I should certainly not have wished to trouble you but this sad illness which has seized her is far beyond natural causes."

The wizard could stand no more of this, but burst out laughing, and said, "Glaucé, what need is there for these excuses to cover the cause which has already betrayed itself? And you, fair Britomart, although dressed in these poor clothes, are no more hidden than the sun in a veil of clouds. You have done well to come to me for help, for I can give it you."

Britomart was quite abashed at finding herself discovered, and grew very red; but the old nurse was not in the least discomfited.

"Since you know all our grief—for what is there that you do not know?"—she said to Merlin, "I pray you to pity our trouble, and grant us relief."

Merlin reflected for a few minutes; then he spoke to Britomart, and told her many things that would happen in the future. He bade her not to be in the least troubled, for all would end well, and it was no misfortune for her to love the most powerful knight that had ever lived.

The man whom she had seen in the magic mirror was Sir Artegall, the champion Knight of *Justice*, and he dwelt in the land of the Faerie Queene. He was a mighty warrior, and would fight many battles for his native country, in which Britomart would aid him. He would win again for himself the crown that was his father's by right, and he would reign with great happiness. His son would succeed him, and after him would come a long race of kings.

When Britomart and her old nurse, Glaucé, had heard all they wanted to know, they both felt very glad and hopeful, and they returned home with much lighter hearts than they had set out.

"Deepe busied 'bout worke of wondrous end,
And writing straunge characters in the grownd."

How Britomart set forth on her Quest

Britomart and her old nurse Glaucé now took counsel together as to the best means of finding Sir Artegall. They thought of one plan after another, and at last the nurse hit upon a bold device. She suggested to Britomart that, as the whole country was now disturbed by war, they should disguise themselves, in armour, and go in search of the Knight. It would be easy for Britomart to do this, for she was tall and strong, and needed nothing but a little practice to render her skilful in the use of spear and sword.

"Truly," said Glaucé, "it ought to fire your courage to hear the poets sing of all the brave women who have come from the royal house to which you belong."

She went on to name a long list of noble Princesses who had fought gallantly against their country's enemies, and bade Britomart follow their example and be equally courageous.

Her stirring words sank deep into the heart of the maiden, and immediately filled her with courage, and made her long to do brave deeds. She resolved to go forth as an adventurous knight, and bade Glaucé put all things at once in readiness.

It happened fortunately for them that only a few days before, a band of Britons riding on a foray had taken some rich spoil from the enemy. Amongst this was a splendid suit of armour which had belonged to the Saxon Queen, Angela. It was all fretted with gold, and very beautiful. This, with the other ornaments, King Ryence had caused to be hung in his chief church, as a lasting memorial of his victory. Glaucé, remembering this, led Britomart there late one evening, and, taking down the armour, dressed her in it. Beside the arms stood a mighty spear, which had been made by magic; no living person could sit so fast in the saddle but it could hurl him to the ground. Britomart took this spear, and also a shield which hung near.

When Glaucé had dressed the maiden she took another suit of armour, and put it on herself, so that she could go forth with her young mistress and attend her carefully as her squire. Then they lightly

"In th' evening late old Glaucé hither led
Faire Britomart, and, that same Armory
Downe taking, her therein appareled
Well as she might." . . .

mounted their horses, which were ready for them, and rode away in the darkness of night, so that none should see them.

They never rested till they reached the 'land of the Faerie Queene, as Merlin had directed them. There they met with the Knight from Queen Gloriana's court, as we have already seen, with whom they had much pleasant conversation, but especially about the gallant Sir Artegall. When they came at last to the place where they had to part, the Knight and Britomart, who greatly liked each other, promised always to remain true friends, and Britomart then rode on alone with Glaucé in search of Sir Artegall.

What her companion had told her about Artegall made her long all the more to see him, and she fashioned in her mind a thousand thoughts as to what he would be like, picturing him in her fancy everything that was noble and lovable—"wise, warlike, handsome, courteous, and kind." But these thoughts, instead of soothing her sorrow, only made it worse, till it seemed that nothing but death could drive away the pain. So she rode forth, restless and unrefreshed, searching all lands, and every remotest part, with nothing but her love to guide her.

How Britomart came to the Castle of the Churl Malbecco

One night, as Britomart was riding on her way, a fearful storm came on, great blasts of wind and a pelting shower of hall. Seeing a Castle in front of her, she went up to it, and earnestly begged to be let In. But the Castle belonged to a miserly churl, called Malbecco, who, because of his jealous and peevish disposition, refused to allow any strangers to enter his doors. He cared nothing what men said of him, good or bad; all his mind was set upon hoarding up heaps of ill-gotten gain. He was old and ugly, and lacking in all kindness and courtesy. Instead of opening his doors to all wandering knights, as was the custom of the time, he kept them close-barred, and even in the midst of the terrible tempest which was then raging, Britomart was flatly refused entrance. She was greatly displeased at this, and determined when the time came to punish the churl for his discourtesy.

But, in order to escape the fury of the gale, she was compelled to seek some refuge near. Beside the Castle gate was a little shed, meant for swine, but when she tried to enter she found it already full of guests. Another party of knights had been refused admittance at the Castle, and were forced to fly there for shelter. These would not at first allow Britomart to enter, whereupon she grew very angry, and declared she would either lodge with them in a friendly fashion, or she would turn them all out of the shed, whether they were willing or not, and then she challenged them to come forth and fight.

The knights would now have been willing to let her come in, but her boastful tone irritated them; one of them, Paridell by name, was especially annoyed,. and hastily mounting his steed he rode forth to fight with her. Their spears met with such fury that both man and horse were borne to the ground, and Paridell was so sorely bruised that he could scarcely arise to continue the combat on foot, with swords, as was then the custom.

But his companion, Sir Satyrane (who was the good Knight who had formerly befriended Una in the forest), stepped forward to prevent Britomart and Paridell from fighting further, and his, wise speeches soon soothed their anger. When peace was restored, they agreed to join together to punish the unmannerly churl, who had acted so ungraciously in refusing them shelter from the tempest, and they went towards the gates to burn them down.

Malbecco, seeing that they were really resolved to set fire to the building, rail frantically, and called to them from the castle wall, beseeching them humbly to have patience with him, as being ignorant of his servants' rudeness and inattention to strangers. The

knights were willing to accept his excuses, though they did not believe them, and they did not refuse to enter.

They were brought into a beautiful bower, and served with everything needful, though their host secretly scowled at them, and welcomed them more through fear than charity. They took off their wet garments, and undid their heavy armour, to dry themselves at the fire. Britomart, like the rest, was forced to disarray herself. When she lifted her helmet, and her golden locks fell like a cloud of light to the ground, they were all amazed to find the valiant stranger was a beautiful maiden. They stood gazing at her, silent with astonishment, for eve had never seen a fairer woman, but chiefly they marvelled at her chivalry and noble daring. They longed to know who she might be, yet no one questioned her, and every one loved her on the spot.

Supper was then served, and when the meal was over the Lady Hellenore, wife of Malbecco, invited all the knights to tell their name and

kindred, and any deeds of arms they had done. They talked so long about their various strange adventures, and the daring feats and many dangers they had passed through, that old Malbecco grew quite impatient. He took no interest in conversation of this kind. At last, when the night was half spent, he persuaded them to go to rest; so they all retired to the rooms prepared for them.

The next day, as soon as the sun shone in the sky, Britomart rose up and set forth on her journey. Sir Satyrane went with her, but Paridell pretended to have been so much hurt by his fight with Britomart that he must stay behind at the Castle till his wounds were cured.

How Britomart walked through Fire

Britomart and Sir Satyrane had not long left the Castle of the churl Malbecco when they saw in front of them a huge Giant chasing a young man. Filled with anger, Britomart immediately galloped to the rescue, and Sir Satyrane followed close behind. Seeing them approach, the Giant quickly resigned his prey, and fled to save himself. He ran so fast that neither of them could overtake him, and presently he came to a great forest, where he hid himself. It was not Sir Satyrane he feared so much as Britomart, for some instinct told him that his evil nature would be powerless to fight against any one so good.

Britomart and Sir Satyrane entered the wood, and searched everywhere for the Giant, and, each going a different way, they soon got separated. Britomart went deep into the forest, and at last came to a fountain by which lay a Knight. He had tossed aside his coat and mail, his helmet, his spear, and his shield, and had flung himself face downwards on the grass. At first, Britomart would not disturb him, for she thought him asleep, but, while she stood still looking at him, she presently heard him sob and sigh as if his heart would break.

Filled with pity, Britomart begged him to say what was the matter, as perhaps she might be able to help him. The Knight, whose name was Scudamour, did not think this at all likely, and would scarcely speak, but, after some further gentle words from Britomart, he told her that he was in such deep sorrow because the lady he loved had been seized by a wicked enchanter called Busirane, and shut up in a horrible dungeon, from which no living power could release her. The enchanter had done this because he wanted to marry her himself, and when she refused, and declared she would never forsake her own true Knight, he had taken this cruel revenge.

Then Britomart bade him take courage, for she would either deliver the Lady Amoretta from her dungeon, or she would die with her.

"Ah, gentlest Knight alive," cried Scudamour, "how brave and good you are! But keep your happy days and use them to better purpose. Let me die that ought. One is enough to die."

"Life is not lost by which is bought endless renown," said Britomart.

Thus she persuaded Sir Scudamour to rise and go with her to see what success would befall him in this fresh attempt. She gathered up his armour, which he had flung away in despair, and helped him to put it on, and she fetched his steed, which had wandered to some distance.

Then they went forth together, and soon arrived at the place where their venture was to be made. There they dismounted, drew their weapons, and boldly marched up to the Castle. Here they found no gate to bar their passage, nor any warder, but in the porch, which greatly terrified them, was a huge flaming fire, mixed with smoke and sulphur, which choked all the entrance, and forced them to go back.

Britomart was dismayed at this, and did not know what to do, for it seemed useless danger to attempt to brave the fire, which prevented any one going near. Turning back to Scudamour, she asked what course he thought it would be safest to take, and how they should get at their foe to fight him.

"This is the reason why I said to you at first the quest was hopeless," replied Scudamour, "for this fire cannot be quenched either by strength or cunning, nor can it be moved away, so mighty are the enchantments that keep it here. What else is to be done but to stop this useless labour, and leave me to my former despair? The Lady Amoretta must stay in her wicked chains, and Scudamour die here with sorrowing."

"No, indeed," said Britomart, "for it would be a shameful thing to abandon a noble enterprise at the mere sight of peril, without even venturing. Rather let us try the last chance than give up our purpose out of fear."

So saying, resolved to try her utmost, she threw her shield in front of her face, and, holding the point of her sword straight in front of her, she advanced to the fire. The flames immediately gave way, and parted on either side, so that she walked through without hindrance.

When Scudamour saw Britomart safe and untouched on the other side of the fire, he also tried to pass, and bade the flames make way for him; but the fire would not obey his threatening command, and only raged the more fiercely, forcing him to retire all scorched and painfully burnt. Furious at his failure, more even than at the pain of his burns, he flung himself impatiently down on the grass, but Britomart had now passed the first door and entered the Castle.

The first room she came to was splendid to see, for it was all hung round with rich tapestry, woven with gold and silk. Beautiful pictures, representing well-known fables and stories, were worked in the tapestry, and at the upper end of the room was a great Image which the people of the house were accustomed to worship. This image was made of massive gold, and had wings that shone with all the colours of the rainbow. It was blindfolded, and held in its hand a bow and arrows, which it seemed to shoot at random; some of the arrows were tipped with lead, some with pure gold. A wounded dragon lay under its feet.

Britomart was so amazed at this wonderful figure, that she kept gazing at it again and again, though its brightness quite dazzled her. But, casting her eyes round the room, to discover every secret of the place, she saw written over the door these words:—

"Be bold."

She read this over and over, but could not think to what it could refer; but, whatever it might mean, it did not in the least discourage her from following out her first intention, so she went forward with bold steps into the next room.

This second room was even fairer and richer than the first one, for it was not hung round with tapestry, but was all overlaid with pure gold carved into the most curious and grotesque figures.

Britomart marvelled much to see all this wealth and luxury, but, still more, that there was no trace of living person—nothing but wasteful emptiness and solemn silence over all the place; it seemed strange that there was no one to possess such rich belongings, nor to keep them carefully.

"Her ample shield she threw before her face,
And her swords point directing forward right
Assayld the flame; the which eftsoones gave place,
And did it selfe divide with equall space."

And as she looked about she saw how over that door, too, was written "*Be bold, be bold*;" and everywhere, "*Be bold.*" She meditated much over this, but could not understand it. At last, at the upper end of the room, she saw another iron door, on which was written

"Be not too bold,"

but, though she bent all her wise mind to the subject, she could not tell what it might mean.

Thus she waited there until evening, yet saw no living creature appear. And now gloomy shadows began to hide the world from mortal view and wrap it in darkness. Britomart did not dare to take off her tiring armour, nor to go to sleep, for fear of secret danger, but she held herself in readiness, and saw that all her weapons were in good order.

What Britomart saw in the Enchanted Chamber

As darkness fell, Britomart heard the sound of a shrill trumpet, the sign of an approaching battle or a victory gained. This did not in the least daunt her courage, but rather strengthened it, while she expected each moment to see some foe appear.

Then arose a hideous storm of wind, with thunder and lightning, and an earthquake as if it would shake the foundations of the world. This was followed by a horrible smell of smoke and sulphur, which filled the whole place. Yet still the brave Princess was not afraid, but remained steadfast.

Suddenly a whirlwind swept through the house, banging every door, and bursting open the iron wicket. Then stepped forth a grave-looking person, in costly raiment, and bearing in his hand a branch of laurel. Advancing to the middle of the room, he stood still, as if he had something to say, and beckoned with his hand to call for silence. After making various other signs, as if he were explaining some play that was going on, he softly retired, and then his name could be seen written on his robe in golden letters—"*Ease.*"

Britomart, still standing, saw all this, and marvelled what his strange intention could be.

Then through the iron wicket came a joyous band, minstrels and poets playing and singing the sweetest music, and after them followed a number of strange figures in curious disguise, marching all in order like a procession.

The first was *Fancy*, like a lovely boy. His garment was neither silk nor stuff, but painted plumes, such as wild Indians deck themselves with. He seemed as vain and light as these same plumes, for he walked along as if he were dancing, bearing in his hand a great fan, which he waved to and fro. At his side marched *Desire*. His dress was extravagant, and his embroidered cap was all awry. He carried in his two hands some sparks, which he kept so busily blowing that they soon burst into flame.

Next after these came *Doubt*, in a faded cloak and hood, with wide sleeves. He glanced sideways out of his mistrustful eyes, and trod carefully, as if thorns lay in his path; he supported his feeble steps with a broken reed, which bent whenever he leant hard on it. With *Doubt* walked *Danger*, clothed in a ragged bear's skin, which made him more dreadful, though his own face was grisly enough, and needed nothing to make it more so. In one hand was a net, in the other a rusty blade—Mischief and Mischance. With the one he threatened his foes, with the other he entrapped his friends.

After Danger walked *Fear*; he was all armed from top to toe, yet even then did not think himself safe. He was afraid of every shadow, and when he spied his own arms glittering, or heard them clashing, he fled fast away. His face was pale as ashes, and he kept his eyes fixed on Danger, against whom he always bent a brazen shield, which he held in his right hand.

Side by side with Fear marched *Hope*, a handsome maid, with a cheerful expression and lovely to see. She was lightly arrayed in silken samite, and her fair locks were woven up with gold. She always smiled, and in her hand she held a little phial of dew, from which she sprinkled favours on anyone she chose. She showed a great liking to many people, but true love to few.

After them, *Dissembling* and *Suspicion* marched together, though they were not in the least alike; for Dissembling was gentle and mild, courteous to all, and seemingly gracious, well adorned, and handsome.

"After all these there marcht a most faire Dame,
Led of two grysie Villains, th' one Despight,
The other cleped Cruelty by name."

But all her good points were painted or stolen; her deeds were forged, her words false. In her hand she always twined two clues of silk.

Suspicion was ugly, ill-favoured, and grim, for ever looking askance under his sullen eyebrows. While Dissembling constantly smiled at him, he scowled back at her, showing his nature by his countenance. His rolling eyes never rested in one place, but wandered all round, for fear of hidden mischief; he held a screen of latticework in front of his face, through which he kept peering.

Next him came *Grief* and *Fury*, fit companions—Grief clad in sable, hanging his dull head, carrying a pair of pincers, with which he pinched people to the heart; Fury all in rags, tossing in her right hand a firebrand. Then followed *Displeasure*, looking heavy and sullen, and *Pleasure*, cheerful, fresh, and full of gladness. Displeasure had an angry wasp in a bottle, and Pleasure a honey-laden bee.

After these six couples came a beautiful lady, led by two villains, *Spite* and *Cruelty*. She looked pale as death, and very ill, but in spite of this was most lovely and graceful. Her feeble feet could scarcely carry her, but the two wretches held her up, and kept urging her forward.

Then the Tyrant of the Castle appeared—the winged figure of *Love*, whom Britomart had already seen in the first room as a golden image. He rode on a ravenous lion, and had unbound his eyes, so that he might gloat over the distress of the lovely lady, which seemed to please him greatly. He looked round him with stern disdain, and, surveying his goodly company, marshalled them in order. Then he shook the darts that he carried in his right hand and clashed his rainbow-coloured wings, so that every one was terrified.

Behind him came his three chief attendants, *Reproach*, *Repentance*, and *Shame*, and after them flocked a rude, confused crowd, who owned him as master—*Strife* and *Anger*, *Care* and *Unthriftiness*, *Loss of Time* and *Sorrow*, fickle *Change*, false *Disloyalty*, *Rioting*, *Poverty*, and, lastly, *Death-with-infamy*.

All these and many other evil followers passed in disguise before Britomart, and, having thrice marched round the enchanted chamber, returned to the inner room whence they had come.

How Britomart rescued a Fair Lady from a Wicked Enchanter

As soon as the strange procession had passed into the inner room, the door shut tight, driven by the same stormy blast with which it had first opened. Then the brave maiden, who all this while had remained hidden in shadow, came forth, and went to the door to enter in, but found it fast locked. In vain she thought to open it by strength when charms had closed it, and, finding force of no avail, she determined to use art, resolving not to leave that room till the next day, when the same figures would again appear.

At last the morning dawned, calling men to their daily work, and Britomart, fresh as the morning, came out from her hiding-place. All that day she spent in wandering and in gazing at the adornment of the chamber, till again the second evening spread her black cloak over everything. Then at midnight the brazen door flew open, and in went bold Britomart, as she had made up her mind to do, afraid neither of idle shows nor of false charms.

As soon as she entered, she cast her eyes round to see what had become of all the persons she had seen in the outside room the night before, but, lo! they had all vanished. She saw no living mortal of that strange company except the same hapless lady, whose two hands were bound fast, and who had an iron chain round her small waist, fastened to a brazen pillar by which she stood.

In front of her sat the vile Enchanter, drawing in blood strange characters of his art, to try to make her love him. But who could love the cause of all her trouble? He had already tried a thousand charms, but a thousand charms could not alter the lady's steadfast heart.

As soon as the Enchanter saw Britomart, he hastily overthrew his wicked books, not caring to lose his long labour, and, drawing a knife out of his pocket, ran fiercely at the lady, thinking, in his villainy, to kill her. But Britomart, leaping lightly to him, withheld his wicked hand, and overpowered him.

Then, turning the weapon from the one whom he had first meant it, he struck at Britomart and wounded her. The hurt was slight, but it so enraged the maiden that she drew her sword, and smote fiercely at the tyrant. He fell to the ground half dead, and the next stroke would have slain him, had not the lady who stood bound called to Britomart not to kill him. If she did so, the prisoner's pain would be without rem-

edy, for no one but the Enchanter who had put the spell on her could take it off again.

Then Britomart unwillingly stayed her hand, for she grudged him his life, and longed to see him punished.

"Thou wicked man," she said to him, "whose huge mischief and villainy merit death or worse than death, be sure that nothing shall save thee, unless thou immediately restore the lady to health and to her former condition. This do and live, or else thou shalt undoubtedly die."

The Enchanter, glad to live, for he had expected nothing but death, yielded willingly, and, rising, began at once to look over the wicked book, in order to reverse his charms. He read aloud many dreadful things, so that Britomart's heart was pierced with horror. But all the time he read, she held her sword high over him, in case he tried to do further mischief.

Presently the house began to quake, and all the doors to rattle. Yet this did not dismay her nor make her slacken her threatening hand. But, with steadfast eye and stout courage, she waited to see what would be the end. At last the mighty chain which was wound round the lady's waist fell down, and the great brazen pillar broke into small pieces. Gradually her look of terrible suffering passed, and she became restored to perfect health, as if she had never been ill.

When she felt herself unbound, and quite well and strong, she threw herself at the feet of Britomart.

"Ah, noble Knight!" she said, "what recompense can a wretched lady, freed from her woeful state, yield you for your gracious deed? Your virtue shall bring its own reward, even immortal praise and glory, which I, your vassal, freed by your prowess, shall proclaim throughout the world."

But Britomart, lifting her from the ground, said, "Gentle lady, this I ween is reward enough for many more labours than I have done, that now I see you in safety, and that I have been the means of your deliverance. Henceforth, fair lady, take comfort, and put away remembrance of your late trouble. Know, instead, that your loving husband has endured no less grief for your sake."

Amoret, for that was the lady's name, was much cheered to hear this mention of Sir Scudamour, for she loved him best of all living people.

Then the noble champion laid her strong hand on the Enchanter who had treated Amoret so cruelly, and, with the great chain with which he had formerly kept prisoner the hapless lady, she now bound himself, and led him away captive.

Returning the way she came, Britomart was dismayed to find that the goodly rooms which she had lately seen so richly and royally adorned had utterly vanished, and all their glory had decayed. Descending to the perilous porch, she found also that the dreadful flames, which had formerly so cruelly scorched all those who tried to enter, were quenched like a burnt-out torch. It was now much easier to pass out than it had been to come in. The Enchanter, who had framed this fraud to compel the love of the fair lady, was deeply vexed to see his work all wasted.

But when Britomart arrived at the place where she had left Sir Scudamour and her own trusty squire (her old nurse, Glaucé), she found neither of them there. At this she was sorely astonished, and, above all, Amoret, who had looked forward to seeing her own dear Knight, being deprived of this hope, was filled with fresh alarm.

Sir Scudamour, poor man, had waited long in dread for Britomart's return, but not seeing her, nor any sign of her success, his expectation turned to despair, for he felt sure that the flames must have burnt her. Therefore he took counsel with her old squire, who mourned her loss no less deeply, and the two departed in search of further aid.

What Strange Meetings befell on the Way

Leaving the Enchanter's Castle behind them, Britomart and Amoret started in search of Sir Scudamour and Glaucé.

As they went, Amoret told Britomart the story of how she came into the power of the wicked Busirane. On the very day of her marriage to Sir Scudamour, at the wedding feast, while all the guests were making merry, Busirane found means to introduce the strange procession which had so amazed Britomart in the enchanted chamber. Amoret was persuaded in sport to join it, and was carried away quite unknown to any one. Seven months she had been kept in cruel imprisonment, because she would not consent to give up her own dear husband and become the wife of the wicked Enchanter. Now, at last, she was free, and when she discovered that her deliverer was not after all a knight, but in reality a beautiful maiden like herself, her heart overflowed with love and gratitude, and she and Britomart speedily became the best and dearest friends.

In the course of their journey they presently saw two knights in armour coming to meet them, each with what seemed at that distance a fair lady riding beside him. But ladies they were not, although in face and outward show they seemed so. Under a mask of beauty and graciousness they hid vile treachery and falsehood, which were not apparent to any but the wise and cautious.

One was the false Duessa, who had formerly beguiled the Red Cross Knight and Sir Guyon. She had changed her usual appearance, for she could put on as many different shapes as a chameleon can new colours.

Her companion was, if possible, worse than herself Her name was Até, *Mother of Strife*, cause of all dissension both among private men and in public affairs of state. False Duessa, knowing that she was just the most fitting person to aid her in mischief, had summoned her from her dwelling under the earth, where she wasted her wretched days and nights in darkness. Her abode was close to the Kingdom of Evil, where plagues and harms abound to punish those who do wrong. It was a gloomy dell, far under ground, surrounded with thorns and briars, so that no one could easily get out; there were many ways to enter, but none by which to leave when one was once in; for it is harder to end discord than to begin it.

All the broken walls inside were hung with the ragged memorials of past times, which showed the sad effects of strife. There were rent robes and broken sceptres, sacred things ruined, shivered spears, and shields torn in twain, great cities ransacked, and strong castles beaten down, nations led into captivity, and huge armies slain—relics of all these ruins remained in the house of Até. All the famous wars in history found a record here, as well as the feuds and quarrels of private persons too many to mention.

Such was the house inside. Outside, the barren ground was full of poisonous weeds, which *Strife* herself had sown; they had grown great from small seeds—the seeds of evil words and wrangling deeds,

which, when they come to ripeness, bring forth an infinite increase of trouble and contention, often ending in bloodshed and war. These horrible seeds also served Até for bread, and she had been fed upon them from childhood, for she got her life from that which killed other people. She was born of a race of demons, and brought up by the Furies.

Strife was as ugly as she was wicked; she could speak nothing but falsehood, and she never heard aright. She could not even walk straight, but stumbled backwards and forwards; what one hand reached out to take, the other pushed away, or what one hand made, the other destroyed. Great riches, which had taken many a day to collect, she often squandered rapidly, dismaying their possessors; for all her study and thought was how she might overthrow the things done by Concord. So far did her malice surpass her might that she tried to bring all the world's fair peace and harmony into confusion. Such was the odious creature that rode with Duessa.

The two knights who escorted them, Blandamour and Paridell, were young and handsome, but both equally foolish, fickle, and false. When they saw Britomart and the lovely Lady Amoret approaching, Blandamour jestingly tried to make his companion attack Britomart, so that he might win Amoret for himself. But Paridell remembered how he had already fought with a knight bearing those arms and that shield, outside the castle of the churl Malbecco, and he had no desire to provoke a new fight.

"Very well," said Blandamour; "I will challenge him myself;" and he rode straight at Britomart.

But he had soon cause to repent his rashness, for Britomart received his advance with so rude a welcome that he speedily left his saddle. Then she passed quietly on, leaving him on the ground much hurt, an example of his own folly, and as sad now as he had formerly been merry, well warned to beware in future with whom he dared to interfere.

Paridell ran to his aid and helped him to mount again, and they marched on their way, Blandamour trying as well as he could to hide the evil plight he was in. Before long they saw two other knights coming quickly to meet them, and Blandamour was enraged to see that one was Sir Scudamour, whom he hated mortally, both because of his worth, which made all men love him, and because he had won by right the Lady Amoret. Blandamour was greatly vexed that his bruises prevented his wreaking his old spite, and he immediately spoke thus to Paridell:—

"Fair sir, let me beg of you in the name of friendship, that, as I lately ventured for you and got these wounds, which now keep me from battle, you will now repay me with a like good turn, and justify my cause on yonder Knight."

Paridell willingly agreed, and sped at the stranger like a shaft from a bow, but Sir Scudamour was on his guard, and prepared himself to give him a fitting welcome. So furiously they met that each hurled the other from his horse, like two billows driven by contrary tides, which meet together, and rebound back with roaring rage, dashing on all sides and filling the sea with foam. So fell these two, in spite of all their pride.

But Scudamour soon raised himself, and upbraided his foe for lying there so long.

Blandamour, seeing the fall of Paridell, taunted Sir Scudamour as a traitor, and heaped abuse on him, saying that he only attacked knights who were too weak to defend themselves.

Scudamour gave no answer to this, trying to restrain his indignation; but then Duessa and Até both chimed in, wickedly doing all they could to, rouse his passion.

They spoke jeering words, and said they wondered Sir Scudamour should care to fight for any lady, for Amoret was faithless, and had forgotten him and gone off with another Knight.

This Knight, we know, was in reality the Princess Britomart; but Sir Scudamour did not know this. He swore, in a fearful rage, to be revenged; he even threatened to kill the squire, Glaucé, who was still with him, since fie could not get hold of his master. In vain the poor old nurse tried to appease him, for she dared not disclose Britomart's secret. Three times Sir Scudamour lifted his hand to kill Glaucé, and three times he drew back, before at last he became a little pacified.

How Sir Satyrane proclaimed a Great Tournament

The fickle and quarrelsome couple, Blandamour and Paridell, having been defeated by Britomart and Sir Scudamour, next fell in with a party of two knights and two masked ladies. They sent their squire to find out who these were, and he brought back word that they were two doughty knights of dreaded name, Cambell and Triamond, and the two ladies were their wives, Cambina and Candace. All four were very famous people, and the dearest friends possible. They had had many wonderful adventures of their own, about which perhaps you will read some day.

Blandamour, in his usual vainglorious spirit, would gladly have tested his strength against the knights, but he was still sore from the late unlucky fight with Britomart. However, he went up to them, and began to abuse and insult them, thinking in this way to will admiration from the ladies. Of course this enraged the two knights, who were both bent on punishing Blandamour for his base behaviour. But Cambina, wife of Cambell, soothed them with her mild words, so, for the present, they were reconciled.

The whole party rode on together, talking of daring deeds and strange adventures, and, among other things, of the great tournament to which they were then all bound

This tournament had been set on foot by Sir Satyrane, the same woodland knight who had formerly befriended Una, and who had met Britomart at the castle of the churl Malbecco. Some time before, ranging abroad in search of adventure, he had come to the sea-coast, where he was horrified to find a vile monster, something like a hyena, feeding on the dead body of a milk-white palfrey. He knew the horse at once as the one on which Florimell was accustomed to ride, and, moreover, he found beside it her golden girdle. This girdle had fallen from her in flight, for Florimell had escaped in a small boat; but Sir Satyrane did not know this-he thought she had been killed by the savage brute. Filled with fury, he fell on the creature. He was unable to slay it, for it was protected by the magic spells of its mistress, a wicked witch; but he led it away captive for the time, though it afterwards escaped.

The golden girdle which Sir Satyrane found he kept as a sacred treasure, and wore for the sake of Florimell. But when she herself was lost and gone, many knights who also loved her dearly were jealous that Sir Satyrane alone should wear the ornament of the lost lady, and began to bear much spite against him. Therefore, to stop their envy, he caused a solemn feast, with public tourneying, to be proclaimed, to which every knight was to bring his lady. She who was found fairest of them all was to have the golden girdle as a reward, and she was to bestow it on the stoutest knight.

Now it happened after the flight of Florimell, that the wicked witch from whom she had escaped made up another person to represent her, in order to deceive people. This imitation maiden was most beautiful to see. The substance of which her body was made was purest snow frozen in a mass, and mixed with virgin wax, tinted with vermilion; her eyes shone like stars, her hair was yellow gold. Any one who saw her would surely say it was Florimell herself, or even fairer than Florimell, if such a thing could be.

But this false Florimell had a wicked and deceitful spirit, full of fawning guile, and she excelled in all manner of wily cunning.

In the course of her wandering, this creature, who was known by the name of the "Snowy Lady," came across Braggadochio, whom you may remember as the cowardly boaster that stole Sir Guyon's horse and armour. But as she rode along with Braggadochio the latter was attacked and beaten by another knight, who thought the lady was the real Florimell. He in turn was vanquished by Blandamour, who also imagined that she was the true Florimell, and was very proud of himself for getting possession of such a paragon. Though he was so false himself, and had deceived hundreds of others, he was no match for the "Snowy Lady" in cunning, and was completely taken in by her.

When Blandamour heard of the great tournament held by Sir Satyrane in honour of Florimell's golden girdle, he immediately determined to go there and claim the prize on behalf of its rightful owner, whom he then believed to be under his protection. Thus it came to pass that the false Florimell journeyed with Blandamour and the others to the tournament.

Not long after Cambell and Triamond, with their wives, Cambina and Candace, had joined the party, they saw a man in bright armour, with spear in rest, riding towards them as though he meant to attack them. Paridell immediately prepared his own weapons, whereupon the other slackened his pace, and seemed to alter his intention, as if he meant nothing but peace and pleasure now that he had fallen by chance into their fellowship. Seeing this, they greeted him civilly, and he rode on with them.

This man was Braggadochio. When his eyes fell on the false Florimell, he remembered her as the lady who had been taken from

"He sett upon her Palfrey, tired lame,
And slew him cruelly ere any reskew came."

him not long before. He therefore began to challenge her as his own prize, and threatened to seize her again by force.

Blandamour treated his words with much disdain, saying, "Sir Knight, since you claim this lady, you shall win her, as I have done, in fight. She shall be placed here, together with this hideous old hag, Até (*Strife*), that whoso wins her may have her by right. But Até shall go to the one that is beaten, and he shall always ride with her till he gets another lady."

That offer pleased all the company, so the false Florimell was brought forward with Até, at which every one began to laugh merrily. But Braggadochio now tried to back out of his challenge. He said he never thought to imperil his person in fight for a hideous old creature like that. If they had sought to match the lady with another one equally fair and radiant, he would then have spent his life to justify his right.

At this vain excuse they all began to smile, scorning his unmanly cowardice. The Snowy Lady reviled him loudly for refusing to venture battle for her sake when it was offered in such knightly fashion, and Até secretly taunted him with the shame of such contempt. But nothing did he care for friend or foe, for in the base mind dwells neither friendship nor enmity.

But Cambell jestingly stopped them all, saying, "Brave knights and ladies, certainly you do wrong to stir up strife when most we need rest, so that we may keep ourselves fresh and strong against the coming tournament, when every one who wishes to fight may fight his fill. Postpone your challenge till that day, and then it shall be tried, if you will, which one shall have Até and which one still hold the lady."

They all agreed, and so, turning everything to sport and pleasantness, they passed merrily on their way, till at length, on the appointed day, they came to the place where the tournament was to be held.

What befell on the First and Second Days of the Tournament

On arriving at the scene of the tournament, the little company divided, Blandamour and those of his party going to one side and the rest to the other side but boastful Braggadochio, from vain-glory, chose rather to leave his companions, so that men might gaze more on him alone. The rest disposed themselves in groups, as seemed best to each one, every knight with his own lady.

Then, first of all, came forth Sir Satyrane, bearing the precious relic in a golden casket, so that no evil eyes should profane it. Then softly drawing it out of the dark, he showed it openly, so that all men might mark it—a gorgeous girdle of marvellous workmanship, curiously embossed with pearls and precious stones of great value. It was the same girdle which Florimell had lately lost. Sir Satyrane hung it aloft in open view, to be the prize of might and beauty. The moment it was uncovered, the glorious sight attracted every one's gaze and stole the hearts of all who looked on it, so that they uttered vain vows and wishes. Thrice happy, it seemed to them, would be the lady and knight who gained such a splendid reward for their peril and labour.

Then the bold Sir Satyrane took in his hand a great spear, such as he was accustomed to wield, and, advancing forward from all the other knights, set his shield in place, showing that he was ready for the fray. The warriors who fought on his side were called the "Knights of Maidenhood." They were the challengers, and their aim was to keep the golden girdle in their own possession.

Against him, from the other side, stepped out a Pagan knight, well skilled in arms, and often tried in battle. He was called "Bruncheval the Bold." These two met together so furiously that neither could sustain the other's force, and both champions were felled to the ground, where they lay senseless.

Seeing this, other knights rode quickly to their aid, some fighting on one side and some on the other. Only Braggadochio, when his turn came, showed no desire to hasten to the help of his party, but stood still as one who seemed doubtful or dismayed. Then Triamond, angry to see him delay, sternly stepped forward and caught away his spear, with which he so sorely assailed one of the knights that he bore both horse and rider to the ground. To avenge his fall one knight after another pressed forward, but Triamond vanquished them all, for no one seemed able to withstand his power.

By this time Sir Satyrane had awakened from his swoon. When he looked around and saw the merciless havoc that Sir Triamond had wrought to the knights of his party, his heart was almost broken with bitterness, and he wished himself dead rather than in so bad a plight. He began at once to gather up his scattered weapons, and, as it happened, he found his steed ready. Like a flash of fire from the anvil, he rode fiercely to where Triamond was driving his foes before him, and, aiming his spear at him, he pierced his side badly. Triamond could scarcely keep from falling, but he withdrew softly from the field as well as he could, so that no one saw plainly what had happened.

Then the challengers—the Knights of Maidenhood—began to range the field anew, and pride themselves on victory, since no one dared to maintain battle against them. By that time it was evening, which forced them to refrain from fighting, and the trumpets sounded to compel them to cease.

So Sir Satyrane was judged to be the best knight on that first day.

The next morning the tournament began anew. Satyrane, with his gallant band, was the first to appear, but Sir Triamond was unable to prepare for battle, because of his wound. This grieved him much, and Cambell, seeing this, and eager to win honour on his friend's behalf, took the shield and armour which were well known to belong to Triamond, and without saying a word to any one, put them on and went forth to fight.

There he found Satyrane lord of the field, triumphing in great joy, for no one was able to stand against him. Envious of his glory, and eager to avenge his friend's indignity, Cambell at once bent his spear against him. After a furious battle, he overthrew Sir Satyrane; but, before he could seize his shield and weapons, which were always the reward of the victor, a hundred knights had pressed round him to rescue Satyrane, and in the hope of taking Cambell prisoner. Undismayed, the latter fought valiantly, but what could one do against so many? At last he was taken captive.

When news of this was brought to Triamond, he forgot his wound, and, instantly starting up, looked for his armour. But he sought in vain, for it was not there—Cambell had taken it. Triamond therefore threw on himself Cambell's armour, and nimbly rushed forward to take his chance. There he found the warrior band leading away his friend-a sorry sight for him to see.

He thrust into the thickest of that knightly crowd, and smote down all between till he came to where he had seen Cambell, like a captive thrall, between two other knights. Triamond attacked them so fiercely that they were obliged to let their prisoner go, and then the two friends, fighting together, scattered their foes in alarm, as two greedy wolves might a flock of sheep. They followed in pursuit till the sound of the trumpet warned every one to rest.

Then all with one consent yielded the prize of this second day to Triamond and Cambell as the two best knights. But Triamond resigned it to Cambell, and Cambell gave it back to Triamond, each trying to advance the other's deed of arms, and make his praise preferred before his own.

So the judgment was deferred to another day.

How Britomart did Battle for the Golden Girdle

The last day of the tournament came, when all the knights again assembled to show their feats of arms. Many brave deeds were done that day, but Satyrane above all the other warriors displayed his wondrous might; from first to last he remained fighting, and though sometimes for a little while fortune failed him, yet he always managed to retrieve his honour, and with unwearied power he kept the prize secure for his own party.

The field was strewn with shivered spears, and broken swords, and scattered shields, showing how severe the fight had been; there might be seen also loose steeds running at random, whose luckless riders had been overthrown, and squires hastening to help their wounded masters. But still the Knights of Maidenhood came off the best, till there entered on the other side a stranger knight.

Whence he came no man could tell. He was in a quaint disguise, hard to be discovered, for all his armour was like a savage dress, decked with woody moss, and his steed had trappings of oak-leaves, that seemed fit for some savage mortal. Charging the enemy, this stranger smote down knight after knight, till every one began to shun the dreadful sight of him. They all wondered greatly who he was and whence he came, and began to ask each other his name; but when they could not learn it anyhow, it seemed most suitable to his wild disguise to term him the *Savage Knight*.

But, truly, his right name was otherwise. Though known to few, he was called Sir Artegall, the champion of *Justice*, the doughtiest and the mightiest Knight then living.

Sir Satyrane and all his band were so dismayed by his strength and valour that none of them dared remain in the field, but were beaten and chased about all day till the evening. Then, as the sun set, out of the thickest rout rushed forth another strange knight, who put the glory of the "Savage Knight" to shame—so can nothing be accounted happy till the end.

This strange Knight charged his mighty spear at Artegall. in the midst of his pride, and smote him so sorely on the visor that he fell back off his horse, and had small desire to rise again. Cambell, seeing this, ran at the stranger with all his might and main, but was soon likewise to be seen lying on the field. Triamond thereupon was inwardly full of wrath, and determined to avenge the shame done to his friend; but by his friend he soon found himself lying, in no less need of help. Blandamour had seen everything from beginning to end, and when he beheld this he was sorely displeased, and thought he would soon mend matters but he fared no better than the rest before him.

Many others likewise ran at the Knight, but in like manner they were all dismounted; and of a truth it was no wonder. No power of man could stay the force of that enchanted spear, for the stranger was no other than the famous Britomart.

Thus the warrior Princess restored that day to the Knights of Maidenhood the prize which was well-nigh lost, and bore away the prize of prowess from them all.

Then the shrill trumpets began to bray loudly, and bade them leave their labour and long toll for the joyous feast and other gentle play, for now the precious golden girdle was to be awarded to the most beautiful lady.

Through all ages it has been the custom that the prize of Beauty has been joined with the praise of arms and Chivalry. And there are special reasons for this, for each relies much on the other; that Knight who can best defend a fair Lady from harm, is surely the most fitting to serve her; and that Lady who is fairest and who will never swerve from her faith, is the most fitting to deserve his service.

So after the proof of prowess well ended came next the contest of the sovereign grace of beauty, in which the girdle of Florimell should fall to her who most excelled. Many wished to win it only from vanity, and not for the wondrous virtues which some said it possessed. For the girdle gave the gift of constant and loyal love to all who wore it; but whosoever was false and fickle could never keep it on, for it would loosen itself, or else tear asunder. It was said to be of magic origin, and Florimell, to whom it had been given long ago, held it dear as her life. No wonder, then, that so many ladies sought to win it, for she who wore it was accounted to be peerless.

The feast, therefore, being ended, the selected judges went down into the late field of battle to decide this doubtful case, for which all the ladies contended. But, first, inquiry was made as to which of those knights who had lately tourneyed had won the wager. Then it was judged that Satyrane had done best on the first day, for he ended last, having begun first; the second day was adjudged to Triamond, because he saved the victor from disaster, for Cambell was in all men's sight the victor till by mishap he fell into the hands of his foemen; the third day's prize was adjudged to the stranger knight, whom they all termed the "Knight of the Ebony Spear," and it was given by good right to Britomart, for she had vanquished the "Savage Knight," who until then was the victor, and appeared at the last unconquered for the last is deemed best.

To Britomart, therefore, the fairest lady was adjudged as a companion.

But Artegall greatly grudged this, and was much vexed that this stranger had forestalled him both of honour and of the reward of victory. He could not dispute what was decreed, but he inwardly brooded over the disgrace, and awaited a fit time to be avenged.

This matter being settled and every one agreed, it next followed to decide the Paragon of Beauty, and yield to the fairest lady her due prize.

"He at his entrance charg'd his powrefull spear
At Artegall, in middest of his pryde,
And therewith smote him on his umbriere
So sore, that tombling back, he downe did slyde."

How the Golden Girdle was awarded to the False Florimell

Then each Knight in turn began to claim the golden girdle on behalf of his own lady. First, Cambell brought to their view his fair wife, Cambina, covered with a veil. The veil being withdrawn at once revealed her surpassing loveliness, which stole all wavering hearts. Next, Sir Triamond uncovered the face of his dear Candace, which shone with such beauty that the eyes of all were dazzled as with a great light. After her, Paridell produced his false Duessa. With her forged beauty, Duessa entrapped the hearts of some who considered her the fairest; and, after these, a hundred more ladies appeared in turn, each one of whom seemed to excel the others.

At last Britomart openly showed her lovely Amoret, whose face uncovered seemed like the heavenly picture of some bright angel. Then all who saw her thought that Amoret would surely bear away the prize.

But Blandamour, who imagined that he had the real, true Florimell, now displayed the Snowy Lady, and the sight, once seen, dismayed all the rest.

For all who had seemed bright and fair before, now appeared base and contemptible; compared with her, they were only like stars in comparison with the sun. Every one who saw her was ravished with wonder; they thought she could be no mortal, but must be some celestial being. They were all glad to see Florimell, yet thought Florimell was not so fair as this lady. Like some base metal overlaid with gold, which deceives those who see it, was this false image who passed for the true Florimell. Thus do forged things sometimes show the fairest.

Then, by the decision of all, the golden belt was granted to her as to the fairest lady; and, bringing it to her, they thought to place it round her waist, as became her best. But this they could by no means do, for every time they fastened the girdle, it grew loose and fell away, as if there were some secret fault in her. Again and again she put it round her waist, but again and again it fell apart. All the people wondered at the strange sight, and each one thought according to his own fancy.

But the Snowy Lady herself thought it was some spiteful trick, and it filled her with wrath, and shame as a thing devised to bring disgrace on her.

Then many other ladies likewise tried to put on the girdle, but it would stay on none of them. As soon as they thought it fast, immediately it was untied again.

Seeing this, a scornful knight began to just and sneer, saying it was a pity that, among so many beautiful ladies, not one was found worthy to wear the girdle. All the knights began to laugh and all the ladies to frown, till at last the gentle Amoret also essayed to prove the girdle's power. She set it round her waist, and immediately it fitted perfectly, with no difficulty whatever.

The others were very envious, and the Snowy Lady was greatly fretted. Snatching the belt angrily from Amoret, she again tied it round her own body, but none the more would it fit her.

Nevertheless, to her, as her due right, was the girdle yielded, for every one thought she was the true Florimell, to whom it really belonged. And now she had to choose her companion knight. Then she adjudged the prize to the "Knight of the Ebony Spear," who had won it in fight. But Britomart would not assent to this, nor give up her own companion, Amoret, for the sake of that strange lady, whose wondrous beauty she esteemed less than the wisdom and goodness of Amoret.

When the other knights saw Britomart refuse, they were all very glad, for each hoped Florimell would choose himself. But the judges said that after Britomart she must next choose the second best, and that was the "Savage Knight." But Sir Artegall had already left in displeasure because he had not won the prize. Then she was offered Triamond, but Triamond loved Candace, and no one else. Then Sir Satyrane was adjudged to Florimell, and he was right glad to gain so goodly an award; but Paridell and Blandamour and many other knights were very angry, and wanted to fight Sir Satyrane. The hideous old woman, Até, with her wicked words, stirred them all up to demand and challenge Florimell as their right, the recompense which they deserved for their peril.

Amongst the rest, with boastful, vain pretence, Braggadochio stepped forward and claimed her as his thrall, having won her in battle long ago. He called the Snowy Lady herself to witness this, and being asked, she confessed that it was the case.

Thereupon all the other knights were more angry than ever, and they were quite ready to prepare anew for battle. But Sir Satyrane hit on a plan to appease them. He suggested that the Lady herself should choose which knight she preferred, and all the others should abide by her choice. This they agreed to. So Florimell was placed in the midst of them all, and every knight hoped she would choose him. Then, having looked a long time at each one, as though she wished to please them all, the Snowy Lady walked up to Braggadochio, and the two went off together.

Britomart took no part in the struggle for Florimell, for as soon as she saw that discord had arisen, she left the place. Taking with her the lovely Amoret, who was still looking for Sir Scudamour, Britomart rode off on her first quest, to seek her beloved Knight, Sir Artegall, whose image she had seen in the magic mirror. Little did she know that he was the "Savage Knight" with whom she had so lately fought, and who was even now waiting to be revenged on her. Unlucky maid, to seek her enemy! Unlucky maid to seek far and wide for him whom, when he was nearest, she could not discover because of his disguise!

How Sir Scudamour came to the House of Care

Thus Britomart, with much toll and grief, still sought the Knight whom she had seen in the magic mirror, and in all her sad misfortunes she found her fellow-wanderer, Amoret, a great comfort. But the gentle Scudamour, whose heart the malicious Até had filled with jealous discontent, was bent on revenge-on revenge against the blameless Princess. The wicked tale told by Até pricked his jealous heart like a thorn, and pierced his soul like a poisoned arrow. Nothing that Glaucé could do or say would alter his feeling; the more she tried to excuse Britomart, the worse it fretted and grieved him night and day, so that nothing but dire revenge might abate his anger.

Thus as they travelled, night, gloomy with cloud and storm and bitter showers, fell upon th em before its usual hour. This forced them to seek some shelter where they might hide their beads in quiet rest. Not far away, unfitting for any guest, they spied a little cottage, like some poor man's dwelling. It was placed under a steep hillside, where the mouldering earth had hollowed out the bank. A small brook of muddy water, bad-smelling as a puddle, passed close to it, bordered by a few crooked willows.

When Sir Scudamour and Glaucé came nearer, they heard the sound of many iron hammers ceaselessly beating in turn, so that it seemed as though some blacksmith dwelt in that desert place. Entering, they found the good man himself bent busily at work. He was a wretched, worn creature, with hollow eyes and wasted cheeks, as if he had been long pent in prison. His face was black and grisly-looking, smeared with smoke that nearly blinded his eyes. He had a ragged beard and shaggy hair, which he never cut nor kept in order. His garment was rough and all torn to rags; he had no better, nor cared for any better. His hands were blistered and burnt from the cinders, all unwashed, with long nails fit to rend the food on which he lived.

This creature was called *Care*. He was a blacksmith by trade, who never ceased working, day or night, but made iron wedges of small use. (These are unquiet thoughts, that invade anxious minds.)

He kept six servants hard at work, always standing round the anvil with great huge hammers, who never rested from battering stroke on stroke. All six were strong men, but each was stronger than the one before, so they went up, as it were, in steps. So likewise the hammers which they bore succeeded, like bells, in due order of greatness. The last servant far exceeded the first in size; he was like some monstrous giant. So dreadfully did he beat the anvil that it seemed as if he would soon drive it to dust. So huge was his hammer, and so great his energy, that it seemed as though he could break and rend asunder a rock of diamond if he cared to try.

Sir Scudamour greatly wondered at the manner of their work and weary labour, and having beheld it for a long time, at last inquired the cause and end of it. But all his questions were in vain, for they would not stop from their work for anything, nor listen to what he said. Even the gusty bellows blew fiercely, like the north wind, so that no one could hear. "*Sadness*" moved them, and the bellows were "*Sighs*."

The warrior, seeing this, said no more, but lay down to rest in his armour. To rest he lay down on the floor—in olden days the best bed for adventurous knights—and thought to have refreshed his weary limbs. And the aged nurse, Glaucé, his faithful squire, also laid her feeble joints down, for her age and weakness much needed rest after so long and tiring a journey.

There lay Sir Scudamour, long expecting the moment when gentle sleep would close his weary eyes, turning often from side to side, and

"Whereto approaching nigh they heard the sound
Of many yron hammers beating ranke."

often choosing a new place where it seemed he might repose better. And often in wrath he again rose from there, and often in wrath lay down again. But wherever he disposed himself, he could by no means obtain the desired ease; every place seemed painful, and each alteration useless.

And evermore when he thought to sleep, the sound of the hammers jarred his nerves, and evermore when he began to get drowsy, the noise of the bellows disturbed his quiet rest. All night the dogs barked and howled around the house, scenting the stranger-guest; and now the crowing cock, and now the owl shrieking loudly, fretted his very soul.

If by fortune a little drowsiness chanced to fall on his heavy eyelids, immediately one of the villains rapped him on the head with his iron mallet, so that he awoke at once and started up quickly, as one afraid, or as if one had suddenly called him. Thus he was often roused, and then he lay musing on the unhappy cause that had led him to the House of Care.

At last his weary spirit, too tired to resist further, gave place to rest; yet even now he was troubled with bad dreams. Then the wicked creature, the master-smith, took a pair of red-hot iron tongs and nipped him in the side, so that his heart quite quaked at the pain. Thereupon, he started up to be avenged on the person who had broken his quiet slumber, but looking round about him he could see no one, yet the smart remained, though the giver of it fled.

In such disquiet and heart-fretting pain, Sir Scudamour passed all that long night, and now the day began to peep over the earth, sprinkling the morning grass with pearly dew. Then up he rose, like a heavy lump of lead, and one could plainly read in his face, as in a looking-glass, signs of the anguish he had gone through.

He mounted his war-horse and set forth again on his former journey, and with him also went Glaucé, the aged squire, ready to share whatever pain and peril might be in store.

How the "Savage Knight" met the "Knight with the Ebony Spear"

The day after Sir Scudamour left the House of Care, as he rode sadly on his way, he unexpectedly saw an armed Knight sitting in the shade on the edge of a forest, while his steed grazed beside him. Directly this Knight saw Scudamour, he mounted and rode eagerly towards him, as if he intended mischief; but, as soon as he saw the arms borne by him, he lowered his spear and turned aside. Sir Scudamour wondered at this, but the other said, "Ah, gentle Scudamour, I submit myself to your grace, and ask pardon of you for having this day almost done you an injury."

Whereupon Scudamour replied, "Small harm is it for any warrior to prove his spear, without malice, on a venturous knight. But, sir, since you know my name, pray tell me what is your own?"

"Truly, you must excuse me from making known my right name now, for the time has not yet come for it," was the reply; "but call me the *Savage Knight*, as others do."

"Then tell me, Sir Savage Knight," said Scudamour, "do you dwell here, within the forest, which would answer well with your array?—Or have you put it on for some special occasion, as seems more likely, as you shun known arms?

"The other day a stranger Knight brought shame and dishonour on me," replied the Savage Knight. "I am waiting to revenge the disgrace whenever he shall pass this way, by day or night."

"Shame be his reward who purposes shame!" said Scudamour. "But what is he by whom you were shamed?"

"A stranger Knight, unknown by name, but known by fame and by all ebony spear, with which he bore down all who met him. He, in an open tourney lately held, stole away from me the honour of the game, and having felled me (already weary), reft me of the fairest lady, whom he has ever since withheld."

When Scudamour heard mention of the spear, he knew right well it was Britomart, who also, as he imagined, had taken Amoret from himself. Then his jealous heart swelled with rage, and he said sharply, "And that is not the first unknightly act which that same knight has done to other noble warriors, for he has lately stolen my lady from me, for which he shall pay dearly before long; and if to the vengeance decreed by you this hand call supply any help or succour, it shall not fail whensoever you need it."

So they both agreed to wreak their wrath on Britomart.

While they thus talked together, lo! far away they saw a Knight gently riding towards them. He was attired in foreign armour and strange array, and when he came near they saw plainly he was the same for whom they waited.

Then said Scudamour, "Sir Savage Knight, let me beg this, that since I was the first to be wronged, let me be the first to requite it, and if I happen to fail, you shall recover my right."

This being yielded, Sir Scudamour prepared his spear for battle, and ran fiercely against Britomart. But she gave him so rude a welcome that she smote both man and horse to the ground, from which they were in no hurry to rise. The sight of his mischance added fresh fuel to Artegall's burning rage, and thrusting forward his steel-headed lance at a venture, he rode against Britomart; but his evil intention recoiled on himself, for unawares he suddenly left his saddle, and in great amazement found himself on the ground.

Starting up lightly, he snatched forth his deadly blade, and assailed Britomart with such vigour that, although she was mounted and he on foot, she was forced to give ground. As they darted here and there, it chanced in her wheeling round that one stroke fell on her horse and wounded him so badly that Britomart was forced to alight.

Now she could no longer use her enchanted spear. Casting it from her, she betook herself to her sword and shield, and fought so valiantly that even now she was almost a match for Sir Artegall; but towards the end, while his strength seemed to get greater, hers grew less. At last, he raised his hand, and gathering all his force, struck such a terrible blow that it seemed as if nothing but death could be her fate.

The stroke fell on her helmet, and with its force sheared off the visor, and from there glanced harmlessly downwards, and did her no more injury.

With that, her angel face, unseen before, shone forth radiant as the dawn; and round about it her yellow hair, loosed from its usual bands, appeared like a golden border, cunningly framed in a goldsmith's forge. Yet goldsmith's cunning never knew how to fashion such subtle wire, so clear and shining; for it glistened like the golden sand which the bright water of Pactolus throws forth on the shore around him.

As Sir Artegall again lifted up his hand, thinking to work his utmost vengeance on her, his powerless arm, benumbed with secret fear, shrunk back from his revengeful purpose, and his cruel sword fell from his slack fingers to the ground; as if the steel had sense and felt some compassion that his hand lacked, or as if both of them thought to do obedience to such divine beauty. And Artegall himself, gazing long thereon, at last fell humbly down upon his knee; and imagining he saw some angelic being—for he did not know what else it could be—he besought her to pardon his error, which had done her such infinite wrong, while trembling horror seized him, and made every limb quake and his brave heart quail.

Britomart, nevertheless, full of wrath for that last stroke, kept her angry hand uplifted all the while; she stood over him, with a stern look, threatening to strike, unless he prevented her, and bidding him rise, or he should surely die. But die or live, nothing would make Sir Artegall stand up. He prayed more earnestly that the warrior-maiden would either pardon him or do with him as she chose, because of the great wrong he had done her.

When Scudamour saw this, where he stood not far away he was wondrously dismayed, and, drawing near and seeing plainly this peerless image of perfection, he too was terrified, and did homage to Britomart as to some celestial vision.

But Glaucé, seeing all that happened, knew well how to put right their error. Glad at such a good ending, and rejoiced to see Britomart safe after her long toll, she advanced, and saluted her with a hearty greeting. Then she besought her, as she was dear to her, to grant truce for awhile to these warriors, which being yielded, they lifted their beavers and showed themselves to her such as indeed they were.

How Britomart ended her Quest

When Britomart, with keen, observant eye, beheld the beautiful face of Artegall, tempered with sternness, strength, and majesty, her mind at once recalled it as the same which in her father's palace she had seen long since in that enchanted mirror. Then her wrathful courage began to falter, and her haughty spirit to grow tame, so that she softly withdrew her uplifted hand. Yet she tried again to raise it, as if feigning the anger which was now cold; but always when she saw his face, her hand fell down, and would no longer hold the weapon against him. Then having tried in vain to fight, she armed her tongue, and thought to scold him. Nevertheless, her tongue would not obey her will, but when she would have spoken against him, brought forth mild speeches instead.

Sir Scudamour, glad at heart because he had found all his jealous fears false, now exclaimed jestingly, "Truly, Sir Artegall, I rejoice to see you bow so low, and that you have lived to become a lady's thrall, who formerly were wont to despise them!"

When Britomart heard the name of Artegall, her heart leaped and trembled with sudden joy and secret fear. She flushed deeply, and thought to hide her agitation by again feigning her former angry mood.

Then Glaucé began wisely to put all matters right. First, she told both the knights not to marvel any more at the strange part Fate had made Britomart play; then she bade Sir Artegall not to lament because he had been conquered by a woman, for love was the crown of Knighthood; and, lastly, she entreated Britomart to relent the severity of her anger, and, wiping out the remembrance of all ill, to grant pardon to Artegall, if he would fulfil the penance she would impose on him. "For lovers' happiness is reached by the path of sorrow," she added.

At this, Britomart blushed, but Sir Artegall smiled to himself and rejoiced in his heart; yet he dared not speak too suddenly of the love he bore her, for her grave and modest face and royal bearing still kept him in awe.

But Scudamour, whose heart hung all this while in suspense between hope and fear, longing to hear some glad and certain news of his Lady Amoret, now addressed Britomart. "Sir, may I ask of you tidings of my love, my Amoret, since you freed her from her long and woeful captivity? Tell me where you left her, so that I may seek her, as is fitting."

"Indeed, Sir Knight, what has become of her, or if she has been stolen away, I cannot rightly tell you," replied Britomart. "From the time I freed her from the Enchanter's captivity, I have preserved her from peril and fear, and always kept her from harm, nor was there ever any one whom I loved more dearly; but one day, as we travelled through a desert wild, both being weary, we alighted and sat down in the shadow, where I fearlessly lay down to sleep. When I awoke, I did not find Amoret where I had left her, but thought she had wandered away or got lost. I called her loudly, I sought her near and far, but nowhere could find her, nor hear any tidings of her."

When Scudamour heard this bad news his heart was thrilled with fear, and lie stood dazed and silent. Glaucé tried to comfort him, bidding him not give way to needless dread until he was certain what had happened, "for she may yet be safe, though she has wandered away," she said. "It is best to hope the best, though afraid of the worst!"

But he took no heed of her cheerful words, till Britomart said, "You have, indeed, great cause of sorrow, sir; but take comfort, for by the light of heaven I swear not to leave you, dead or living, till I find your Lady, and be avenged on him who stole her!"

With that he was contented.

So, peace being established amongst them all, they took their horses and rode forward to some resting-place, guided by Sir Artegall. Here a hearty welcome greeted them, with daily feasting, both in bower and hall, until their wounds were well healed, and their weary limbs recovered after their late rough usage.

And all the time Sir Artegall and Britomart grew more and more in love with each other, though Britomart did all she could to hide her feeling. But so winningly did Sir Artegall woo her that at last she was obliged to listen to him, and to relent. She consented to be his wife, and the marriage took place.

But their happiness was not yet complete. Sir Artegall was all this while bound upon a hard adventure, which had still to be fulfilled, and when a fitting time came, he had to depart on his quest. Poor Britomart would scarcely let him go, though he faithfully promised to return directly he had achieved his task, which would probably take him not longer than three months. With that she had to be appeased for thc present, however unhappy she really felt; and early the next morning Sir Artegall started. Britomart went with him for a while on his journey. She could not bear to part from him, but all the way kept trying to find excuses for delay. Many a time she took leave, and then again invented something to say, so unwilling was she to lose his company. But at last she could find no further excuse, so, with a sad heart, she left

him and returned to Scudamour, whom she had promised to aid in his search for Amoret.

Sir Scudamour and Britomart went back to the desert forest, where the latter had lately lost Amoret. They sought her there, and inquired everywhere for tidings, yet found none.

But by what hapless fate or terrible misfortune the Lady Amoret had been conveyed away is too long to tell here. In another story may be read the adventures that befell her after she parted from Britomart.

The Squire of Low Degree

The Giant with Flaming Eyes

BRITOMART, the Warrior Princess, having rescued the fair lady Amoret from the wicked Enchanter, then started forth with her to find her husband, the good Knight Scudamour. Riding through a forest, they alighted to rest, and here Britomart, overcome with weariness, lay down to sleep.

Amoret, meanwhile, fearing nothing, roamed at pleasure through the wood. Suddenly from behind, some one rushed out, who snatched her up and bore her away. This was a huge, hideous savage, who killed and ate all the beautiful maidens he could get hold of. He carried Amoret fainting in his arms, right through the forest, till he came to his dwelling, a horrible cave, far from all people's hearing. Into this he flung her, and went off to see if he could secure any other victims.

Amoret was roused by her fall, but when she looked about and found nothing around her but darkness and horror, she almost fainted again, and did not know whether she were above or under the ground. Then she heard some one close by sighing and sobbing, and found this was another beautiful lady whom the savage had taken prisoner.

Amoret asked her who she was, and the lady told her sad story.

She said her name was Emilia; she was the daughter of a great lord, and everything went joyously with her till she happened to fall in love with a gentle youth, a Squire in her father's household. He was gallant and worthy enough for any lady to love, but he was not of noble birth like herself, and her father refused to let her marry him, and was angry with her for her folly. Nothing, however, would make her alter her mind, and rather than forsake her faithful Amyas she resolved to leave friends and family, and fly with him. A meeting-place in the wood was arranged, to which she came, but there, instead of her gallant Squire, she found the savage monster, who pounced on her like an eagle, and carried her to his cave.

While Emilia and Amoret were talking of their troubles, the hideous villain who was the cause of them came rushing back, rolling away the stone which he used to stop the entrance, in order that no one might go out. Directly he entered, Amoret slipped past him, and escaped from the cave with a loud scream of horror. Fast she fled, but he followed as swiftly. She did not feel the thorns and thickets prick her tender feet; neither hedge, nor ditch, nor hill, nor dale could stop her; she overleaped them all like a deer, and made her way through the thickest brushwood. And whenever she looked back with anxious eyes and saw the grisly monster approaching, she quickened her pace, spurred on by fear.

Long she fled thus, and long he followed, and it seemed as if there were no living aid for her on earth. But it chanced that the glorious Huntress-Queen, Belphœbe, with her companions the wood-nymphs, were that day chasing the leopards and the bears in that wild forest. A gentle squire, who was also one of the party, got separated from the others, and he came in sight of Amoret just as she was overtaken by the savage, who carried her away under his arm, grinning, and yelling with laughter.

The squire immediately attacked the savage, but it was difficult to do him any harm, for the latter held Amoret all the while as a shield, and the squire was afraid of hurting her. But at last he did succeed in wounding the wretch, who then flung Amoret rudely on the ground, and flew at the squire so fiercely that he forced him back.

In the midst of their battle, Belphœbe drew near. The robber, seeing her approach with bow in hand and arrows ready bent, would no longer stay to fight, but fled away in ghastly fear, for he knew she was the only one who could kill him. But fast as he flew, Belphœbe kept pace with him, and before he reached his den she sent forth an arrow with mighty force which caught him in the very doorway and slew him.

Amoret and Emilia were now safe, and they lived together in the wood for some time; but both were very ill—Emilia from having been kept so long a prisoner in the cave, where she was nearly starved, and Amoret from the hurts she had received in the rough handling of the savage.

One day it chanced that through this wood rode Prince Arthur, and he came to the place where the two ladies dwelt. He was greatly grieved to see the sad state in which they were, especially Amoret, who looked as if she could not live long. He immediately drew forth some of that precious liquor which he always kept about him, and which had the power of healing all wounds. It was the same wonderful medicine that he had long ago given to the Red Cross Knight, when he rescued him from the dungeon of Giant Pride. Prince Arthur sprinkled a few drops of this on Amoret's wounds, and she soon recovered her strength.

When the ladies were well, Prince Arthur began to ask what evil guide had brought them there, and how their harms befell. They told him all that had happened, and how they had been released from thraldom by the beautiful Belphœbe. Then the Prince said he would restore them safely to their friends, and placing them both on his warhorse, he went beside them himself on foot, to shield them from fear.

Thus, when they had passed out of the forest they spied far away a little cottage, to which they came before nightfall. But entering, they found no one dwelling there, except one old woman who sat upon the ground in tattered raiment, her dirty locks scattered all about her, while she gnawed her nails with cruelty and rage. She was a hideous creature to see, and no less hateful by nature, for she was stuffed full with rancour and spite, which often broke forth in streams of poison, bitterness, and falsehood against all who held to truth or virtue. Men called her name *Slander*.

"A Squire came galloping, as he would flie,
Bearing a little Dwarfe before his steed,
Whom after did a mightie man pursew,
Ryding upon a Dromedare on hie,
Of stature huge, and horrible of hew."

It was Slander's nature to abuse all goodness, and continually to invent crimes of which to accuse guiltless people, so that she might steal away their fair name. No knight was ever so bold, nor any lady so good and loyal, but what Slander strove to defame them falsely; never thing was done so well but she would blot it with blame, and deprive it of due praise. Her words were not, as common words are meant, to express the meaning of the mind, but they were sharp and. bitter to pierce the heart and grieve the soul; like the stings of asps that kill with their bite, her spiteful words pricked and wounded inwardly.

Such was the hag, unfit to receive these guests, whom the greatest Prince's court would have been glad to welcome; but their necessity bade them look for no better entertainment. It was, besides, an age which despised luxury. People were accustomed to hardness and homely fare, which trained them to warlike discipline, and to endure carelessly any hard fortunes or luckless mishaps which might befall them.

All that evening, then, welcomed with cold and cheerless hunger, they spent together, and found no fault, except that the hag scolded and railed at them for lodging there without her consent. But they mildly and patiently endured it all, regardless of the unjust blame and bitter reviling of such a worthless creature.

Directly it was daylight they prepared again for their journey, and went forth, Amoret and Emilia as before riding on the horse, and the Prince walking beside them. As soon as they departed, wicked old Slander followed, reviling them, and calling them bad names. The more they were vexed at this, the worse she raged and railed; and even when they had passed cut of sight and hearing she did not stop her spiteful speeches, but railed anew against the stones and trees, until she had dulled the sting that grew in the end of her tongue.

As the travellers went slowly on their way, they saw galloping towards them, as if in flight, a Squire who bore before him on his steed a little dwarf, shrieking loudly for help. They were pursued by a mighty man, riding on a dromedary, huge of stature, and horrible to behold. From his terrible eyes came two fiery beams, sharper than needles' points, which had the power of working deadly poison to all who looked on him without good heed, and of secretly slaying his enemies.

All the way he raged at the Squire, and hurled threats at him, but the latter fled so fast he could not overtake him. Seeing the Prince in his bright armour, the Squire called to him to pity him and rescue him from his cruel foe.

Then Prince Arthur at once took down the two ladies from his war-horse, and mounting in their place came to the Squire. In another moment the Giant was upon them. He aimed a furious blow at the Squire, which would certainly have killed him, had not the noble Prince defeated the stroke by thrusting forward, and meeting it on his own shield. It fell with such force that it drove the shield aside, and knocked both the Squire and the dwarf to the ground. Then Prince Arthur, enraged, smote at the Pagan with all his might and main, and killed him.

When the Squire saw his foe dead he was indeed glad, but the dwarf howled aloud to see his lord slain, and tore his hair, and scratched his face for grief.

Then the Prince began to inquire about everything that had happened, and who he was whose eyes flamed with fire. And all this the Squire then told him:—

"For his Friend's Sake"

"This mighty man whom you have slain," said the Squire, "is the son of a huge giantess. By his strength he gained rule to himself and led many nations into thraldom, conquering them, however, not in battle, by armies of men with waving banners, but by the power of his malignant eyes, with which he killed all who came within his control. Never before was he vanquished, but always vanquished all with whom he fought. Nor was there any man so strong but what he bore him down, nor any woman so fair but he made captive of her; for his chief desire was to make spoil of strength and beauty, and utterly to destroy them. Because of his wicked eyes, which cast flakes of fire into the hearts of those who looked at him, he was rightly called *Corflambo*.

He has left one daughter who is named the fair Pœana, who seems outwardly as fair as living eye ever yet saw; and if her virtue were as bright as her beauty, she would be as fair as any one on earth. But she is too much given to folly and pleasure, and is also too fickle and too fanciful.

"Well, as it happened, there was a gentle Squire who loved a lady of noble birth; but because his low rank forbade his hoping to marry so high, her friends sagely counselled her against letting herself down to his level. But Emilia would not break the promise she had given Amyas, for she loved him truly, and holding firmly to her first intention, she resolved to marry him, in spite of all her friends. They appointed, therefore, a time and place of meeting, but when accordingly the Squire repaired there, a sad misadventure happened. Instead of finding his fair Emilia, he was caught unawares by Corflambo, who carried his wretched captive, dismayed with despair, to his dungeon, where lie remained unaided, and unsought by any one.

"The Giant's daughter came one day in glee to the prison, to view the captives who lay in bondage there. Among the rest she chanced to see this gallant youth, the Squire of low degree. She took a great liking to him, and she promised that if he would love her in return he should have his liberty.

"Amyas, though plighted to another lady to whom he firmly meant to keep his faith, thought he had better take any means of escape offered by fortune, and therefore pretended to like Pœana a very little, in order to win her favour and get his liberty. But the Giant's daughter still kept him in captivity, fearing that if she set him free he would leave at once and forget her. Yet she showed him so much favour above the other prisoners that he was allowed sometimes to walk about her pleasure gardens, having always a keeper with him, The keeper was this dwarf, her pet menial, to whom as a special favour she commits the keys of all the prison doors. He can, at his will, release those whom he chooses, and those also whom he chooses he can reserve for more severe punishment.

When tidings of this reached me, I was deeply grieved because of the great love I bear to Amyas, and I went to the Castle of Corflambo. There I concealed myself for a long time, till one day the dwarf discovered me, and told his mistress that her Squire of low degree had secretly

"This Gyant's daughter came upon a day
Unto the prison in her joyous glee,
To view the thrals which there in bondage lay."

stolen out of prison; for he mistook me for Amyas, because no two people were ever more alike.

"I was taken and brought before the Giant's daughter, who being also beguiled by the likeness, began to blame me for seeking to escape by flight from one who loved me so dearly; and then she ordered me again to prison. Glad of this, I did not contradict her, nor make any resistance, but suffered that same dwarf to drive me to the dungeon.

"There I found my faithful friend in heavy plight and sad perplexity, for which I was sorry, yet bent myself to comfort him again with my company. But this, I found, grieved him the more; for his only joy in his distress, he said, was the thought that Emilia and I were free. He loved Emilia well, as I could guess, and yet he said his love for me was even greater.

'But I reasoned with him and showed him how easy it would be to manage a disguise because of our likeness, so that either we could change places or his freedom might be gained. He was most unwilling to agree, and would not for anything consent that I, who was free and out of danger, should willfully be brought into thraldom. Yet, overruled at last, he consented.

"The next day, at about the usual hour, the dwarf called at the door of the dungeon for Amyas to come directly to his lady's bower. Instead of Amyas, I—Placidas—came forth, and, undiscovered, went with him. The fair Pœana received me with joy, and gave me an affectionate greeting, thinking that I was Amyas. Not having any former love of my own, I was quite willing to accept her kindness and favour, as indeed it was expedient to do. I pretended to make excuses for my former coldness, and promised to be more amiable in future. All this I did, not for my own sake, but to do good to my friend, for whose liberty alone I staked love and life.

"Thenceforward I found more favour at Pœana's hand. She bade the dwarf who had charge of me lighten my heavy chains and grant me more scope to walk abroad. So, one day, as I played with him on the flowery bank of a stream, finding no means of gaining our freedom unless I could convey away the dwarf, I lightly snatched him up and carried him off.

"He shrieked so loudly that at his cry the tyrant himself came forth and pursued me. Nevertheless I would not give up my prey, and hither by force I have brought him."

As Placidas spoke thus to Prince Arthur, the two ladies, still doubtful through fear, came near, wishing to hear tidings of all that had happened.

Directly Emilia spied her captive lover's friend, young Placidas, she sprang towards him, and throwing her arms round him, exclaimed, "Does Amyas still live?"

"He lives," said Placidas, "and loves his Emilia."

Not more than I love him," she cried. "But what misfortune has kept him so long from me?"

Then Placidas told her how Amyas had been taken captive. It filled her tender heart with pity to hear of the misery in which he had lain so long, and she eagerly begged Prince Arthur to set him free. This the Prince readily consented to do, and well he performed his work.

The Giant's Daughter

Of all human affection the love of one friend for another is surely the noblest and most unselfish; and this true friendship Amyas, and Placidas had for each other—not even their affection for kindred or fairest lady could shake their loyalty. For though Pœana were as beautiful as the morning, yet Placidas, for his friend's sake, scorned her offered favours. His only thought was what he could do to set Amyas free.

Now after Prince Arthur had promised to succour the Squire who had lain so long in prison, he next began to consider how best he could effect his purpose. Taking up the dead body of the Giant, he firmly bound it on the dromedary, and made it so to ride as if it were alive. Then he took Placidas and placed him in front of Corflambo, as if he were a captive; and he made the dwarf (though very unwillingly) guide the beast till they drew near the castle. When the watchman who kept continual guard saw them thus coming home, he ran down, without doubt or fear, and unbarred the gate, and the Prince following passed in with the others.

There in her delicious bower he found the fair Pœana playing on a rote, complaining of her cruel lover, and singing all her sorrow in music. So sweet and lovely she seemed that the Prince was half-entranced, but wisely bethinking himself of what was right, he caught her unawares and held her captive.

Then he took the dwarf and compelled him to open the prison door, and to bring forth the thralls which he kept there. Over a score of unknown knights and squires were brought to him, all of whom he freed from their bitter bondage, and restored to their former liberty. Among the rest came the Squire of low degree, all weak and wan. As soon as Emilia and Placidas beheld him they both ran and embraced him, holding him fast between them, and striving all they could to comfort him.

The Giant's daughter, seeing this, envied them both, and bitterly railed at them, weeping with rage and jealousy. But when they had been for some time together, talking over their adventures, although Pœana had often seen Amyas and Placidas separately, she began to doubt which was really the captive Squire whom she had loved so dearly; for they appeared so alike in face and person that it was difficult to discover which was which. So also Prince Arthur was amazed at their resemblance, and gazed long in wonder, as did the other knights and squires who saw them.

Then they began to ransack the Giant's castle, in which they found great store of hoarded treasure, which the tyrant had gathered by wicked means. Prince Arthur took possession of this, and afterwards remained a little while at the castle to rest himself, and refresh the ladies Amoret and Emilia, after their weary toll. To these also he gave part of the treasure.

To add to the rejoicing, he set free the captive lady, the fair Pœana, and placed her in a chair of state with the rest, to feast and frolic. But she would show no gladness nor pleasant glee, for she was grieved for the loss both of her father and of her lands and money. But most of all she deeply grieved for the loss of the gentle Squire Placidas, whom she now really loved.

But Prince Arthur, with his accustomed grace, charmed her to mild behaviour from the sullen rudeness which spoilt her. With gentle

"There did he find in her delicious bower
The fair Pœana playing on a rote."

words and manner he calmed her raging temper, and softened the bitterness that gnawed at her heart and kept her from the feast; for although she was most fair to see, she spoilt all her beauty by cruelty and pride. And in order to end everything with friendly love—since love was the cause of her grief—Prince Arthur wisely urged the trusty Squire Placidas not to despise without better trial the lady who loved him so dearly, but to accept her to be his wedded wife. Placidas was quite willing to marry Pœana; so all their strife came to an end.

From that day forth they lived long together in peace and happiness. no private quarrel nor spite of enemies could shake the calm security of their position. And she whom Nature had created so fair that she could match the fairest of them all, and vet who had spoilt it by her own wayward folly, henceforth reformed her ways, so that all men marvelled at the change, and spoke in praise of her.

Thus having settled these friends, Amyas and Placidas, in peace and rest (for Amyas, of course, married his dear Emilia), Prince Arthur again went on his way; and with him went the Lady Amoret, for she had still to find her husband, the good Knight Scudamour.

The Adventures of Sir Artegall

"The champion of true Justice, Artegall."
"Wise, warlike, personable, courteous, and kind."

The Sword of Justice and the Iron Man

ONE of the noblest heroes at the Court of the Faerie Queene was Artegall, the champion of *Justice*. After his marriage with Britomart, it may be remembered, he started on a hard adventure, which led him into much peril. This was to succour a distressed lady whom a strong tyrant unjustly kept captive, withholding from her the heritage which she claimed. The lady was called Irene (*Peace*), and the Tyrant, Grantorto (*Great Wrong*).

When Irene came to the Faerie Queene to beg redress, Queen Gloriana, whose delight it was to aid all poor suppliants, chose Artegall to restore right to her, because he seemed the best skilled in righteous learning.

Even from his cradle Artegall had been brought up to justice; for one day when he was a little child playing with his companions, he had been found by a great and wonderful lady called Astræa, who, while she dwelt here among earthly men, instructed them in the rules of justice. Seeing that the boy was noble and fit for her purpose, she persuaded him to go with her. She took him far away to a lonely cave, in which she brought him up, and taught him all the discipline of justice. She taught him, to weigh equally both right and wrong, and where severity was needed to measure it out according to the line of conscience. For want of mankind she caused him to practise this teaching on wild beasts which she found in the woods wrongfully oppressing others of their own kind. Thus she trained him, and thus she taught him to judge skilfully wrong and right till he reached the years of manhood, so that even wild beasts feared him, and men admired his overruling might. Nor was there any living person who dared withstand his behest, much less match him in fight. To make him more dreaded, Astræa gave Artegall a wonderful sword, called "Chrysaor," which excelled all other swords. It was made of most perfect metal, tempered with adamant, all garnished with gold upon the blade, whereby it took its name. It was no less powerful than famous, for there was no substance so firm and hard but it could pierce or cleave, nor any armour that could guard off the stroke, for wherever it lighted, it cut completely through.

In course of time Astræa left this world, and went to live among the stars, from which she had first come. But she left behind her on earth her servant, an Iron Man, who always attended on her to execute her Judgments, and she bade him go with Artegall and do whatever he was told. The man's name was Talus; he was made of iron mould, immovable, irresistible, unchanging; he held in his hand an iron flail, with which he threshed out falsehood and unfolded the truth.

Talus, therefore, went with Sir Artegall on this new quest, to aid him, if he chanced to need aid, against the cruel tyrant who oppressed

. . . "For want there of mankind,
She caused him to make experience
Upon wyld beasts, which she in woods did find
With wrongfull powre oppressing others of their kind."

the Lady Irene and kept the crown from her. Nothing is more honourable to a knight, nor better becomes brave chivalry, than to defend the feeble in their right, and redress the wrongs of those who go astray. So the heroes of old won their greatest glory, and herein this noble Knight excelled, who now went forth to dare great perils for the sake of justice.

As Artegall and Talus went on their way they chanced to meet the servant of Florimell, who told the good news that his lady was safe and well, and engaged to be married to her own true knight, Marinell. Sir Artegall was very glad to hear this, and asked when the wedding was to take place, for if he had time he would like to be present to do honour to the occasion.

"The wedding will be within three days," said the man, "at the Castle of the Strand; at which time, if nothing hinders me, I shall be there to do her service, as I am bound. But in my way, a little beyond here, dwells a cruel Saracen who keeps with strong hand the passage of a bridge. He has killed there many a knight-errant, wherefore all men, out of fear, shun the passage."

"What sort of person, and how far away, is he who does such harm to travellers?" asked Artegall.

"He is a man of great defence, expert in battle and in deeds of arms," was the answer; "and he is made much bolder by the wicked spells with which his daughter supports him. He has got large estates and goodly farms by oppression and extortion, with which he still holds them. His crimes increase daily, for he never lets any one pass that way over his Bridge, be he rich or poor, without paying him toll-money. His name is called Pollenté, because he is so strong and powerful; he: conquers every one,—some by his strength, and some also he circumvents by cunning. For it is his custom to fight on the bridge, which is very narrow, but exceedingly long, and in this bridge are fixed many trap-falls, through which, not noticing, the rider falls down. Underneath the bridge flows a swift and dangerously deep river, into which falls headlong, destitute of help, any one whom the Saracen overthrows. But the tyrant himself, because of his long practice, leaps forth into the flood, and there assails his foe, confused by his sudden fall, so that horse and main are both equally dismayed, and either drowned or treacherously slain. Then Pollenté robs them at will, and brings the spoil to his daughter, who dwells hard by. She takes everything that comes, and fills her wicked coffers, which she has heaped so high by wrong-doing that she is richer than many a prince, and has purchased all the country lying near with her ill-gotten revenue. Her name is Munera.

"She is very beautiful and richly attired; her hands are made of gold, and her feet of silver. Many great lords have wished to marry her, but she is so proud that she despises them all."

"Now by my life, and with Heaven to guide me," said Sir Artegall, "no other way will I take this day but by that bridge where the Saracen abides; therefore lead me thither."

The Adventure of the Saracen's Bridge

Sir Artegall soon came to the place where he saw the Saracen ready armed on the bridge, waiting for spoil. When he and Talus drew near to cross it, an ugly-looking rascal came to them to demand passage-money, according to the custom of the law. "Lo, there are your wages!" said Sir Artegall, and smote him so that he died.

When the Pagan saw this he grew very angry, and at once prepared himself for battle; nor was Sir Artegall behind, so they both ran at each other with levelled spears. Right in the middle, where they would have met breast to breast, a trap was let down to make them fall into the river. The wicked wretch leaped down, knowing well that his foe would fall; but Sir Artegall was on his guard, and also leaped before he fell.

Then both of them being in the stream they flew at each other violently, the water in no way cooling the heat of their temper but rather adding to it. But there the Saracen, who was well used to fighting in the water, had great advantage, and often almost overthrew Sir Artegall. The charger, also, which he rode could swim like a fish.

When Sir Artegall saw the odds against him, he knew there was no way but to close hastily with his foe, and driving strongly at Pollenté he gripped him fast by his iron collar, and almost throttled him. There

they strove and struggled together, each trying to drag the other from his horse, but nothing could make Artegall slacken his grip. At length he forced Pollenté to forsake his horse's back, for fear of being drowned, and to betake himself to his swimming. There Pollenté had no advantage, for Artegall was skilful in swimming, and dared venture in any depth of Water. So every knight exposed to peril should be expert in swimming and able to make his way through water,

For some time the end of the contest was doubtful, for besides being skilled in that exercise, both were well trained in arms and thoroughly tried Artegall, however, kept his breath and strength better, so that his foe could no longer withstand him, nor bear himself upright, but fled from the water to the land. Artegall, wit h his bright sword, Chrysaor, pursued him so closely that Pollenté had scarcely set foot on shore before his head was cut off.

This done, Sir Artegall took his way to the castle in which Munera dwelt, guarded by many defenders Artegall sought entrance, but was refused and defied with a torrent of evil abuse. He was also beaten with stones flung down from the battlements, so that he was forced to retire, and he bade his servant Talus invent some way by which he could enter without danger.

Then Talus went to the castle gate, and let fly at it with his iron flail, so that it sorely terrified all the warders, and made those stoop who had borne themselves so proudly. He battered and banged on the door, and thundered strokes so hideously that he shook the very foundations of the building, and filled all the house with fear and uproar.

At this noise the Lady Munera appeared on the castle wall. When she saw the dangerous state in which she stood, she feared she would soon be destroyed, and began with fair words to entreat the Iron Man below to cease his outrage; for neither the force of the stones which they threw, nor the power of charms which she wrought against him could make him stop.

But when she saw him proceed, unmoved by pity or by prayers, she tried to bribe him with a goodly reward. She caused great sacks with countless riches to be brought to the battlements, and poured over the castle wall, so that she might gain some time, though dearly bought, whilst he gathered up the gold.

Talus was not in the least moved or tempted by this, but still continued his assault with the iron flail, so that at length he rent down the door, and made a way for his master. When Artegall entered, it was no use for any one to try to withstand him. They all fled; their hearts failed them, and they hid in corners here and there; and their wicked lady herself, half-dead, hid in terror. For a long time no one could find her, but Talus, who, like a bloodhound, could track out secret things, at length found her where she Jay hidden under a heap of gold, and dragged her forth. Sir Artegall himself pitied her sad plight, but he could not change the course of justice. Like her father, Munera had to be punished, in order to warn all mighty people who possess great power that they must use it in the right way, and not oppress the feeble. The Tyrant's daughter was thrown into the water, and the stream washed her away.

Then Talus took all the ill-gotten gold and treasure which her father had scraped together by hook and crook, and burning it into ashes, poured it into the river. Lastly, he pulled down the castle to its very foundation, and broke up all the hewn stones, so that there could be no hope of its being restored, nor memory of it among any nation. All which Talus having thoroughly performed, Sir Artegall reformed the evil fashion and wicked customs of the bridge; and this done, he returned to his former journey.

The Giant with the Scales

After travelling a long, weary way, Sir Artegall and Talus came near the sea, and here one day they saw before them an immense crowd of people, stretching out as far as the eye could reach. They were much astonished at this great assembly, and therefore approached to ask what had brought them together. There they beheld a mighty giant standing on a rock, and holding high in his hand a great pair of scales, with which he boasted in his presumption that he would accurately weigh the whole world, if he had anything to match it in the other scale. He said he would take up all the earth, and all the sea, divided from each other; so would he also make one balance of the fire, and one of air, without wind or weather; then he would balance heaven and hell together, and all that was contained within them, and would not miss a feather of their weight-any surplus of each that remained over he would restore to its own part, For, said he, they were all unequal, and had encroached on each other's share, like the sea which had worn the earth, as the fire had done the air. So all the rest took possession of each other's parts, and thus countries and nations had gone awry. All of which he undertook to repair in the way they had anciently been formed, and everything should be made equal. He would throw down the mountains and make them level with the plain; the towering rocks he would thrust down into the deepest sea; he would suppress tyrants,

so that they should no longer rule; and all the wealth of the rich men he would take away and give to the poor.

All the silly ignorant folk flocked about the giant, and clustered thick to hear his vain delusions, like foolish flies round a jar of honey;

for they hoped to gain great benefits by him, and uncontrolled freedom. When Artegall saw and heard how he misled the simple people, he disdainfully drew near, and thus spoke to him without fear:—

"You that presume to weigh the world anew, and restore all things to an equality, it seems to me show great wrong instead of right, and boast far more than you are able to perform." And then he went on to rebuke the giant for his folly and presumption, and showed him that if he could not understand nor weigh properly even the things that he saw, how much less could he attempt to balance unseen matters, or call into account the works of the great Ruler of the universe.

But the giant would not listen to reason, for he had no real desire for the right, and he still tried to continue his false and wicked teaching. Talus, therefore, seeing his mischievous ignorance, came up, and toppled him over into the sea, where he fell with a great splash and was drowned.

When the people who had long waited there saw his sudden destruction, they began to gather in a turbulent mob, and tried to stir up strife, because of the loss of all their expectations. For they had hoped to get great good, and wonderful riches, by the giant's new schemes, and resolving to revenge his death, they rose in arms, and stood in order of battle.

When Artegall saw this lawless multitude advancing in hostile fashion, he was much troubled, and did not know what to do; for he was loath to soil his hands by killing such a rascally crew, and yet he feared to retire, lest they should follow him with shame. Therefore he sent Talus to them to inquire the cause of their array, and to request a truce. But as soon as they saw him coming they began to attack him with their weapons, and rudely struck at him on every side yet they could not in the least hurt or dismay him. Then Talus lay about him with his flail and overthrew them like a swarm of flies. Not one of them dared come in his way, but they flew here and there, and hid themselves out of his sight in holes and bushes. When Talus saw that they all forsook the field and none of the rascal rout were left, he returned to Sir Artegall, and they went on together.

Borrowed Plumes, and the Fate of the Snowy Lady

After long storms and tempests the sun's face again shines forth joyfully, so when fortune has shown all her spite some blissful hours at last must needs appear. So it was with the Lady Florimell. After escaping from the cruel hyena that killed and devoured her milk-white palfrey, she met with many troubles and misfortunes; but they were all over now, and she was happily betrothed to her own true Knight, Marinell.

The time and place of the bridal were blazed far and wide, and solemn feasts and tournaments were arranged, to which a countless throng of lords and ladies resorted from all directions, nor was there any brave knight absent. It would need the tongue of a herald to tell the glory of the feast that day-the splendid service, the brilliant variety of entertainments, the pomp of the bridegroom, the richness of the bride's array, the crowd of noble ladies and gallant knights, the royal banquets, and the general rejoicing. When all the people had sufficiently feasted, they began to prepare themselves for deeds of arms and contests of chivalry.

Then first of all rode forth Sir Marinell, and with him six more knights, to challenge all on behalf of Florimell, and to maintain that she excelled all other ladies. Against them came every one that cared to joust, from every coast and country under the sun no one was debarred; all had leave who chose. Many brave deeds were done that day, and many a knight unhorsed, but little was lost or won. All that day the greatest praise redounded to Marinell. So also the second day. At the end of the fighting the trumpets proclaimed that Marinell was the best.

The third day came, which would test all the others, and the warriors met together to finish the tournament. Then Marinell again showed great valour, and flew like a lion through the thickest of the press, so that every one fled from the danger, and was amazed at his might. But the greater the prowess, the greater the peril; Marinell pressed so far into the ranks of the enemy that they closed up behind him, so that he could by no means make a way out. He was taken prisoner, and bound with chains, and would have been led away, forsaken of all, had not some succour overtaken him in time.

It happened that while Marinell was thus sorely beset, Sir Artegall came into the tilt-yard, with Braggadochio, whom he had lately met on the way with the false Florimell, the "Snowy Lady." When Artegall heard the bad fortune that had betided Marinell, he was much excited at his undeserved disgrace. He immediately. begged the braggart with whom he was riding to change shields with him, in order that he might be the better concealed, and thus armed he went forth, and soon overtook the knights who were leading Marinell away. There were a hundred of them altogether. Half of them set upon Sir Artegall, and half stayed behind to guard the prey. Artegall was not long in beating the first fifty, and soon snatched the prisoner from the other fifty. Then he quickly armed Marinell again, and together they overcame all the rest of the knights, and were left lords of the field. So Marinell was rescued from his foes.

Having done this, Sir Artegall restored his shield to Braggadochio, who all this while had remained in the background. Then the trumpets sounded, and the judges rose, and all the knights who had borne armour that day came to the open hall to listen to whom the honour of the prize should be adjudged.

There also in open sight came the fair Florimell into the public hall, to give his guerdon to every knight, and the best to him to whom the best should fall. Then they loudly called for the stranger Knight, to whom they should yield the garland, but he came not forth; but instead of Sir Artegall came Braggadochio, and showed his shield, which bore the device of the sun, broadly blazoned on a golden field.

The sight filled them with gladness, so to him they adjudged the prize of all that triumph. Then the shrill trumpets thrice resounded the name of Braggadochio, and thus courage lent a cloak to cowardice. Then the beautiful Florimell came to Braggadochio, and spoke graciously in praise of his gallantry, and gave him a thousand thanks for so well defending her cause.

To this the boaster (which filled all knights with utter contempt for him) made scornful answer that what he did that day he did, not for her, but for his own lady's sake, who excelled both her and every one else; and he added further bragging and unseemly speeches. His words much abashed the gentle lady, and she turned aside, ashamed to hear what he said.

Then he brought forth his snowy Florimell, who was standing near, in charge of Trompart, covered with a veil from people's gaze; and when they had thoroughly eyed her they were stupefied with great amazement, saying that it was surely Florimell, or if it were not, then she surpassed Florimell herself. Such feeble skill have the vulgar with respect to perfect things!

Marinell, likewise, when he beheld, was exceedingly amazed, not knowing what to think or to do. He stood for a long time lost in astonishment, his eyes fixed fast on the Snowy Maid, whom the more he looked at, the more he thought was the true Florimell.

When Artegall, who stood all this while close covered in the crowd, saw everything that passed, and the boasting and ungrateful cheating of Braggadochio, he could stand it no longer, but came forth, and showed himself openly to every one, and said to the boaster—

"Base wretch, thou hast defaced another's worth with thy lies and decked thyself with borrowed plumes; when they are all restored, thou shalt be left in disgrace. That shield which thou bearest was indeed the one which saved the day's honour to Marinell; but that was not the arm, nor thou the man who did that service to Florimell. For proof, show forth thy sword, and let it tell what strokes, what dreadful battle it stirred up this day. Or show the wounds which befell you!

"But *this* is the sword which wrought such havoc; and this the arm which bore that shield; and these the signs" (he pointed to his wounds) "by which it is apparent the glory was got. As for that lady which he shows here," he continued, turning to the others, "it is not Florimell at all, but some worthless creature, fit for such a mate, who has fallen into his hand by misfortune;" and for proof he bade them call the true Florimell.

So the noble Lady was brought, adorned with honour and all comely grace, blushing with modesty, so that the roses mixed with the lilies in her lovely face, for she still felt deep shame at the rude words which Braggadochio had flung at her. And when the people saw her they shouted aloud, and all showed signs of gladness.

Then Sir Artegall placed her by the Snowy Lady, like a true saint beside some painted image, to make trial of their beauty, and to see which should get the honour. Straightway, as soon as they were both met together, the enchanted damsel vanished into nothing. Her body of snow melted as with heat, and nothing remained of all her goodly appearance except the empty girdle, which had been clasped round her waist.

When the people present beheld this, they were struck with astonishment, and their hearts quailed with horror, to see the thing which seemed so excellent stolen away, so that no one understood what became of it. Braggadochio himself was so daunted with despair that he stood immovable, like a lifeless body.

But Artegall took up the golden belt, the only thing reft of all the spoil, which was not the Snowy Lady's, as many mistakenly believed, but Florimell's own girdle reft from her when she fled from the vile monster; unbuckling it, he presented it to Florimell, who fitted it perfectly round her slender waist. The girdle possessed the magic power of breaking or becoming unfastened when it was put on by any unworthy person. Many ladies had often tried to wear it, but it fitted no one till it came into the hands of its rightful owner, Florimell.

How the Good Horse Brigadore knew his own Master

While every one was busied about Florimell, and in hearing the truth about Braggadochio, Sir Guyon, as it befell, came forward from the thickest of the crowd to claim his own good steed, which Braggadochio had stolen long ago. Seizing the golden bit with one hand, he drew his sword with the other, for he meant to smite the thief heavily, and had he not been held he would certainly have done so.

Then a great hurly-burly rose in the hall because of that war-horse, for Braggadochio would not let him pass, and Sir Guyon was quite resolved to have him, or to put the matter to the proof over his dead body. The uproar being perceived by Artegall, he drew near to stay the

"Streight-way, so soone as both together met,
Th' enchaunted Damzel vanisht into nought,
Her snowy substance melted as with heat,
Ne of that goodly hew remayned ought."

tumult, and began to ask how the steed had been taken away, whether extorted by might or stolen by cunning.

Then Sir Guyon told him about the Knight and the Lady, whom he and the Palmer had found, and to avenge whom he had gone on his quest against the wicked enchantress, Acrasia. He described how, when he had gone into the thicket to help the dying lady, his horse had been purloined by craft, for which he now challenged the thief to fight. But Braggadochio would by no means consent to this, for he hated such doings, and would rather lose than make trial of his right by an appeal to arms.

Sir Artegall, hearing this, might then have handed over the horse to Sir Guyon, for according to knightly custom there was no need to try one's cause by the law of arms, if a foe refused to meet one in the field. But wishing to establish Guyon's claim properly, he asked him to describe any secret token borne by the horse.

"If that will satisfy you," said Sir Guyon, "there is within his mouth a black spot, shaped like a horse's shoe, for any one who cares to seek for it."

In order to test this, some one took hold of the horse, to look into his mouth; but the creature immediately struck at him so savagely with his heels that he broke his ribs to pieces. Another, who seemed to have a little more sense, took him by the bright embroidered headstall, but the horse bit him so sharply on the shoulder that he was quite disabled. Nor would he open his mouth to a single person until Sir Guyon himself spoke to him, and called him by his name, "Brigadore."

The instant the horse understood his voice he stood stock-still, and allowed every one to see the secret mark; and when his master called him by name he broke all his fastenings with joy, and gleefully followed him, frisking, and prancing, and bending his head in submission. Thereupon Sir Artegall plainly saw to whom he belonged, and said—

"Lo, there, Sir Guyon, take to yourself the steed, arrayed as he is in his golden saddle, and let that worthless fellow fare hence on foot, until he has gained a horse."

But the vain braggart began to rate and revile Sir Artegall for giving such an unjust judgment against him. The Knight was so incensed at his insolence that he was tempted to punish him, and thrice he laid his

"And out of court him scourged openly;
So ought all faytours that true knighthood shame,
And armes dishonour with base villanie,
From all brave knights be banisht with defame."

hand on his sword to slay him. But Sir Guyon pacified Sir Artegall, saying it would only dishonour him to wreak his wrath on a churl like that. It would be punishment enough that every one saw his disgrace.

Then Talus seized the boaster, and dragging him out of the hall inflicted this punishment on him, First he shaved off his beard; then he took his shield, and turned it upside down, and blotted out the device; and then he broke his sword in two, and scattered all his armour. After that he openly scourged him out of the court.

So should all traitors who shame true chivalry be banished with infamy from among brave knights, for their evil doings often bring disgrace on just merit.

The Adventure of the Two Brothers and the Coffer

When the wedding festivities of Marinell and Florimell were over, Sir Artegall left the Castle of the Strand, to follow his first quest; and the only person who went with him to help him was his servant Talus, the Iron Man.

As he passed along the sea-shore he chanced to come where two comely squires were having an angry quarrel. They were brothers, but were just now stirred up by some matter of debate. Two good-looking damsels stood beside them, trying by every means to soothe their ire—now by fair words, but words did little good—now by threats, but threats only made them angrier. Before them stood a strong coffer, fast bound on every side with iron bands, but seeming to have received much injury either by being wrecked upon the shore, or by being carried far from foreign lands. It appeared as if it were for this coffer the squires were fighting; and though the ladies kept interfering to prevent their furious encounter, yet they were firmly resolved to try their rights by dint of sword. Thus they both stood ready to meet in cruel combat when Sir Artegall, happily arriving, stopped for awhile their greedy bickering till he had inquired the cause of their dispute. To whom the elder made this answer:—

"You must know, sir, we are two brothers, to whom our father, Milesio by name, equally bequeathed his land, two islands, which you see there before you, not far off in the sea. Of these the one appears but like a little mount, of small size, yet it was as great and wide, not many years ago, as that other island, which is now so much larger.

"But the course of time, which destroys everything, and this devouring sea, which spares nothing, have washed away the greater part of my land, and thrown it up to my brother's share, so his is increased but mine is lessened. Before which time I loved, as it happened, the maid over there, called Philtera the Fair, with whom I should have received a goodly dower, and to whom I was to have been married.

"At that time my younger brother, Amidas, loved the other damsel—Lucy—to whom but little dower was allotted. Her virtue was the dowry that delighted—and what better dowry can a lady possess? But now when Philtera saw my lands decay, and my former livelihood fail, she left me, and went over to my brother, who, taking her from me, completely deserted his own love.

"Lucy, seeing herself forsaken, in despair flung herself into the sea, thinking to take away her grief by death. But see how her purpose was foiled! Whilst beaten to and fro amidst the billows, hovering between life and death, she chanced unawares to light upon this coffer, which offered to her, in her danger, hope of life.

"The wretched maiden, who had formerly desired death, now that she had had a taste of it began to repent that she had been so foolish, and caught hold of the sea-beaten chest, which after long tossing in the rough waves, at last rested on my island. Here I, wandering by chance on the shore, espied her, and with some difficulty helped to save her from the jaws of death, which threatened to swallow her up. In recompense for this she then bestowed on me those goods which fortune had given her, together with herself, a free gift—both goodly portions, but herself the better of the two.

"In this coffer which she brought with her we found great treasure, which we took as our own, and so considered it. But this other damsel, Philtera, my brother's wife, pretends now that the treasure belongs to herself, that she transported the same by sea, to bring it to her newly made husband, but suffered shipwreck by the way. Whether it be so or not. I cannot say. But whether it indeed be so or not, this I do say, that whatsoever good or ill Providence or fortune throws to me, not purposely wronging any one else, I hold as my own, and will so hold it still. And though Amidas first won away my land, and then my love (though now that matters little), yet he shall not also make prey of my good luck, but I will defend it as long as ever I can."

Bracidas, the elder brother, having thus spoken, the younger one followed on.

"It is quite true what my brother here has declared to you about the land; but the dispute between us is not for that, but for this treasure, thrown upon his shore, which I can prove, as shall appear by trial, to belong to this lady, to whom I am married. It is well known by good marks and perfect witnesses, and therefore it ought to be rendered to her without denial."

When they had thus ended, the Knight spoke:—

"Truly it would be easy to reconcile your strife, if you would submit it to some just man."

"Unto yourself!" they both cried. "We give you our word to abide the judgment you pronounce to us."

"Then in token that you will accept my verdict, let each lay down his sword under my foot," said Sir Artegall, "and then you shall hear my sentence."

So each of them laid down his sword out of his hand.

Then Artegall spoke thus to the younger brother:—

"Now tell me, Amidas, if you can, by what good right do you withhold to-day that part of your brother's land which the sea has plucked away from him, and laid on your share?"

"What other right," quoth Amidas, "would you deem valid, except that the sea laid it to my share?"

"Your right is good," said Sir Artegall, "and so I judge it. That which the sea sent unto you should be your own."

Then, turning to the elder brother, he spoke thus:—

"Now, Bracidas, let this likewise be plain: your brother's treasure, which has strayed from him, being well known to be the dowry of his wife—by what right do you claim this to be your own?"

"What other right," quoth Bracidas, "would you deem valid, except that the sea has thrown it unto me?"

"Your right is good," said Sir Artegall, "and so I judge it. That which the sea sent unto you should be your own; for equal things have equal rights. What the mighty sea has once possessed and quite plucked from its owner's hands—whether by the rage of the unresting waves, or tempest, or shipwreck—it may dispose of by its imperial might to whomever it chooses, as a thing left at random. So in the first place, Amidas, the land was declared to be yours; and so, in like manner, Bracidas, the treasure is yours by right."

When Sir Artegall had thus pronounced sentence, both Amidas and Philtera were displeased, but Bracidas and Lucy were very glad, and immediately took possession of the treasure, in accordance with the judgment.

So their discord was appeased by this sentence, and each one had his right; and Sir Artegall, having stopped their contention, went on his way.

Radigund, Queen of the Amazons

As Sir Artegall travelled on his way he saw far off a crowd of many people, to whom he hastened, in order to discover the cause of such a large assembly. When he came near he saw a strange sight-a troop of women clad in warlike fashion, with weapons in their hands, as if ready to fight; and in the midst of them he saw a Knight, with both hands pinioned behind him, and round about his neck a halter tight, ready prepared for the gallows. His head was bare and his face covered, so that it was not easy to distinguish him. He went along with a heavy heart, grieved to the soul, and groaning inwardly that he should die so base a death at the hands of women. But they, like merciless tyrants, rejoiced at his misery, and reviled him, and sorely reproached him with bitter taunts and terms of disgrace.

When Artegall, arriving at the place, asked what cause had brought the man to destruction, the women swarmed eagerly around him, meaning to lay their cruel hands on him, and to do him some unexpected mischief. But he was soon aware of their evil mind, and drawing back defeated their intention. He was ashamed to disgrace himself by fighting with women, so he sent Talus to punish them for their rash folly. With a few strokes of his iron flail the latter speedily dispersed their troop, and sent them home to tell a piteous tale of their vain prowess turned to their own injury.

The wretched man doomed to death they left behind them, glad to be quit of them. Talus soon set him at liberty, and released him from his horror at such a shameful death, unfitting a knight, which he dreaded more than loss of life; and uncovering his face, he brought him to his master, who then knew him at once.

"Sir Terpin!" cried Artegall. "Hapless man, what are you doing here? Have you lost yourself and your senses? Or have you, who can boast of subduing men, yielded to the oppression of women? Or what other deadly misfortune has fallen on you, that you have run so foolishly far astray as to lead yourself to your own destruction?"

The man was so confused, partly with shame, partly with dismay, that he stood lost in astonishment, and could find little to say in excuse.

"You may justly term me hapless, who am brought to this shame, and am to-day made the scorn of knighthood," was his only answer. "But who can escape Fate? The work of Heaven's will surpasses human thought."

"True," said Sir Artegall, "but faulty men often attribute their own folly to Fate, and lay on Heaven the guilt of their own crimes. But tell me, Sir Terpin—and do not let your misery daunt you—how you fell into this state."

"Since you needs will know my shame," said the Knight, "and all the ill which has lately chanced to me, I will briefly relate it, and do not turn my misfortune to my blame.

"Being desirous, as all knights are, to try deeds of arms through hard adventures, and to hunt after fame and honour, I heard a report which flew far abroad that a proud Amazon lately bade defiance to all brave knights, and wrought them all the villainy her malice could devise, putting some to shame, and doing many of them to death.

"The cause of her hate is for the sake of a Knight called Bellodant the Bold, whom a short time ago she liked greatly, and tried in every way to attract; but finding nothing of any avail, her love turned to hatred, and for his sake she vowed to do all the ill she could to other knights,—which vow she now fulfils.

"For all those knights whom by force or guile she subdues she treats shamefully. First she despoils them of their armour, and clothes them in women's garments; then with threats she compels them to work to earn their food—to spin, to card, to sew, to wash, to wring. She gives them nothing to eat but bread and water, or some such feeble food, to disable them from attempting revenge.

"But if with manly disdain any of them withstand her insolent commands, she causes them to be immediately hanged on that gibbet over there, in which condition I stood just now; for being conquered by her in fight, and put to the base service of her band, I chose rather to die than to live that shameful life, unworthy of a knight."

"What is the name of that Amazon?" asked Artegall. "And where, and how far hence does she live?"

"Her name is called Radigund," replied Sir Terpin, "a princess of great power, and greater pride, Queen of the Amazons, well tried in arms and sundry battles, which she has achieved with great success, and which have won her much glory and fame."

"Now, by my faith," said Sir Artegall, "I will not rest till I have tested her power, and avenged the shame that she shows to knights. Therefore, Sir Terpin, throw from you those squalid clothes, the pattern of despair, and go with me, that you may see and know how Fortune will repair your ruined name and knighthood, whose praise she would tarnish."

Sir Terpin joyfully threw off his iron fetters, and eagerly prepared to guide the way to the dwelling of the Amazon, which was not more than a mile or two distant—a goodly and a mighty city, called after her own name Radigone.

On their arrival they were immediately espied by the watchman, who warned all the city of the appearance of three warlike persons, of whom one seemed like a Knight fully armed, and the other two likely to prove dangerous. The people ran at once to put on their armour, swarming in a cluster like bees, and before long their Queen herself, looking half like a man, came forth into the crowd, and began to set them in array.

And now the Knights, being arrived near, beat upon the gates to enter in; threatening the porter, who scorned them for being so few, to tear him to pieces if they won the city. When Radigund beard them her heart was torn with rage. She bade her people to unbar the gates at once, and to make way for the knights with well-prepared weapons.

As soon as the gates were set open the Knights pressed forward to make an entrance, but midway they were met by a sharp shower of arrows, which stopped them. Then all the mob attacked them savagely, heaping strokes so fast on every side, and with such a hail of arrows, that the Knights could not withstand them. But Radigund herself, when she espied Sir Terpin freed from her cruel doom, was suddenly seized with a fit of fury, and flying at him like a lioness, smote him so fiercely that he fell to the ground. Then she leaped to him, and placed her foot on his neck.

When Sir Artegall saw the Knight's peril, he sprang at once to his rescue, and assailed Radigund with such vigour that he drove her back. For a moment she was stunned, but as soon as she collected her senses she turned on Sir Artegall, half-mad with revengeful anger and pride, for she had never suffered such a rebuff. But before they could meet in fight her maidens flocked round her so fast that they parted them, in spite of their valour, and kept them far asunder. But amongst the others the fight lasted till the evening.

And all the while the great Iron Man sorely vexed the Amazons with his strange weapon, to which they had never been accustomed in war. He chased and outran them, and broke their bows, and spoilt their shooting, so that not one of them all dared to go near him. They scattered like sheep before a wolf, and fled before him through all the fields and valleys.

But when the daylight grew dim with the shadows of night, Radigund, with the sound of a trumpet, caused her people to cease fighting, and gathering them to the gate of the city, made them all enter, and had the weak and wounded conveyed in, before she would retreat herself.

When the field was thus empty and all things quiet, Sir Artegall, weary with toil and travel, caused his pavilion to be richly prepared in full view of the city gate. He himself, together with Sir Terpin, rested here in safety all that night; but Talus was accustomed, in times of jeopardy, to keep a nightly watch for fear of treachery.

Radigund, full of heart-gnawing grief for the rebuke she had met that day, could take no rest nor relief, but tossed about in her mind in what way she could revenge her disgrace. Then she resolved to try her fortune in single fight herself, rather than see her people destroyed, as she had seen that day.

She called to her a trusty maid, named Clarinda, whom she thought fittest for the business, and said to her—

"Go, damsel, quickly; get ready to do the message which I shall tell you, Go you to the stranger Knight who yesterday drove us to such distress; tell him that to-morrow I will fight with him, and try in a fair field which is the mightier.

"But these conditions you must propound to him—that if I vanquish him he shall obey my law, and ever be bound to do my bidding And so will I, if he vanquish me, whatever he shall like to do or say. Go straight, and take with you as witness six of your companions of the highest rank; and carry with you wine and rich delicacies, and bid him eat: henceforth he shall often sit hungry."

The damsel instantly obeyed, and putting all in readiness went forth to the town gate, where, sounding a trumpet loudly from the wall, she sent warning to the warrior Knights. Then Talus, issuing from the tent, took his way fearlessly to the wall, to know what that sounding of the trumpet meant, whereupon the damsel called to him, and explained that she wished to parley with his lord.

Then he conducted them at once to his master, who gave them a cordial greeting, and to whom they told their message, word for word. Sir Artegall, gladly accepting it, entertained them with fitting courtesy, and gave them rich and handsome gifts. So they turned their steps homeward again, but Artegall went back to rest, that he might be fresher against the next day's fight.

How Sir Artegall threw away his Sword

As soon as day dawned, the noble warriors, mindful of the fight before them, duly prepared themselves, the Knight as beseemed a knight, and the Amazon in the way she liked best to dress.

She wore a light loose robe of purple silk, woven with silver, quilted upon white satin, and plentifully trimmed with ribbons; not to hinder her movements it was tucked up to her knee, but could when she liked be lowered to her heel, Over that she wore for defence a small coat of mail. Oil her legs were painted buskins, laced with bands of gold; her scimitar was lashed at her thigh in an embroidered belt; and on her shoulder hung her shield, decked with glittering stones, so that it shone like the full moon.

Thus she came forth, stately and magnificent, from the city gate, guarded with many damsels who waited on her to defend her, playing on shalms and trumpets, the sound of which reached high into heaven; and so she marched into the field, where there was a rich pavilion ready prepared to receive her, until it was time to begin the fight.

Then forth from his tent came Artegall, armed from head to foot, and first entered the lists. Radigund soon followed, cruel of mind, and with a fierce countenance, fully bent on daring the utmost trial of battle. The lists were shut fast, to prevent the mob from rudely pressing to the centre, and they circled round in huge crowds to see how fortune would decide the dangerous problem.

The trumpets sounded, and the fight began—bitterly it began and ended. The Amazon flew at Sir Artegall frantic with fury, but the more she raged the more resolute he stood. She hewed, she thrust, she lashed, she laid on every side. At first the Knight bore her blows, and forbore to return them; but presently in his turn he began to attack, and so mightily did his strokes fall on her steel armour, that flakes of flame were seen flashing all round her as if she had been on fire. But Radigund with her shield so well warded off the danger of his keen weapon that she safely guarded her life, until at last, with one stroke of his blade, Sir Artegall cut away half her shield.

This so enraged Radigund that she flew at Artegall with her sharp scimitar, like a bear on her prey, and wounded him badly in the thigh. Thereupon she began to boast of her triumph, and taunt the Knight with spiteful speeches, as if she had already got the prize.

Indignant at her idle vaunting, Sir Artegall struck at her again with such power that he shattered the other half of her shield, and then he smote on her helmet so that she sank senseless on the grassy field.

When he saw her lying on the ground, he sprang towards her, and unlaced her helmet, thinking to cut off her head; but when he had uncovered her face such a miracle of loveliness shone forth that he was dazzled with astonishment. His heart was so pierced with pity that he threw away his sharp sword, reviling his hand that had done injury to such a vision of beauty.

Radigund meanwhile awakened from her swoon, and stared about her in confusion. As soon as she saw the Knight standing there beside her with no weapon in his empty hands, she flew at him with fresh cruelty, and though he kept retiring she laid on him huge redoubled strokes. The more he meekly entreated her to stay her hand from greedy vengeance, the more she increased her merciless attack.

Sir Artegall could do nothing but shun her angry onslaught, and ward off with his shield alone, as well as he could, the fierceness of her rage. He begged her to stay her strokes, and said that he would yield himself; yet she would not hearken, nor give him time to breathe, till he had delivered to her his shield, and submitted himself to her mercy in the open field.

Thus was Sir Artegall overcome—though indeed he was not overcome, but yielded of his own accord. Yet was he justly doomed by his own judgment when he had said unwarily that he would be her thrall

and do her service. For though he first gained the victory, yet afterwards, by abandoning his sword, he wilfully lost that which before he had attained.

Then Radigund struck him with the flat of her sword, in token of true subjection to her power, and as a vassal took him to thraldom. But the more hapless Terpin she caused to be pinioned and led away to the cruel fate from which he had but lately been rescued.

But when the Amazons thought to lay hands on Talus, he thundered amongst them with his iron flail, so that they were glad to let him escape, for the heaps of those he stew and wounded, besides the rest which he dismayed, were too many to number. But all this while he did not once attempt to rescue his own lord, for he thought it just to obey.

Then Radigund took this noble Knight, left at her disposal by his own wilful blame, and caused him to be disarmed of all the knightly ornaments with which he had formerly won great fame. In place of these she had him shamefully dressed in woman's clothes, and put on him a white apron instead of a cuirass.

Thus clad, she brought him from the battlefield into a long, large chamber, decked with memorials of the ruin of many knights whom she had subdued; amongst these she caused his armour to be hung on high, to betray his shame, and she broke his sword for fear of further harm.

Entering, he saw round about him many brave knights whose names he knew well, who were there bound to obey the Amazon's arrogant law, all spinning and carding in an orderly row, so that Sir Artegall's brave heart loathed the unseemly sight. But the captive knights were forced through hunger and want of food to do the work appointed them, for nothing was given them to eat or drink, but what their hands could earn by twisting linen twine.

Radigund placed Sir Artegall the lowest among them all, and gave a distaff into his hand, that he should spin thereon flax and tow—a sordid office for so brave a mind; thus hard is it to be the slave of a woman!

Yet Sir Artegall took it even in his own despite, and obeyed her without murmuring, since he had plighted his faith to become her vassal if she won him in fight.

The House of Guile

Thus for a long while Sir Artegall continued obediently serving proud Radigund, however much it galled his noble heart to obey the dictates of a tyrannous woman. Having chosen his lot, he could not now change.

As the days went by, the Amazon Queen began to have a great liking for her strange captive, but for a long time she kept this carefully concealed, for her pride would not allow her to own to such a feeling for her lowly vassal. At last, when she could bear it no longer, she sent for her trusted maid, Clarinda, and told her to. devise some means by which to discover whether there were any chance of Sir Artegall's loving her, if she gave him his liberty. Clarinda promised to do her best, and tried by all the means in her power to win favour with the Knight, but the more she saw of him the better she liked him herself, so she ended by being false both to her mistress and to Sir Artegall. To the Queen she pretended that Sir Artegall was very stern and obstinate, and scorned all her offers of kindness and gentler treatment; and to the Knight she declared that she had earnestly besought Radigund to grant him freedom, but the Queen would by no means be persuaded, and had ordered instead that he should be more harshly treated and laden with iron chains. This command, however, Clarinda said she would not carry out, because of her own regard for the Knight, and she further promised that if she found favour in his sight she would devise some means of setting him free

Sir Artegall, glad to gain his liberty, answered her civilly, but determined in his heart that nothing should make him forsake his own true love, Britomart; and deceitful Clarinda had not the least intention of freeing him from bondage, but considered rather how she might keep him more securely. Therefore every day she unkindly told her mistress that the Knight spurned her offers of goodwill, and Sir Artegall she told that the Queen refused him his freedom. Yet in order to win his affection, she showed him this much friendship, that his scanty fare was improved, and his work lessened.

Thus for a long while Sir Artegall remained there in thraldom.

Britomart, meanwhile, waited and longed for news of her absent lord, and when the utmost date assigned for his return had passed, a thousand fears assailed her doubting mind. Sometimes she feared lest a terrible misfortune had befallen him; sometimes lest his false foe had entrapped him in a snare; at other times a jealous fear troubled her that perhaps Sir Artegall had forgotten her, and found some other lady whom he loved better. Yet she was loath to think so ill of him as this. One moment she blamed herself; another, condemned him as faithless and untrue; then, trying to cheat her grief, she pretended she had reckoned the time wrong, and began to count it all over a different way.

When months went on, and still he never came back, she thought of sending some one to seek him, but could find no one so fitting to do this as her own self.

One day, unable to rest quietly in any place, she came to a window opening to the west, which was the way Sir Artegall had gone. There, looking forth, she felt many vain fancies disquiet her, and sent her winged thoughts swifter than wind to carry her heart's message to her love. As she looked long, she spied some one coming hastily towards her. Then she knew well before she saw him plainly, that it was some one sent from Sir Artegall; and as he drew near, she found it was his servant, Talus. Filled with hope and dread she ran to meet him, exclaiming—

"And where is he, thy lord, and how far hence? Tell me at once. And has he lost or won?"

Then Talus told the whole story of Sir Artegall's captivity.

Britomart listened bravely to the end, and then a sudden fit of wrath and grief seized her. Without waiting to make any answer, she got ready at once, donned her armour, and mounting her steed, bade Talus guide her on.

So she rode forth to seek her Knight; sadly she rode, speaking no word good or bad, and looking neither to the right or left. Her heart burned with rage to punish the pride of that woman who had pent her lord in a base prison, and had tarnished his great honour with such infamous disgrace.

Thus riding, she chanced to meet towards evening a knight strolling on the plain as if to refresh himself. He seemed well on in years, and inclined rather to peace than to needless trouble, his raiment and his modest bearing both showing that he meant no evil. Coming near, he began to salute Britomart in the most courteous fashion. Though the

Princess would rather have remained mute than joined in commonplace conversation, yet sooner than despise such kindness she set her own wishes aside, and so returned his greeting in due form. Then the other began to chat further about things in general, and asked many questions, to which she gave careless answer. For she had little desire to talk about anything, or to hear about anything, however delightful; her mind was wholly possessed by one thought, and there was no place for any other.

When the stranger observed this, he no longer forced her to talk unwillingly, but begged her to favour him, since the skies were growing dark and wet, by lodging with him that night, unless good cause forbade it. Britomart, seeing night was at hand, was glad to yield to his kind request, and went with him without any objection.

His dwelling was not far away, and soon arriving, they were received in the most gracious and befitting manner, for their host gave them excellent good cheer, and talked of pleasant things to entertain them. Thus the evening passed well, till the time came for rest. Then Britomart was brought to her bower, where attendants waited to help her to undress. But she would not for anything take off her armour, although her host warmly besought her; for she had vowed, she said, not to lay aside this warrior garb till she had wrought revenge on a mortal foe for a recent wrong; which she would surely perform, let weal or woe betide her.

When their host perceived this, he grew very discontented, for he was afraid lest he should now miss his purpose; but taking leave of her, he departed.

Britomart remained all night restless and comfortless, with deeply grieved heart, not allowing the least twinkle of sleep to refresh her. In sorrowful thoughts she wore away the weary hours, now walking softly about, now sitting still, upright. Neither did Talus let sleep close his eyelids, but kept continual guard, lying in much discomfort outside her door, like a spaniel, watching carefully lest any one should by treachery betray his lady.

Just at cock-crow Britomart heard a strange noise in the hall below, and suddenly the bed, on which she might have been lying, by a false trap was let to fall down into a lower room; then immediately the floor was raised again, so that no one could spy the trap.

At the sight of this, Britomart was sorely dismayed, plainly perceiving the treason which was intended; yet she did not stir, in case of more, but courageously kept her place, waiting what would follow.

It was not long before she heard the sound of armed men coming towards her chamber, at which dreadful peril she quickly caught her sword, and bound her shield about her. As she did so, there came to her door two knights, all armed ready to fight, and after them a rascally mob, rudely equipped with weapons.

As soon as Talus spied them he started up from where he lay on the ground, and caught his thresher ready in his hand. They immediately let drive at him, and pressed round in riotous array, but as soon as he began to lay about with his iron flail, they turned and fled, both the armed knights and the unarmed crowd. Talus pursued them wherever he could spy them in the dark, then returning to Britomart, told her the story of the fray, and all the treason that was intended.

Though greatly enraged, and inwardly burning to be avenged for such an infamous deed, Britomart was compelled to wait for daylight. She therefore remained in her chamber, but kept wary heed, in case of any further treachery.

The cause of this evil behaviour was unknown to Britomart, but this is how it was.

The master of the house was called Dolon (*Guile*), a subtle and wicked man; in his youth he had been a knight, and borne arms, but gained little good and less honour by that warlike kind of life; for he was not in the least valorous, but with sly shifts and wiles got the better of all noble and daring knights, and brought many to shame by treachery.

He had three sons, all three like their father treacherous, and full of fraud and guile. The eldest, named Guizor, had, through his own guilty cunning, been slain by Artegall, and to avenge him, Dolon, with his other two sons, had lately devised many vile plots. He imagined by several tokens that his present guest was Artegall, but chiefly on account of the Iron Man who was always accustomed to remain with Artegall. Dolon, therefore, meant surely to have slain the Knight, but by the grace of heaven and her own good heed, Britomart was preserved from the traitor.

The next morning, as soon as it was dawn, she came forth from the hateful chamber, fully intending to punish the villain and all his family. But coming down to seek them where they dwelt, she could not see father, nor sons, nor any one. She sought in each room, but found them all empty; every one had fled in fear, but whither neither she nor Talus knew.

She saw it was in vain to stay there longer, so took her steed, and lightly mounting, started again on her former way. She had not ridden the distance of an arrow's flight before she saw in front of her the two false brethren on the perilous Bridge, where Sir Artegall had fought with the Saracen. The passage was narrow, like a ploughed ridge, so that if two met, one must needs fall over the edge.

There they thought to wreak their wrath on her, and began to reproach her bitterly, accusing her of murdering Guizor by cunning. Britomart did not know what they meant, but she went forward without pausing till she came to the perilous Bridge. There Talus wanted to prepare the way for her, and scare off the two villains, but her eyes sparkled with anger at the suggestion. Not staying to consider which way to take, she put spurs to her fiery steed, and making her way between them, she drove one brother at the point of her spear to the end of the Bridge, and hurled the other brother over the side of it into the river.

Thus the Warrior Princess slew the two wicked sons of Goodman Guile.

The Battle of Queen Radigund and Britomart

That night Britomart spent in the great Temple of Isis, which was dedicated in days of old to the worship of justice. Here in her sleep she had a wondrous vision, which at first filled her with dread. But when she described it next morning to the priests in the Temple, they told her that her dream had a good meaning, and that everything would end well. Greatly relieved to hear this, she bestowed rich rewards on the priests, and made royal gifts of gold and silver to the Temple. Then taking leave of them, she went forward to seek her love, never resting and never relenting till she came to the land of the Amazons.

When news of her approach was brought to Radigund she was filled with courage and glee instead of being dismayed. Glad to hear of fighting, of which she had now had none for a long time, she bade them open the gates boldly, so that she might see the face of her new foe; but when they told her of the Iron Man who had lately slain her people, she bade them hold them shut.

So there outside the gate, as seemed best, her pavilion was pitched, in which brave Britomart rested herself, while Talus watched at her door all night. All night, likewise, those of the town, in terror, kept good watch and ward upon their wall.

The next morning, as soon as it was dawn, the warlike Amazon peeped out of her bower, and caused a shrill trumpet to sound to warn her foe to hasten to the battle. Britomart, who had long been awake and arrayed for contest, immediately stepped haughtily from the pavilion, ready for the fight, and on the other side her foe soon appeared.

But before they lifted hand, Radigund began to propound the strict conditions with which she always fettered her foes—that Britomart should serve her as she had bound the rest to do. At this, Britomart frowned sternly, in disdain of such indignity, and would no longer parley, but bade them sound the advance, for she would be tied by no other terms than those prescribed by the laws of chivalry.

The trumpets sounded, and they rushed together with greedy rage, smiting with their falchions; neither sought to shun the other's stroke, but both savagely hacked and hewed, furious as a tiger -and a lioness fighting over the same prey. So long they fought that all the grassy floor was trampled with blood. At last Radigund, having espied some near advantage, let drive at Britomart with all her might, thus taunting her with savage scorn—

"Bear this token to the man whom you love so dearly, and tell him you gave your life for his sake!"

The cruel stroke glanced on Britomart's shoulder plate, and bit to the bone, so that she could hardly hold up her shield for the smart of it. Yet she soon avenged it, for the furious pain gave her fresh force, and she smote Radigund so rudely on the helmet that it pierced to the very brain, and felled her to the ground, where with one stroke Britomart killed her.

When Radigund's warrior band saw this dreadful sight they all fled into the town, and left Britomart sole victor. But they could not retreat so fast but that Talus could overtake the foremost. Pressing

"Thence forth unto the Idole they her brought;

* * * * * *

To which the Idole, as it were inclining,
Her wand did move with amiable looke,
By outward shew her inward sense designing."

through the mob to the gate, he entered in with them, and then began a piteous slaughter; for all who came within reach of his iron flail were soon beyond the skill of any doctor.

Then the noble Conqueror herself came in, and though she had sworn a vow of revenge, yet when she saw the heaps of dead bodies slain by Talus, her heart was torn with pity, and she bade him slack his fury. Having thus stayed the massacre, she inquired for the iron prison where her love lay captive. Breaking it open with indignant rage, she entered, and went all over it; when she saw the strange and horrible sight of the men dressed up in womanish garb, her heart groaned with compassion for such unmanly and disgraceful misery.

When at last she came to her own Knight, whom the like disguise had no less disfigured, abashed with shame she turned aside her head, and then with pity and tender words she tried to comfort him. She caused the unsightly garments to be immediately taken off, and in their stead sought for other raiment, of which there was great store, as well as bright armour reft from many a noble knight whom the proud Amazon had subdued. When Sir Artegall was clad anew in this apparel Britomart's spirits revived, and she rejoiced in his gallant appearance.

They remained for awhile in the city of Queen Radigund, so that Sir Artegall might recover his strength, and Britomart be healed of her wounds. During this time Britomart reigned as a Princess, and changed all the order of government. The women were deposed from the rule which they had usurped, and true justice was dealt them, so that, worshipping Britomart as a goddess, they all admired her wisdom and listened to her teaching. All those knights who had long been hidden in captivity, she freed from their thraldom, and made magistrates of the city, giving them great wealth and authority. And in order that they should always remain faithful, she made them swear fealty to Artegall.

As the latter Knight was now fully recovered, he proposed to proceed upon the first adventure which had called him forth, the release of the: Lady Irene from the villain Grantorto. Very sad and sorrowful was Britomart at his departure, yet wisely moderated her own grief, seeing that his honour, which she put above all things, was much concerned in carrying out that adventure. For a little while after lie had gone she remained there in the city, but finding her misery increase with his absence, and hoping that change of air and place would somewhat ease her sorrow, she too departed, to appease her anguish in travel.

The Adventure of the Damsel, the Two Knights, and the Sultan's Horses

As Sir Artegall rode forth on his way, accompanied only by Talus, he saw far off a damsel on a palfrey flying fast in terror before two knights, who pursued her. These in turn were themselves pursued by another knight, who pricked after them with all his might, his spear ready levelled. At length. the latter overtook the hindmost of the two knights, and compelled him to turn and face him; but the other still pursued the maid, who flew as fast in front of him, and never stopped till she saw Sir Artegall. To him she ran at once, in glad haste, hoping to get help against her enemy; and Artegall, seeing her approach, went forward to relieve her fear, and to prevent her foe from hurting her.

But the pursuing knight, greedy as a hound after his prey, still continued his course, thinking to overthrow Sir Artegall with his spear. Thus alike sternly resolved they met fiercely. But Artegall was the stronger, and better skilled in tilt and tournament, and he hurled the other out of his saddle quite two spears' lengths. The Pagan knight, unluckily for himself, pitched on his head, broke his neck, and was killed on the spot.

Meanwhile the third Knight had defeated and slain the second of the villains, and leaving him there dead, he ran on to overtake his companion. Instead of him he found Sir Artegall, and not knowing he was also on the side of the damsel, he ran at him without thinking; and the latter, seeing him approach so fiercely, made against him again. So they met, and struck strongly, and broke their spears; yet neither was dismounted, though they both shook to and fro, and tottered like two towers quaking in a tempest.

But when they had recovered their senses they drew their swords, meaning to make amends with them where their spears had failed. When the damsel, who had seen the end of both her foes, now beheld her friends beginning for her sake a more fearful fray, she ran to them in haste, crying to them to stay their cruel hands until they both heard what she had to say to them.

"Ah, gentle Knights," she cried, "why do you thus unwisely wreak on yourselves another's wrong? I am the injured one whom both of you have aided. Witness the two Pagan knights whom ye may see dead on the ground! What more revenge, therefore, do you desire? If more, then I am she who was the root of all. End your revenge on me."

When they heard her speak thus, and saw that their foes were indeed dead, they immediately stayed their hands, and lifted up their visors to look at each other; and then Sir Artegall saw that his adversary was none other than Prince Arthur himself.

Filled with admiration for his gallant and noble bearing, and touched with the deepest affection, he drew near, and prayed pardon for having unknowingly wronged him, offering to yield himself to the Prince for ever, or to any penance he chose to inflict.

To whom the Prince replied—

"Truly, I need more to crave the same pardon, for having been so misled by error as to mistake you for the dead man. But since it pleases you that both our faults shall be forgotten, amends can soon be made, since neither is much damaged thereby."

Thus their perfect friendship was easily restored, and they embraced lovingly, each swearing faithfully on his blade never thenceforth to nourish enmity against the other, but always mutually to maintain each other's cause.

Then they called the damsel, and asked her who were the two foes from whom she was flying so fast, and who she was herself, and what was the reason why she was pursued by them.

The maiden, whose name was Samient, replied that she was in the service of a great and mighty queen called Mercilla, a Princess of great power and majesty. She was known above all for her bounty and sovereign grace, with which she supported her royal crown, and strongly beat down the malice of her foes, who envied her, and fretted, and frowned at her happiness. In spite of them she grew greater and greater, and even to her foes her mercies increased.

Amongst the many who maligned her was a mighty man dwelling

near, who, with cruel spite and hatred, did all in his power to undermine her crown and dignity. Her good knights, of whom she had as brave a band as any Princess on earth, he either destroyed, if they stood against him, or else tried to bribe slyly to take his part. And not content with this, he was always trying by treacherous plots to kill Queen Mercilla.

"He is provoked to all this tyranny, they say, by his bad wife, Adicia," continued Samient, "who counsels him, because of his strength, to break all bonds of law and rule of right; for she professes herself a mortal foe to justice, and always fights against it, working deadly woe to all who love it, and making her knights and people do so likewise.'

"My liege lady, seeing this, thought it best to deal with Adicia in a friendly fashion, in order to put an end to strife, and to establish rest both for herself and her people. She therefore sent me on a message to treat with her, by way of negotiation, as to some final peace and fair arrangement, which might be concluded by mutual consent.

"At all times it is customary to afford safe passage to messengers who come on a just cause, but this proud dame, disdaining all such rules, not only burst into bitter words, reviling and railing at me as she chose, but actually thrust me like a dog out of doors, miscalling me by many a bitter name, who never did any ill to her. Then lastly she sent those two knights after me to work me further mischief, but thanks to Heaven and your valour, they have paid the price of their own folly."

So said the damsel, and showed herself most grateful to Prince Arthur and Sir Artegall for their aid.

The Knights, having heard of all the wrongs done by the proud dame Adicia, were very indignant, and eagerly desired to punish her and her husband, the Sultan. But thinking to carry out their design more easily by a counterfeit disguise, they arranged this plot: first, that Sir Artegall should array himself like one of the two dead knights, then that he should convey the damsel Samient as his prize to the Sultan's court, to present her to the scornful lady, who had sent for her.

This was accordingly done.

Directly the Sultan's wife saw them, as she lay looking out of the window, she thought it was the Pagan knight with her prey, and sent a page to direct him where to go. Taking them to the appointed place, the page offered his service to disarm the Knight, but Sir Artegall refused to take off his armour, fearing to be discovered.

Soon after, Prince Arthur arrived, and sent a bold defiance to the Sultan, requiring of him the damsel whom he held as a wrongful prisoner. The Sultan, filled with fury, swearing and cursing, commanded his armour to be brought at once, and mounted straight upon a high chariot, dreadfully armed with iron wheels and hooks, and drawn by cruel steeds, whom he fed with the flesh of slaughtered men.

Thus he came forth, clad in a coat of mail, all red with rust. The Prince waited ready for him in glistering armour, right goodly to see, that shone like the sun. By the stirrup Talus attended, playing his page's part, as his master had directed.

So they went forth to battle, both alike fierce, but with different motives. For the proud and presumptuous Sultan, with insolent bearing, sought only slaughter and revenge; but the brave Prince fought for right and honour against lawless tyranny, on behalf of wronged weakness; trusting more to the truth of his cause than in his own strength.

The Sultan in his folly thought either to hew the Prince in pieces with his sharp wheels, or to bear him down under his fierce horses' feet, and trample him in the dust. But the bold Knight, well spying that peril if he came too near the chariot, kept out of the way of the flying horses. Yet as he passed by, the Pagan threw a dart with such force that, had he not shunned it heedfully, it would have transfixed either himself or his horse. Often Prince Arthur came near, hoping to aim some stroke at him, but the Sultan was mounted so high in his chariot, and his wing-footed coursers bore him so fast away, that before the Prince could advance his spear, he was past and gone; yet still he followed him everywhere, and in turn was followed by him.

Again the Pagan threw another dart, which, guided by some bad spirit, glided through Prince Arthur's cuirass, and made a grisly wound in his side. Furious as a raging lion, the Prince sought to get at his foe; but whenever he approached, the chariot wheels whirled round him, and made him fly back again as fast; and the Sultan's horses, like hungry hounds hunting after game, so cruelly chased and pursued him that his own good steed, although renowned for courage and hardy race, dared not endure the sight of them, but fled from place to place.

Thus for a long while they rushed to and fro, seeking in every way to find some opening for attack; but the Prince could never get near enough for one sure stroke. Then at last from his victorious shield he drew the veil which hid its magic light, and coming full before the horses as they pressed upon him, flashed it in their eyes.

Like the lightning which burns the gazer, so did the sight of the shield dismay their senses, so that they turned back upon themselves and ran away with their driver. Nor could the Sultan stay their flight with reins or accustomed rule, as he well knew how; they did not fear him in the least—their only fear was that from which they fled dismayed, like terrified deer. Fast as their feet could bear them they flew over hill and dale. In vain the Pagan cursed and swore and railed, and dragged with both hands at the reins; he called and spoke to them, but nothing availed. They heard him not, they forgot his training, they went which way they chose, heedless of their guide. Through woods and rocks and mountains they drew the iron chariot, and the wheels tore the Sultan, and tossed him here and there from side to side, crying in vain to those who would not hear his crying.

And all the while Prince Arthur pursued closely behind, but could find no means of smiting his foe.

At last the horses overthrew the chariot, which was turned topsy-turvy, and the iron hooks and sharp knives caught hold of the Sultan and tore him all to rags. Nothing was left of him but some bits of his battered and broken shield and armour. These Prince Arthur gathered up and took with him that they might remain as a token, whenever the tale was told, of how worthily that day, by Heaven's decree, justice had avenged herself of wrong, so that all men might take warning by the example.

Therefore, on a tree in front of the tyrant's door, he caused them to be hung in the sight of all men, to be a memorial for ever.

When the Lady Adicia from the castle height beheld them she was appalled, but instead of being overcome with fright, as another woman might have been, she immediately began to devise how to be revenged.

Knife in hand, she ran down, vowing to wreak her vengeance on the maiden messenger whom she had ordered to be kept prisoner by Sir Artegall, mistaking him for her own knight; and coming into her presence she ran at her with all her might. But Artegall, being aware thereof, stayed her cruel hand before it reached Samient, and caught the weapon from her. Thereupon, like one distracted, she rushed forth, wherever her rage bore her, frantic with passion. Breaking out at a postern door, she ran into the wild wood, where, it is said, on account of her malice and cruelty she was transformed into a tiger.

The Adventure at the Den of Deceit

After the defeat of the Sultan and the flight of his wicked wife, Prince Arthur and Sir Artegall wished to hand over the place and all its wealth to Samient to hold for her lady, while they departed on their quest; but the maiden begged them so earnestly to go with her to see Queen Mercilla that at last they consented.

On the way she told them of a strange thing near at hand—to wit, a wicked villain who dwelt in a rock not far off, and who robbed all the country round, and took the pillage home. In this his own wily wit, and also the security of his dwelling-place, both of which were unassailable, were of great assistance. For he was so, crafty both to invent and execute, so light of hand and nimble of foot, so smooth of tongue and subtle in his tale, that any one looking at him might well be taken in. Therefore he was called Deceit.

He was well known for his achievements, and by his tricks had brought many to ruin. The rock, also, where he dwelt was wondrous strong, and hewn a dreadful depth far under ground; within it was full of winding and hidden passages, so that no one could find his way back who once went amiss.

The Knights, hearing this, longed to see the villain where he lurked, and bade Samient guide them to the place. As they came near, they agreed that the best plan would be for the damsel to go on in front, and sit alone near the den, wailing and raising a pitiful uproar. When the wretch issued forth, hoping to find some spoil, they, lying in wait, would closely ensnare him before he could retreat to his den, and thus they hoped to foil him easily.

Samient immediately did as she was directed, and the noise of her weeping speedily brought forth the villain, as they had intended.

He was as dreadful a creature as ever walked on earth, with hollow, deeply set eyes, and long shaggy locks straggling down his shoulders. He wore strange garments all in rags and tatters, and in his hand he held a huge long staff, the top of which was armed with many iron hooks, to catch hold of everything that came within reach of his clutches, and he kept casting looks around in all directions. At his back he bore a great wide net, with which he seldom fished in the water, but which he used to fish for silly folk on the dry shore, and in fair weather he caught many.

When Samient saw close beside her such an ugly creature she was really frightened, and now in earnest cried aloud for help. But when the villain saw her so afraid, he tried guilefully to persuade her to banish fear; smiling sardonically on her, he diverted her mind by talking pleasantly and showing her some amusing tricks, for he was an adept at jugglery and conjuring feats. Whilst her attention was engaged, he suddenly threw his net over her like a puff of wind, and snatching her up before she was well aware, ran with her to his cave. But when he came near and saw the armed Knights stopping his passage, he flung down his burden and fled fast away.

Sir Artegall pursued him, while Prince Arthur still kept guard at the entrance of the den. Up to the rock ran Deceit, like a wild goat leaping from hill to hill, and dancing on the very edge of the craggy cliffs. It was useless for the armed Knight to think of following him, but he sent his Iron Man after him, for Talus was swift in chase.

Then wherever Deceit went Talus pursued him, so that he soon forced him to forsake the heights and descend to the low ground. Now Deceit tried a new plan: he suddenly changed his form. First he turned himself into a fox, but Talus still hunted him as a fox; then he transformed himself to a bush, but Talus beat the bush till at last it changed into a bird, and passed from him, flying from tree to tree, and from reed to reed; but Talus threw stones at the bird, so that presently it changed itself into a stone, and dropped to the ground; whereupon Talus took the stone up in his hand and brought it to the Knights, and gave it to Sir Artegall, warning him to hold it fast for fear of tricks. While the Knight seized it in a tight grip, the stone went unawares into a hedgehog, and pricked him, so that he threw it away; then it began to run off quickly, returning to Deceit's own shape; but Talus soon overtook him and brought him back.

But when he would have changed himself into a serpent, Talus drove at him with his iron flail, and thrashed him so that he died. So that was the end of Deceit the self-deceiver.

" The Damzell straight went, as she was directed,
Unto the rocke; and there upon the soyle
Gan weepe and wayle, as if great grief had her affected.

The cry whereof entering the hollow cave
Eftsoones brought forth the villaine, as they ment."

Leaving his dead body where it fell, the two Knights went on with the maiden to see her Lady, as they had agreed. Presently they beheld a stately palace, mounted high with terraces and towers, and all the tops were glistering with gold, which seemed to outshine the sky, and with their brightness dazzled the eyes of strangers. There alighting, they were directed in by Samient, and shown all that was to be seen. The magnificent porch stood open wide to all men, day and night; yet it was well guarded by a man of great strength, like a giant, who sat there to keep out guile and malice and spite, which often under a feigned semblance works much mischief in Princes' courts. His name was *Awe*.

Passing by him they went up the hall, which was a wide large room, filled with people, making a great din. In the thickest of the press the marshal of the hall, whose name was *Order*, came to them, and commanding peace, guided them through the throng. All ceased their clamour to gaze at the Knights, half terrified at their shining armour, which was a strange sight to them; for they never saw such array there, nor was the name of war ever spoken, but all was joyous peace, and quietness, and just government.

So by degrees they were guided into the presence of the Queen. She sat high up, on a throne of bright and shining gold, adorned with priceless gems. All over her was spread a canopy of state, glittering and gleaming like a cloud of gold and silver, upheld by the rainbow-coloured wings of little cherubs. Thus she sat in sovereign majesty, holding a sceptre in her royal hand, the sacred pledge of peace and clemency. At her feet lay her sword, the bright steel brand rusted from long rest, yet when foes forced it, or friends sought aid, she could draw it sternly to dismay the world. Round about her sat a bevy of fair maidens, clad in white, whilst underneath her feet lay a great huge lion, like a captive thrall, bound with a strong iron chain and collar.

Now at the instant when the two stranger Knights came into the presence of the Queen, she was holding, as it happened, a great and important trial. Having acknowledged their obeisance with royal courtesy, she gave orders to proceed with the trial; and wishing that the Knights should see and understand all that was going on, she bade them both mount up to her stately throne, and placed one on each side of her.

Then there was brought forward as prisoner a lady of great beauty and high position, but who had blotted all her honour and titles of nobility by her wicked behaviour. This was no other than the false Duessa, who had wrought so much mischief by her malice and cunning. Seeing the piteous plight in which she now stood, Prince Arthur's tender heart was touched with compassion; but when he heard the long roll of her crimes read forth, he could no longer wish that she should escape punishment. Sir Artegall, for the sake of justice, was against her, and she was judged guilty by all. Then they called loudly to the Queen to pronounce sentence. Mercilla was deeply moved at the sight of Duessa's wretched plight, and even then would gladly have pardoned her; but in order to save her land from further evil, which would grow if not checked, she was obliged to keep to the stern law of justice. Melting to tears, she suddenly left her throne, unable to speak the words that doomed the prisoner to death; and she never ceased to lament with bitter remorse the fate which the wretched Duessa had brought on herself.

The Adventure of the Tyrant Grantorto

While Prince Arthur and Sir Artegall were staying at the court of Queen Mercilla, there came one day two noble youths to implore aid for their mother, for their father was dead. A cruel tyrant, the son of a giant, had ravaged all her land, setting up an idol of' his own, and giving her dear children one by one to be devoured by a horrible monster. Prince Arthur, seeing that none of the other knights were eager for this adventure, boldly stepped forward, and begged the Queen to let him undertake it. She gladly granted permission, and the, following morning he started on his journey. In due course he reached the land which had been laid waste, fought with the tyrant, and overcame him, slew the vile monster, and restored the lady to her rightful possessions.

Sir Artegall, meanwhile, had started again on his first quest, which was to set free the Lady Irene and punish Grantorto. He fared forward through many perils, with Talus, as usual, his only attendant, till he came at length near the appointed place.

There, as he travelled, he met an old and solitary wayfarer, whom he knew at once as the attendant of Irene, when she came in sorrow to the court of the Faerie Queene to entreat protection. Saluting him by name, Sir Artegall inquired for news of his Lady, whether she were still alive, and if so why he had left her. To whom the aged knight replied that she lived and was well, but had been seized by treachery and imprisoned by the tyrant Grantorto, who had often sought her life. And now he had fixed a day by which, if no champion appeared to do battle for her and prove her innocent of those crimes of which she was accused, she should surely suffer death.

Sir Artegall was much cast down to hear these sad tidings, and sorely grieved that it was owing to his own long delay in captivity that the misfortune had happened.

"Tell me, Sir Sergis," he said, "how long a space hath he lent her to provide a champion?"

"Ten days he has granted as a favour," was the answer; "for he knows well that before that date no one can have tidings to help her. For all the shores, far and wide, which border on the sea, he guards night and day, so that no one could land without an army. Already he considers her as good as dead."

"Now turn again," said Sir Artegall; "for if I live till those ten days are ended, be assured, Sir Knight, she shall have aid, though I spend my life for her."

So he went back at once with Sir Sergis.

Then as they rode together they saw in front of them a confused crowd of people, rudely chasing to and fro a hapless Knight, who was in much danger from their rough handling. Some distance away, standing helpless in the midst of the mob, they spied a lady, crying and holding up her hands to him for aid. Sir Artegall and Talus put to flight the rascally rout who were assailing the Knight, and then inquired of him the cause of his misadventure. He replied that his name was Burbon, and that he had been well known and far renowned till mischief had fallen on him and tarnished his former fame. The lady was his own love, whom the tyrant Grantorto had tried to bribe from him with rich gifts and deceitful words, and now he had sent a troop of villains to snatch her away by open force. Burbon had for a long time vainly tried to rescue her, but was overcome by the multitude of his assailants.

"But why have you forsaken your own good shield?" said Artegall. "This is the greatest shame and deepest scorn that can happen to any knight, to lose the badge that should display his deeds."

"That I will explain to you, lest you blame me for it, and think it was done willingly, whereas it was a matter of necessity," said Sir Burbon, blushing half for shame. "It is true that I was at first dubbed knight by a good Knight—the Knight of the Red Cross, who, when he gave me arms to fight in battle, gave me a shield on which he traced his dear Redeemer's badge. That same I bore for a long time, and with it fought many battles, without wound or loss. With it I appalled Grantorto himself,—and oftentimes made him fall in field before me. But because many envied that shield, and cruel foes greatly increased, to stop all strife and troublous enmity I laid aside the battered scutcheon, and have lately gone without it, hoping thereby to obtain my Lady; nevertheless I cannot have her, for she is still detained from me by force, and is perverted from truth by bribery."

"Truly, Sir Knight," said Artegall, "it is a hard case of which you complain, yet not so hard as to abandon that which contains the blazon of your honour—that is, your warlike shield. All peril and all pain should be accounted less than loss of fame. Die rather than do aught that yields dishonour."

"Not so," quoth Sir Burbon, "for when time serves I may again resume my former shield. To temporise is not to swerve from truth, when advantage or necessity compels it."

"Fie on such forgery!" said Artegall. "Under one hood to hide two faces! Knights should be true, and truth is one in all. Down with all dissembling!"

"Yet help me now for courtesy against these peasants who have oppressed me," said Burbon, "so that my lady may be freed from their hands."

Sir Artegall, although he blamed his wavering mind, agreed to aid him, and buckling himself at once to the fight, with the help of Talus and his iron flail soon dispersed the rabble.

But when they came to where the lady now stood alone, and Burbon ran forward to embrace her, she started back disdainfully, and would listen to nothing he said. The Knights rebuked her for being so fickle and wayward, and Sir Artegall's grave words so abashed her, that she hung down her head for shame, and stood speechless. Seeing this, Burbon made a second attempt, and she allowed him to place her on his steed without resistance. So he carried her off, seemingly neither well nor ill pleased.

Then Sir Artegall took his way to the sea-shore, to see if he could find any shipping to carry him over to the savage island where Grantorto held the Lady Irene captive. As good fortune fell, when they came to the coast they found a ship all ready to put to sea. Wind and weather served them so well that in one day they reached the island, where they found great hosts of men in order of battle ready to repel them, who held possession of the ground and forbade them to land. Nevertheless they would not refrain from landing, but as they drew near, Talus jumped into the sea, and wading through the waves, gained the shore, and chased the enemy away. Then Artegall and the old Knight landed, and marched forward to a town which was in sight.

By this time those who first fled in fear had brought tidings to the tyrant, who summoned all his forces in alarm, and marched out to encounter the enemy. He had not gone far when he met them; he charged with all his might, but Talus set upon the tyrant's troops and bruised and battered them so pitilessly, that he killed many. No one was able to withstand him; he overthrew them, man and horse, so that they lay scattered all over the land, as thick as seed after the sower.

Then Sir Artegall, seeing his rage, bade him to stop, and made a sign of truce. Calling a herald, he sent him to the tyrant to tell him that he did not come thither for the sake of such slaughter, but to try the right of Irene's cause with him in single fight. When Grantorto heard this message, right glad was he thus to stop the slaughter, and he appointed the next morrow for the combat betwixt them twain.

The following morning was the dismal day appointed for Irene's death. The sorrowful maiden, to whom none had borne tidings of the arrival of Artegall to set her free, looked up with sad eyes and a heavy heart, believing her last hour to be near. Rising, she dressed herself in squalid garments fit for such a day, and was brought forth to receive her doom.

But when she came to the place, and found there Sir Artegall in battle array, waiting for the foe, her heart was cheered, and it lent new life to her in the midst of deadly fear. Like a withered rose, dying of drought, which glows with fresh grace when a few drops of rain fall on her dainty face, so was Irene's countenance when she saw Sir Artegall in that array waiting for the tyrant.

At length, with proud and presumptuous bearing, Grantorto came into the field. He was armed in a coat of iron plate, and wore on his head a steel cap, rusty brown in colour, but sure and strong. He bore in his hand a great pole-axe, with which he was accustomed to fight, the blade of which was iron-studded, but not long. He was huge and hideous in stature, like a giant in height, surpassing most men in strength, and had moreover great skill in single fight. His face was ugly, and his expression stern enough to frighten one with the very sight of it; and when he grinned, it could scarcely be discerned whether he were a man or a monster.

As soon as he appeared within the lists he surveyed Artegall with a dreadful look, as if he would have daunted him with fear, and grinning in a grisly fashion flourished his deadly weapon. But the Knight of the Faerie Queene, who had often seen such a sight, was not in the least quelled by his ghastly countenance, but began straight to buckle himself to the fight, and cast his shield in front of him to be in readiness.

The trumpets sounded, and they rushed together with terrific force, each dealing huge and dangerous strokes. But the tyrant thundered his blows with such violence that they rent their way through the iron walls of his enemy's armour. Artegall, seeing this, took wary heed to shun them, and often stooped his head to shield himself; but Grantorto wielded his iron axe so nimbly that he gave him many wounds. But lifting his arm to smite him mortally, the Knight spied his advantage, and slipping underneath, struck him right in the flank. Yet the tyrant's blow, as be had intended, kept on its course, and fell with such monstrous weight that it seemed as if nothing could protect Sir Artegall from death. But betwixt him and the blow he cast his shield, in which the pole-axe buried itself so deep that Grantorto could in no way wrest it back again. He tugged and strove, and dragged the Knight all about the place, but nevertheless he could not free the axe from the shield.

Artegall, perceiving this, let go of his shield, and attacking the tyrant with his sword Crysaor, swiftly cut off his head.

When the people round about saw this they all shouted for joy at his success, glad to be freed from the tyrant who had so long oppressed them. joyously running to the fair Lady Irene, they fell at her feet, doing homage to her as their true liege and princess, while the glory of her champion was sounded everywhere.

Then Sir Artegall led Irene with fitting majesty to the palace where the kings reigned, and established her peaceably therein, and restored her kingdom again to her. And all such persons as had helped the tyrant with open or secret aid he punished severely, so that in a very short space not one was left who would have dared to disobey her. During the time he remained there all his study was how to deal true justice, and day and night he gave his anxious thoughts as to how he might reform the government.

Thus, having freed Irene from distress, he took his leave, and left her sorrowing at his departure.

Sir Calidore, Knight of Courtesy

The Quest of the Blatant Beast

ONE of the best loved knights at the court of the Faerie Queene was Sir Calidore, for even there, where courteous knights and ladies most did throng, not one was more renowned for courtesy than Calidore. Gentleness of spirit and winning manners were natural to him, and added to these, his gallant bearing and gracious speech stole all men's hearts. Moreover, he was strong and tall, and well proved in battle, so that he had won much glory, and his fame had spread afar. Not a knight or lady at the Court but loved him dearly; and he was worthy of their affection, for he hated falsehood and base flattery, and loved simple truth and steadfast honesty.

But like all Queen Gloriana's other knights, Sir Calidore was not allowed to spend his days in slothful ease at the court. He had his task to perform, and the adventure appointed to him was a hard and perilous one.

As he travelled on his way, it happened by chance that he met Sir Artegall, who was returning half sadly from the conquest he had lately made. They knew each other at once, and Sir Calidore was the first to speak.

"Hail, noblest Knight of all that live and breathe!" he cried. "Now tell me, if it please you, of the good success you have had in your late enterprise."

Then Sir Artegall told him the whole story of his exploits from beginning to end.

"Happy man to have worthily achieved so hard a quest!" said Calidore, when he had finished. "It will make you renowned for evermore. But where you have ended I now begin to tread an endless track, without guide or direction how to enter in or issue forth—in untried ways, in strange perils, and in long and weary labour. And even although good fortune may befall me, it will be unseen of any one."

"What is that quest which calls you now into such peril?" asked Sir Artegall.

"I pursue the Blatant Beast," said Sir Calidore, cc and incessantly chase him through the world until I overtake and subdue him. I do not know how or in what place to find him, vet still I fare forward."

"What is that Blatant Beast?" asked Artegall.

"It is a hideous monster of evil race, born and brought up in dark and noisome places, whence he issues forth to be the plague and scourge of wretched men. He has oftentimes annoyed good knight and true lady, and destroyed many, for with his venomous nature and vile tongue he wounds sorely, and bites, and cruelly torments."

"Then, since I left the savage island, I have seen such a beast," said Artegall. "He seemed to have a thousand tongues, all agreeing in spite and malice, with which he barked and bayed at me, as if he would have devoured me on the spot. He was set on by two hideous old hags, *Envy* and *Detraction*. But I, knowing myself safe from peril, paid no regard to his malice nor his power, whereupon he poured forth his wicked poison the more."

"That surely is the beast which I pursue," said Calidore. "I am right glad to have these tidings of him, having had none before in all my weary travels. Now your words give me some hope."

"God speed you!" said Sir Artegall, "and keep you from the dread danger, for you have much to contend against."

So they took a kindly leave of each other, and parted on their several ways.

Sir Calidore had not travelled far when he came upon a comely Squire, bound hand and foot to a tree, who seeing him in the distance called to him for aid. The Knight at once set him free, and then asked him what mishap had brought him into such disgrace. The Squire replied it was occasioned not by his fault, but through his misfortune.

Not far from here, on yonder rocky hill," he said, "stands a strong Castle, where a bad and hateful custom is kept up. For whenever any knight or lady comes along that way (and they must needs go by, for it is the pass through the rocks), they shave away the lady's locks and the knight's beard to pay toll for the passage."

"As shameful a custom as ever I heard of, and it shall be put a stop to!" said Sir Calidore. "But for what cause was it first set on foot?"

The lady who owns the castle is called Briana, and no prouder one lives," replied the Squire. "For a long time she has dearly loved a doughty Knight, and sought to win his love by all the means in her power. Crudor, for that is his name, in his scornful and selfish vanity refuses to return her affection until she has made for him a mantle, lined with the beards of knights and the locks of ladies. To provide this, she has prepared this castle, and appointed a Seneschal, called Maleffort, a man of great strength, who executes her wicked will with worse malice.

"As I came along to-day with a fair damsel, my dear love, he set upon us. Unable to withstand him, we both fled, and first capturing me he bound me to this tree till his return, and then went in pursuit of her. Nor do I know whether he has yet found her."

While they were speaking they heard a piteous shriek, and looking in the direction whence the cry came, they saw the churl dragging the maiden along by her yellow hair. When Calidore beheld the shameful sight he immediately went in pursuit, and commanded the villain to

"Sir Calidore thence travelled not long,
When as by chaunce a comely Squire he found,
That thorough some more mighty enemies wrong
Both hand and foote unto a tree was bound."

release his prey. Hearing his voice, Maleffort turned, and running towards him. more enraged than terrified, said tauntingly—

"Are you the wretch who defies me? And will you give your beard for this maid, whose part you take? Yet it shall not free her locks from ransom."

With that he flew fiercely at him and laid on the most hideous strokes. But Calidore, who was well skilled in fight, let his adversary exhaust his strength, and then attacked him with such fury that the churl's heart failed him, and he took flight to the Castle, where his hope of refuge remained. But just as the warders on the Castle wall opened the gates to receive him, Calidore overtook him in the porch, and killed him, so that his dead body fell down inside the door. Then Calidore entered in and slew the porter,

The rest of the Castle inmates flocked round him, but he swept them all aside. Passing into the hall he was met by the Lady Briana herself, who bitterly upbraided him for what she termed his unknightly conduct in staying her servants.

"Not unto me the shame, but award it to the shameful doer," replied the Knight. "It is no blame to punish those who deserve it. Those who break the bonds of civility and make wicked customs, those are they who defame both noble arms and gentle courtesy. There is no greater disgrace to man than inhumanity. Then for dread of disgrace forego this evil custom which you here keep up, and show instead kindly courtesy to all who pass. This will gain you more glory than that man's love which you thus seek to obtain."

But the Lady Briana only replied to Sir Calidore with the most scornful insolence, and despatching a hasty message to Crudor, bade him come to her rescue. While they waited for the return of the messenger, she treated Sir Calidore with every indignity, so that an iron heart could scarcely have borne it; but the Knight wisely controlled his wrath, and bravely and patiently endured her womanish disdain.

In due course the answer came back that Crudor would succour his lady before he tasted bread, and deliver up her foe, dead or alive, into her hand. Then Briana immediately became quite blithe, and spoke more bitterly than ever, yet Calidore was not in the least dismayed, but rather seemed the more cheerful. Putting on his armour, he went out to meet his foe, and soon spied a Knight spurring towards him with all his might.

He guessed at once this was Crudor, and without staying to ask his name couched his spear and ran at him. The Knights met with such fury that both rolled to the ground; but while Calidore at once sprang lightly again to his feet, it was some time before Crudor rose slowly and heavily. Then the battle was renewed on foot, and after a fierce and terrible struggle Calidore at last brought his foe to the ground. He could easily have killed him, but Crudor, seeing the danger in which he was placed, cried out—

"Ah, mercy, Sir! Do not slay me, but spare my life which fate has laid under your foot."

"And is this the boast of that proud lady's threat, which menaced to beat me from the field?" said Calidore quietly. "By this you may now learn not to treat strangers so rudely. But put away proud looks and stern behaviour, which shall gain for you nothing but dishonour. However strong and fortunate he may be in fight, nothing is more blameful to a Knight, who professes courtesy as well as arms, than the reproach of pride and cruelty. In vain he seeks to suppress others who has not learned first to subdue himself. All flesh is frail and full of fickleness, subject to the chance of ever-changing fortune: what happens to me to-day may happen to you to-morrow. He who will not show mercy to others, how can he ever hope to obtain mercy? To pay each in his own coin is right and just.

"Yet since you now need to crave mercy, I will grant it, and spare your life, on these conditions: First that you shall behave yourself better to all errant knights, wherever they may be; and next, that you aid ladies in every place and in every trouble."

The wretched man, who had remained all this while in dread of death, gladly promised to perform all Sir Calidore's behests, and further swore to marry Briana without any dowry, and to release her from his former shameful conditions. Then Calidore called the Lady, and soothing her terror, told her of the promise he had compelled Crudor to make.

Overcome by his exceeding courtesy, which quite pierced her stubborn heart, Briana threw herself at his feet, and acknowledged herself deeply indebted to him for having restored both life and love to her. Then they all returned to the Castle, and she entertained them joyfully with feast and glee, trying by all the means in her power to show her gratitude and goodwill. To Sir Calidore, for his trouble, she freely gave the Castle, and professed herself bound to him for ever, so wondrously was she changed from what she had been before.

But Calidore would not keep for himself land or fee as wages for his good deed, but gave them at once as a rightful reward to the Squire whom he had lately freed, and to his damsel, in recompense for all their former wrong. There he remained happily with them till he was well and strong from the wounds he had received, and then he passed forth again on his first quest.

The Proud Discourteous Knight

As Sir Calidore rode on his way he saw not far off a strange sight—a tall young man fighting on foot against an armed Knight on horseback; and beside them he saw a fair lady standing alone on foot, in sad disarray. Before he could get near to ask what was the matter, the armed Knight had been killed by the youth.

Filled with amazement, Sir Calidore steadfastly marked the latter, and found him to be a goodly and graceful youth, still only a slender slip, not more than seventeen years old, but tall and fair of face, so that the Knight surely deemed him of noble birth. He was clad in a woodman's jacket of Lincoln green, trimmed with silver lace; on his head he wore a hood with spreading points, and his hunter's horn hung at his side. His buskins were of the costliest leather, adorned with golden points, and regularly intersected with stripes, as was then the fashion for those of gentle family. In his right hand he held a quivering dart, and in his left a sharp boar-spear.

Calidore, having well viewed him, at length spoke, and asked him how it came that he, though not yet a Knight, had dared to slay a Knight, which was plainly forbidden by chivalry.

"Truly," said the youth, "I was loath to break the law of chivalry, but I would break it again rather than let myself be struck by any man. He assailed me first, regardless of what belongs to chivalry."

"By my troth," then said Sir Calidore, "great blame is it for an armed Knight to wrong an unarmed man. But tell me why this strife arose between you?"

Then the youth, whose name was Tristram, told him that, as he was hunting that day in the forest, he chanced to meet this man, together with the lady. The Knight, as Sir Calidore had seen, was on horseback, but the lady walked on foot beside the horse, through thick and thin, unfit for any woman. Yet not content with this, to add to the disgrace, whenever she lagged behind, as she must needs do, he would thump her forward with his spear, and force her to go on, while she vainly wept, and made piteous lament.

"When I saw this, as they passed by," continued Tristram, "I was moved to indignation, and began to blame him for such cruelty. At this he was enraged, and disdainfully reviled me, threatening to chastise me as one would a child. I, no less disdainful, returned his scornful taunts,. whereupon he struck me with his spear, and I, seeking to avenge myself, threw a slender dart at him, which struck him, as it seems, underneath the heart, so that he quickly died."

Sir Calidore inquired of the lady if this were indeed true, and as she could deny nothing, but cleared Tristram of all blame, then said the Knight—

"Neither will I charge him with guilt. For what he spoke, he spoke it for you, Lady; and what he did, he did it to save himself, against both of whom that Knight wrought unknightly shame."

Then turning back to the gallant boy, who had acquitted himself so well and stoutly, and seeing his beautiful face, and hearing his wise words, Sir Calidore was filled with admiration, and felt certain that he came of heroic blood. Then, because of the affection he bore him, he begged the youth to reveal who he was, "for since the day when I first bore arms," added the Knight, "I never saw greater promise in any one."

Then Tristram replied that he was the son of a King, although by fate or fortune he had lost his country and the crown that should be his by right. He was the only heir of the good King Meliogras of Cornwall, but his father dying while he was still a child, his uncle had seized the kingdom. The widowed Queen, his mother, afraid lest ill should happen to the boy, sent him away out of the country of Lyonesse, where he was born, into the land of Queen Gloriana, and here he had dwelt since the time he was ten years old.

His days had not been spent in idleness, for he had been well trained with many noble companions in gentle manners and other fitting ways. His chief delight was in following the chase, and nothing that ranged in the green forest was unknown to him. But now that he was growing older he felt it was time to employ his strength in a nobler fashion, and he besought Sir Calidore to make him a Squire, so that henceforth he might bear arms, and learn to use them aright.

So Sir Calidore caused him to kneel, and made him swear faith to his Knight, and truth to all ladies, and never to be recreant for fear of peril, nor for anything that might befall. So he dubbed him, and called him his Squire.

Then young Tristram grew full glad and joyous, and when the time came for Sir Calidore to depart, he prayed that he might go with him on his adventure, vowing always to serve him faithfully. Sir Calidore rejoiced at his noble heart, and hoped he would surely prove a doughty Knight, yet for the time he was obliged to make this answer to him:—

"Glad would I surely be, my courteous Squire, to have you with me in my present quest, but I am bound by a vow which I swore to my Sovereign, that in fulfilling her behest I would allow no creature to aid me. For that reason I may not grant what you so earnestly beg. But since this lady is now quite desolate, and needs a safeguard on her way, you would do well to succour her from fear of danger."

Tristram gladly accepted this new service, so, taking a courteous leave, the two parted.

Not long after this, Sir Calidore came upon a Knight and a lady sitting in the shade of some trees. Sir Calidore greeted them courteously, and the Knight invited him to sit down beside them, so that they might talk over all their adventures. While they were chatting together, the Lady Serena wandered away into the fields to pluck some flowers. Then suddenly, from the forest near, the Blatant Beast rushed forth, and catching up the lady, bore her away in his great mouth. Starting up, both Knights at once gave chase, and Calidore, who was swiftest of foot, overtook the monster in the midst of his race, and fiercely charging him, made him leave his prey and take to flight.

Knowing that the Knight was close at hand, Sir Calidore did not pause to succour the lady, but quickly followed the brute in his flight.

Full many paths and perils he passed; over hill and dale, through forest and plain; so sharply did he pursue the monster that he never suffered him to rest, day or night. From the court he chased him to the city, from the city to the village, from the village into the country, and from the country back to remote farms.. Thence the Blatant Beast fled into the open fields, where the herds were keeping the cattle, and the shepherds were singing to their flocks.

Coridon and Pastorella

As Sir Calidore followed the chase of the Blatant Beast he came upon a group of shepherds piping to their flocks. In reply to his questions they answered they had never seen the creature, and if there were any such they prayed heaven to keep him far from them. Then one of them, seeing that Calidore was travel-worn and weary, offered him such simple food and drink as they had with them, and the Knight, who was courteous to all men alike, both the lowly and the high-born, accepted their gentle offer.

As he sat amongst these rustics he saw seated on a little hillock, higher than all the rest, a beautiful maiden, wearing a crown of flowers tied with silken ribbons. She was surrounded by the other shepherdesses, as with a lovely garland, but her beauty far excelled theirs, and all united in singing the praises and carolling the name of the "fairest Pastorella." Not one of all the shepherds but honoured her, and many also loved her, but most of all the shepherd Coridon. Yet neither for him nor for any one else did she care a whit; her lot was humble, but her mind was high above it.

As Sir Calidore gazed at her and marked her rare demeanour, which seemed to him far to excel the rank of a shepherd, and to be worthy of a Prince's paragon, all unawares he was caught in the toils of love, from which no skill of his own could deliver him. So there he sat still, with no desire to move, although his quest had gone far before him. He stayed until the flying day was far spent, and the dews of night warned the shepherds to hasten home with their flocks.

Then came to them an aged sire, with silver beard and locks, and carrying a shepherd's crook. He was always supposed to be the father of Pastorella, and she indeed thought it herself. But he was not so, having found her by chance in the open field as an infant. He took her

"Upon a little hillocke she was placed
Higher than all the rest, and round about
Environ'd with a girland, goodly graced
Of lovely lasses."

home, and cherished her as his own child, for he had none other, and in course of time she came to be accounted so.

Melibee, for so the good old man was called, seeing Calidore left all alone and night at hand, invited him to his simple home, which, although only a mud cottage, with everything very humble, was yet better to lodge in than the open fields. The Knight full gladly agreed, this being his heart's own wish, and went home with Melibee. There he was made heartily welcome by the honest shepherd and his aged wife, and after the frugal supper, which they ate with much contentment, Sir Calidore listened half-entranced while Melibee discoursed on all the joys of a pastoral life. So tempting was the picture he painted that Calidore resolved to lay aside for awhile his toilsome quest and the pursuit of glory, and take a little rest in this peaceful spot. If he were allowed to share the cabin and the scanty fare he promised to reward Melibee well, but the good old man refused the offered gift of gold.

"If you really wish to try this simple sort of life that shepherds lead," he said, "make it your own, and learn our rustic ways for yourself."

So Sir Calidore dwelt there that night, and many days after, as long as it pleased him, daily beholding the fair Pastorella, and all the while growing more deeply in love with her. He tried to please her by all the kindly courtesies he could invent, but she, who had never been accustomed to such strange fashions, fit for kings and queens, nor had ever seen such knightly service, paid small heed to them, and cared more for the shepherds' rustic civility than for anything he did.

Sir Calidore, seeing this, thought it best to change the manner of his appearance. Doffing his bright armour, he dressed himself in shepherd's attire, taking in his hand a crook instead of a steel-headed spear. Clad thus, he went every day to the fields with Pastorella, and kept her flocks diligently, watching to drive away the ravenous wolf, so that she could sport and play as it pleased her.

Coridon, who for a long time had loved her, and hoped to gain her love, was greatly troubled, and very jealous of this stranger. He often complained scowlingly of Pastorella to all the other shepherds, and whenever he came near Calidore, would frown and bite his lips, and was ready to devour his own heart with jealousy. The Knight, on the other hand, was utterly free from malice or grudging, never showing any sign of rancour, and often taking an opportunity to praise Coridon to Pastorella. But the maiden, if ever she had cared for her uncouth admirer, certainly did so no longer now that she had seen Calidore.

Once when Calidore was asked to lead the dance with Pastorella, in his courtesy he took Coridon, and set him in his place; and when Pastorella gave him her own flowery garland, he soon took it off and put it on the head of Coridon.

Another time Coridon challenged Calidore to a wrestling match, thinking he would surely avenge his grudge, and easily put his foe to shame, for he was well practised in this game. But he greatly mistook Calidore, for the Knight was strong and mightily tough in sinew, and with one fall he almost broke Coridon's neck. Then Pastorella gave the oaken crown to Calidore as his due right, but he who excelled in courtesy gave it to Coridon, saying he had won it well.

Thus did that gentle Knight bear himself amidst that rustic throng, so that even they who were his rivals could not malign him, but must needs praise him; for courtesy breeds goodwill and favour even amongst the rudest. So it surely wrought with this fair maiden, and in her mind sowed the seeds of perfect love, which at last, after long trial, brought forth the fruit of joy and happiness

But whatever Sir Calidore did to please Pastorella, Coridon immediately strove to emulate; and if the Knight succeeded in winning favour, he was frozen with jealousy.

One day, as they all three went together to the greenwood to gather strawberries, a dangerous adventure befell them. A tiger rose up out of the wood and rushed with greedy jaws at Pastorella. Hearing her cry for help, Coridon ran in haste to rescue her; but when he saw the fiend he fled away just as fast in cowardly fear, holding his own life dearer than his friend. But Calidore, quickly coming to her aid when he saw the beast ready to rend his dear lady, ran at him enraged, instead of being afraid. He had no weapon but his shepherd's crook, but with that he struck the monster so sternly that he fell stunned to the ground, and then, before he could recover, Sir Calidore cut off his head, and laid it at the feet of the terrified maiden.

From that day forth Pastorella grew more and more fond of the Knight, but Coridon she despised, because of his cowardice. Then for a long time Sir Calidore dwelt happily among these shepherd folk, forgetting his former quest, so full of toil and pain, and rejoicing in the happy peace of rustic bliss.

But at last malicious fortune, which envies the long prosperity of lovers, blew up a bitter storm of adversity.

In the Brigands' Den

One day, when Sir Calidore was away hunting in the woods, a lawless tribe of brigands invaded the country where the shepherds dwelt, ravaged their houses; murdered the shepherds, and drove away their flocks. Old Melibee and all his household were led away captive, and with them also was taken Coridon. In the dead of night, so that no one might see or rescue them, the robbers carried their prey to their dwelling. This was on a little island, so covered with dense brushwood that there seemed no way for people to pass in or out, or to find footing in the overgrown grass; for the way was made underground, through hollow caves that no man could discover, because of the thick shrubs which hid them from sight. Through all the inner parts of their dwelling the darkness of night daily hovered; they were not lighted by any window or opening in the roof, but with continual candle-light, which made a dim and uncertain gloom.

Hither the brigands brought their prisoners, and kept them under constant watch and ward, meaning, as soon as they conveniently could, to sell them as slaves to merchants, who would either keep them in bondage or sell them again. But the Captain of the brigands was enchanted with the loveliness of Pastorella, and determined to keep her for himself. When, therefore, the other prisoners were brought forward to be sold, so that the money received for them might be divided equally among the band, he held back Pastorella, saying that she was his prize alone, with whom no one else had anything to do. Besides, he added, she was now so weak and wan through illness that she was worth nothing as merchandise; and then he showed her to them, to prove how pale and ill she was.

The sight of her wondrous beauty, though now worn and faded, and only to be dimly seen by candlelight, so amazed the eyes of the merchants that they utterly refused to buy any of the other prisoners without her, and offered to pay large sums of gold. Then the Captain bade them be silent. He refused to sell the maiden; they could take the rest if they would—this one he would keep for himself.

Some of the other chief robbers boldly forbade him to do this injury, for the maiden, much as it grieved him, should be sold with the rest of the captives, in order to increase their price. The Captain again refused angrily, and, drawing his sword, declared that if any one dared to lay a hand on her, he should dearly rue it, and his death should pay the price.

From words they rapidly fell to blows, and, the candle being soon quenched in the conflict, the fight raged furiously in the dark. But, first of all, they killed the captives, lest they should join against the weaker side or rise against the remnant. Old Melibee and his aged wife were slain, and many others with them; but Coridon, escaping craftily, crept out of doors, hidden in the darkness, and fled away as fast as he could. Unhappy Pastorella was defended all the time by the Captain of the brigands, who, more careful of her safety than of his own, kept his target always stretched over her. At length he was slain, yet, even in his fall, continued with his extended arms to shelter Pastorella, who, wounded with the same stroke, fell to the ground with him.

With the death of the Captain the fray ceased, and the brigands, lighting fresh candles, made search to see who was slain, friends and foes. There they found their Captain cruelly killed, and, in his arms, the dying maiden; but, seeing that life still lingered, they busily applied all their skill to call her soul back to its home, and so well did they work that at last they restored her to life. This done, they placed her in charge of one of the brigands, who kept her in harsh and wretched

"Their Captaine there they cruelly found kild
And in his armes the dreary, dying mayd."

thraldom, scarcely allowing her food or rest, or suffering her wounds to be properly tended.

Sir Calidore, meanwhile, having returned from the wood, and found the cottage despoiled and his love reft away, waxed almost mad with grief and rage. To add to his anguish, there was not a soul of whom he could inquire anything. He sought the woods, but could see no man; he sought the plains, but could hear no tidings. The woods only repeated vain echoes; the plains were waste and empty. Where once the shepherds played their pipes and fed a hundred flocks, there now he found not one.

At last, as he roamed up and down, he saw a man coming towards him, who seemed to he some wretched peasant in ragged clothes, with hair standing on end, as if he fled from some recent danger, which still followed close behind. As he came near, the Knight saw it was Coridon. Running up to him, Sir Calidore asked where were the rest—where was Pastorella?

Bursting into tears, Coridon told how they had been seized by the brigands, and carried to their den. He described how they were to have been sold as slaves, and the quarrel that had arisen over Pastorella. He told how the Captain had tried to defend her. "But what could he do alone against them all?" he added. "He could not save her; in the end she must surely die. I only escaped in the uproar and confusion, and it were better to be dead with them than to see all this place, where we dwelt together in joy, desolate and waste."

Calidore was at first almost distracted at hearing this dreadful news; but presently, recovering himself, he began to cast about in his mind how he might rescue Pastorella if she were still alive, or how he should revenge her death; or, if he were too weak to avenge her, then at least he could die with her.

Therefore, he prayed Coridon, since he knew well the readiest way into the thieves' den, that he would conduct him there. Coridon was still so frightened that at first he refused; but at last he was persuaded by Sir Calidore's entreaties and promises of reward.

So forth they went together, both clad in shepherd's dress and carrying their crooks; but Calidore had secretly armed himself underneath. Then, as they approached the place, they saw upon a hill, not far away, some flocks of sheep and some shepherds, to whom they both agreed to take their way, hoping to learn some news.

There they found, which they did not expect, the self-same flocks which the brigands had stolen away, with several of the thieves left to look after them. Coridon knew quite well his own sheep, and, seeing them, began to weep for pity; but, when he saw the thieves, his heart failed him, although they were all asleep. He wanted Calidore to kill them as they slept and drive away the sheep, but the Knight had another purpose in view. Waking the brigands, he sat down beside them, and began to chat of different things, hoping to find out from them whether Pastorella were alive or slain. The thieves, in their turn, began to question Sir Calidore and Coridon, asking what sort of men they were and whence they came; to which they replied that they were poor herdsmen who had fled from their masters, and now sought hire elsewhere.

The thieves, delighted to hear this, offered to pay them well if they would tend their flocks, for they themselves were bad herdsmen, they said, not accustomed to watch cattle or pasture sheep, but to foray the land or scour the sea. Sir Calidore and Coridon agreed to keep the flocks; so there they stayed all day, as long as the light lasted.

When it grew towards night the robbers took them to their dens, which they soon got to know quite well, and where they sought out all the secret passages. There they found, to their joy and surprise, that Pastorella still lived. Watching their opportunity, one dead of night, when all the thieves were sound asleep after a recent foray, Sir Calidore made his way to the Captain's den. When he came to the cave he found it fast, but he assailed the door with irresistible might and burst the lock. One of the robbers, awaking at the noise, ran to the entrance, but the bold Knight easily slew him. Pastorella, in the meanwhile, was almost dead with fright, believing it to be another uproar such as she had lately seen. But when Sir Calidore came in, and began to call for her, knowing his voice, she suddenly revived, and her soul was filled with rapture No less rejoiced Calidore when he found her, and like one distracted he caught her in his arms and kissed her a thousand times.

By this time the hue and cry was raised, and all the brigands came crowding to the cave; but Calidore stood in the entry, and slew each man as he advanced, so that the passage was lined with dead bodies. Then, when no more could get near him, he rested till the morning, when he made his way into the open light. Here all the rest of the brigands were ready waiting for him, and, fiercely assailing him, fell on him with all their might. But Calidore, with his raging brand, divided their thickest troops and scattered them wide. Like a lion among a herd of deer, so did he fly among them, hewing and slaying all that came near, so that none dared face the danger, but fled from his wrath to hide from death in their caves.

Then, returning to his dear lady, he brought her forth into the joyous light, and did everything he could to make her forget the troubles through which she had passed. From the thieves' den he took all the spoils and treasures of which they had robbed other people, and all the flocks which they had stolen from Melibee he restored to Coridon.

The Beast with a Thousand Tongues

Sir Calidore, having rescued Pastorella from the brigands' den, took her to the Castle of Belgard, where the good Sir Bellamour was lord, and there a strange thing happened.

Years before, Sir Bellamour had secretly married a beautiful maiden, called Claribel, the daughter of a rich and powerful man, known by the name of the "Lord of Many Islands." Her father had hoped, because of his great wealth, that his daughter would marry the Prince of a neighbouring country, and when he found that she loved Sir Bellamour, he was in such a rage that he threw them in two deep dungeons, forbidding them ever to see each other. When Claribel was in prison, a little daughter was born to her; but, fearing lest her father should get hold of it, she entrusted it to her handmaid, Melissa, to have it brought up as a stranger's child. The trusty damsel carried it into an empty field, and having kissed and wept over it, placed it on the ground, and hid herself behind some bushes near, to see what mortal would take pity on the poor little infant. At length a shepherd, who kept his fleecy flocks on the plains around, led by the infant's cry, came to the place, and when he found there the abandoned treasure, he took it up, and wrapping it in his mantle, bore it home to his honest wife, who ever afterwards brought it up as her own child.

Claribel and Bellamour remained a long time in captivity, till at last the "Lord of Many Islands" died, and left them all his possessions. Then the tide of fortune turned, they were restored to freedom, and rejoiced in happiness together. They had lived for a long time in peace and love when Sir Calidore brought Pastorella to the castle. Here they both received the heartiest welcome, for Sir Bellamour was an old friend of Calidore's, and loved him well; and Claribel, seeing how weak and wan Pastorella was after her long captivity, tended her with the greatest love and care.

Now, it happened that before the handmaiden parted with the infant she noticed on its breast a little purple mark, like a rose unfolding its silken leaves. This same maiden, Melissa, was appointed to wait on Pastorella, and one morning, when she was helping her to dress, she noticed on her chest the rosy mark which she remembered well on the little infant, Claribel's daughter. Full of joy, she rail in haste to her mistress, and told her that the beautiful lady was no other than the little child who had been born in prison. Then Claribel ran quickly to the stranger maiden, and finding it was even as Melissa said, she clasped her in her arms and held her close, weeping softly and saying, "And do you now live again, my daughter, and are you still alive whom long I mourned as dead?"

Then there was great rejoicing in the Castle of Belgard.

Meanwhile Sir Calidore was pursuing the quest of the Blatant Beast, seeking him in every place with unresting pain and toil, and following him by his destroying track, for wherever the monster went he left behind him ruin and devastation.

At last, in a narrow place, Sir Calidore overtook him, and, fiercely assailing, forced him to turn. Then the Blatant Beast ran at him with open mouth, huge and horrible; it was all set with a double row of iron teeth, and in it were a thousand tongues of every kind and quality—

"Putting his puissance forth, pursued so hard
That backward he enforced him to fall;
And being down, ere he new help could call,
His shield he on him threw, and far down held."

some were of dogs, that barked day and night; some of cats that yawled; some of bears that growled continually; some of tigers that seemed to grin and snarl at all who passed by; but most of them were tongues of mortal men, who poured forth abuse, not caring where nor when; and among them were mingled here and there the tongues of serpents, with three-forked stings, that spat out poison at all who came within reach, speaking hateful things Of good and bad alike, of high and low, not even sparing kings or kaisers, but either blotting them with infamy or biting them with their baneful teeth.

But Calidore, not in the least afraid of this horrid spectacle, met him with such impetuous might that he checked his violence and beat him back. Then the monster, rearing up, ramped upon him with his ravenous paws, as if his cruel claws would have rent him; but the Knight, being well on guard, cast his shield between, and putting forth all his strength, forced him to fall back; and when he was down, he threw his shield on him and pinned him to the ground. In vain did the Beast rage and roar; for the more he strove, the more firmly the Knight held him, so that he was almost mad with spite. He grinned, he bit, he scratched, he spat out venom, and acted like a horrible fiend.

When the monster saw force was of no avail, he began to use his hundred tongues, and reviled and railed at the Knight with bitter terms of infamy, weaving in many a forged lie, whose like Sir Calidore had never heard or thought of; yet for all that he did not let the creature go, but held him so tight that he nearly choked him.

At last, when he found his strength failing and his rage lessening, Sir Calidore took a strong muzzle of the stoutest iron, made with many a link, with which he fastened up his mouth, shutting up therein his blasphemous tongue, so that he should never more defame gentle knight or wrong lovely lady; and to this he tied a great long chain, with which he dragged him forth in spite of himself. The hideous Beast chafed inwardly at these strange bonds, which no one till then had dared to impose on him; yet he dared not draw back nor attempt to resist the power of the noble Calidore, but trembled before him, and followed like a frightened dog.

All through Faerie Land he followed him thus, as if he had learnt obedience, so that all the people wherever he went thronged out of the town to see Sir Calidore lead the Blatant Beast in bondage, and seeing it were amazed at the sight; and all such people as he had formerly wronged rejoiced to see him a captive, and many wondered at the Beast, but more wondered at the Knight.

Thus was this monster suppressed and tamed by the mastering might of the doughty Calidore, and so for a long time he remained. But at last, either by wicked fate or the fault of men, he broke his iron chain, and got again at liberty into the world; and here he still ranges, barking and biting, sparing no one in his malice, and doing an infinite deal of mischief wherever he goes; and since the days of the good Sir Calidore no man has ever been able to master him.

THE END

Made in the USA
Monee, IL
14 January 2025